BRASS IN THE DESERT

Center Point
Large Print

Also by Richard S. Wheeler and available from Center Point Large Print:

The Two Medicine River
Richard Lamb
The Fate
Easy Street
Anything Goes

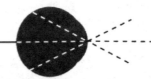

**This Large Print Book carries the
Seal of Approval of N.A.V.H.**

BRASS
IN THE
DESERT

Richard S. Wheeler

CENTER POINT LARGE PRINT
THORNDIKE, MAINE

This Circle Ⓥ Western is published by
Center Point Large Print in the year 2016 in
co-operation with Golden West Literary Agency.

September, 2016
First Edition

Printed in the United States of America
on permanent paper.
Set in 16-point Times New Roman type.

ISBN: 978-1-68324-112-6

Library of Congress Cataloging-in-Publication Data

Names: Wheeler, Richard S., author.
Title: Brass in the desert / Richard S. Wheeler.
Description: First edition. | Thorndike, Maine : Center Point Large Print,
2016. | Series: Circle V Western
Identifiers: LCCN 2016021193 | ISBN 9781683241126
    (hardcover : alk. paper)
Subjects: LCSH: Large type books. | GSAFD: Western stories.
Classification: LCC PS3573.H4345 B73 2016 | DDC 813/.54—dc23
LC record available at https://lccn.loc.gov/2016021193

Chapter One

The vultures were wheeling. That might be bad, or maybe good, depending on what was about to die. For Gladstone Brass it was probably good. He was usually on the side of the vultures.

His father had named him after the prime minister, but woe to anyone who called him Glad. He wasn't glad and never would be.

He squinted at the distant column, spiraling in the morning blue, and headed that way. Things needed checking out. The black burro, Tía María, followed automatically. She was laden with beans and a water cask, mostly empty now. In the parched wastes of central Nevada there wasn't much of either.

Naked rock, lack of vegetation, bitter cold nights, and roasting days kept people out. So did Gladstone. He ruled an empire of emptiness, a vast heartless waste where few souls ventured. That blank place on the maps was his private world, and he felt violated if he encountered any other mortal within its vast confines.

"All right, we'll see who's met his fate," he said to Tía María, who was his sole companion. She was a jenny who was privy to all his secrets. After his mule, Balthazar, had gotten bit by a desert rattler and croaked, he caught Tía María in a desert cañon full of wild burros, and discovered she was a good listener and didn't mock him, the way Balthazar had.

The vultures circled half a mile away, on the far side of a parched basin with gritty gravel underfoot. The whirling column was not far from a seep that had quit running, which was probably the reason someone or something had croaked there. Gladstone knew every spring and seep in the whole desert, the ones that ran year round, the ones that quit in the heat, the ones that leaked lethal waters laced with arsenic or other heavy metals.

When he climbed to the place, a few black vultures reared up and flapped away. They had been feasting on something that was mostly hide and bone. Four legs. *Pity it was a beast instead of a human,* he thought. Vultures deserved to dine on better meat.

But the carcass was encased by a packsaddle. Brass was just absorbing that revelation when a coarse voice crackled from a line of scree just up the slope.

"Bring me that cask, Brass, or you're dead."

Gladstone knew the voice, and knew the dead burro. And knew that the unfriendly black muzzle of a revolver he now spotted poking through the scree would dictate whatever happened next. The weapon was in the hand of the one man Brass despised more than all the rest of mortality combined—Bitter Bowler. A tightening went through him.

"Maybe I won't," he said.

The shot knocked his slouch hat off his head. He gently reached down and picked it up and discovered ventilation in its crown.

"I shot the burro for its blood and I'll drink yours if that's how you want it," Bowler said.

"Before I die, tell me how you got your name," Brass said.

"That's a secret you'll never learn. Now bring the cask."

"What happened, Bowler?"

"My ankle. It's busted. The burro kicked it."

"Ah! There's justice in the world. The devil betrayed you. The only thing wrong is that you still have one good leg."

"Bring me your water or you croak. Right here. Right now."

"So what good will my mostly empty cask do you?"

"It'll buy me a few more days. I'm tired of palaver. Bring the cask."

"Then we'll both run out of water."

Bowler laughed harshly. "That's the idea."

The barrel of the revolver lowered slightly, pointed in the general direction of Gladstone's heart. This might require some negotiation.

"What you need, Bowler, is a crutch. Shoot me, and you have no hope. Give me a little leeway, and I'll make a crutch. There might be something around here you can lean on."

Bowler's gray face and iron-colored beard were visible now. The vultures flapped nearby. They had been waiting for him to abandon life. Brass wished he had arrived an hour later and found the vultures plucking Bowler's eyes out.

"Bring me the cask," Bowler said.

"I'll find something for a crutch. You need a good stick."

An odd silence ensued.

Bowler shot Tía María. The slug drilled through the burro's neck. The little burro folded slowly, a whine rising, a betrayal accomplished, and then she collapsed in a heap.

"So, you ain't going anywhere now," Bowler said. There was a rasp in his voice.

"You've killed my friend. My mother, my sister, my daughter."

"If I'm gonna die, I may as well take you with me."

Vultures were once more settling on the carcass of Bowler's burro. They were mostly silent, but there was a slight gabble as they conversed. They were opportunists, and here was a feast.

"Bring me water," Bowler said.

Gladstone Brass stared at the man he'd fought and outwitted and damned for a dozen years, a man who kept invading his own country, prying gold-laden quartz from his ledges, stealing water from his seeps, and doing his best to kill him.

"All right," he said.

He headed for Tía María, opened the pannier, lifted out the wooden cask, found a metal cup, and carried the cask and cup to Bowler. The man lay on a bed of rubble, his boot off, his right ankle swollen and angry. Bowler was in grave condition, his breath ragged, his eyes bulging. But the revolver was steady.

Gladstone slowly set the cask on the scree and opened the cock and filled the tin cup. It was bad water. It came from the Angel Cliff seep on the north side of the Salt Hills, and was alkaline. The seep was so slow it had taken a whole hour to fill the five-gallon cask.

He handed it to Bitter, who sipped it, kept on sipping, and glared at Gladstone.

"What's this? Don't you know bad water when you see it?"

Gladstone Brass refilled the cup twice more, and Bitter Bowler swallowed it all.

"I didn't think you'd help me," Bitter said.

"I saved the vultures. They'd croak on your rotten flesh."

That might even be true. Bitter Bowler's flesh was as foul as any hanging from any mortal. It exuded rank odors indescribably noxious. It ranged in color from swamp-scum green to chalk. It webbed out from smoldering eyes. It pinched,

9

soft and rubbery, as if there were no substance to it. It announced to any observer that Bitter Bowler had emerged from some prehistoric bog, dried out, and turned into a bag of warped bones. Mosquitoes died when they bit him. Rattlesnakes went limp.

"That's Angel Cliff water, and that's where I'm taking you. That's as much help as you're going to get."

"I cleaned out that pocket before you knew what hit you," Bowler said.

He was referring to a seam of gold-flaked quartz near there that had been Gladstone's source of income for years. Whenever Gladstone needed a few goods in Eureka, he bagged some quartz and rode in, sold it, and bought the flour or salt or whiskey he wanted, and faded into his vast blank space in the map as fast as he could. That's how it went until Bitter Bowler had found his diggings and cleaned out the ledge.

Gladstone had half a dozen other mineral ledges tucked away in his skull, and if he needed something from town, he knew how to get it. But the theft of his best ore rankled. Bowler was a criminal and needed dying.

"You're not taking me anywhere," Bowler said. "You can refill and bring the water here. And bring me a good stick to lean on."

Gladstone ignored him. There were things to figure out. Such as getting Bowler out, or letting him croak. It didn't matter which. He shooed the greedy vultures away and pulled Bowler's packsaddle off what little remained of the man's burro. There was hardly enough wood in the cross buck to make a crutch. There wasn't enough wood in the one on Tía María, either. Bowler needed a stout stick to carry his weight. A crutch. The nearest trees were some bristle cone, amazingly old, up on the peaks to the east. A crutch for Bitter wouldn't form itself out of nothing.

"There's justice in the world, after all," Gladstone said. "You'll have to walk on your busted leg."

"Like I say, go get us some water. Take my canteen and fill it."

Gladstone studied the strewn contents of Bitter's pack. Some spare britches, some mess gear, dry canteen, a grimy box of .38-caliber shells, a battered bag of flour, pickaxe and shovel, hammer, moccasins, one candle and flint and steel, and a burlap sack.

"I'm quitting you. I'll take the canteen. You can eat Tía María until the sun fries you. Save the last round for yourself."

Bowler stared.

Gladstone swore that tears were rising in Bowler's marble eyes, but that was impossible. Bitter Bowler could not shed tears. Some things were impossible, and that was one of them. But the next time Gladstone glanced toward the man,

Bowler's cheeks were wet. And that made Gladstone even grumpier. Men as evil as Bowler had no tear ducts, and men as dehydrated as Bowler had no tears to leak away.

The black vultures sat in a row on the carcass of the burro, enjoying the show.

Gladstone headed out. He didn't know whether he'd make it to Angel Cliff with only a dry canteen and a little flour. From Angel Cliff he would face a tough trip to Eureka. There were some seeps in a few grassy cañons where he might scrape up some water if he was lucky. He wasn't much better off than Bowler, but at least he had both legs under him.

This time of year the heat built up midday, but the evenings and mornings weren't bad. He would walk to water. He bulled through the hot afternoon, pushed into evening, with a sky so clear and air so dry that he felt he was on the road to infinity. Massed ahead were the ridges that harbored Angel Cliff, but that was still miles distant. He felt hungry, but he was used to that and pushed ahead. The seep actually released enough moisture to succor a patch of green. There was brush, a few stunted cottonwoods, some grass for a pack animal, and sometimes some berries. It would be a good place to rest.

It would be a good place to hack a few limbs and turn one of them into a crutch for Bitter Bowler, but the hell with him. He wasn't going to fashion a crutch and walk all the way back to that skunk and then help him hobble to water. Let him put the last bullet into his rank body and donate himself to the vultures.

But the thought troubled him. If he could find the right cottonwood limb, and he could somehow whittle a crutch with his belt knife, he might go back with a crutch and full canteen and help the man who had made his life miserable for years. But maybe not. He didn't know what he would do. Rescuing Bitter was like rescuing a rabid skunk.

The long, hard hike wore him out. He was older and grayer than Bitter Bowler, and he hurt most of the time. The sun had stained him the color of an old saddle, and the dry wind had cut furrows into his face and neck. He wore his hair long, as a sunshade. His hands were scarred and broken, mauled by digging out ore with a pick hammer and pike. He rested on a sun-soaked hot rock now and then, but didn't quit. The ridges loomed higher, and soon after twilight he lost his way, but a rising moon saved him, and he found the right gulch. He could swear he smelled smoke, but maybe it was nothing but the stench of Bitter Bowler's flesh caught in his nostrils. Late in the evening, he rounded a wide bend in the dry gulch, and beheld the flicker of a fire, and smelled wood smoke for sure. He spotted a man sitting there, absorbing the light like some damned fool.

Another greenhorn invader in his country, another intruder to push out.

There was no escaping what he had to do.

"Hello the camp!" he yelled.

Chapter Two

The man at the seep whirled, drew a flashy six-gun, and crouched. Gladstone Brass watched, amused. Anyone with any sense of self-preservation would have ducked into shadow. But the firelight con-tinued to play on the man, who was facing an unknown party out in the dark.

"Hold your horses, fella, I need water and I'm coming in," Gladstone said. He started edging in, and kept jabbering. "Now I'm coming in for a little water, and you can put that shooter away."

"Come here, then," the man said.

Gladstone stepped toward the light, and the man half-heartedly lowered the revolver a notch. It was a shiny nickel-plated one. The younger man looked Gladstone over, seeing a thin, grizzled, gray-bearded, creased desert rat.

"There now, fella, that wasn't so bad, was it?"

"Speak slowly. My English is not yet perfected," the man said.

"Where you from?"

"Alsace-Lorraine," the man said. "The city of Metz."

"Wherever that might be," Gladstone said.

"France, sometimes Germany, who knows?"

Gladstone surveyed the camp. A black mule was tethered in the brush and was chewing it. A clean pack lay on the ground unopened. A kettle on a tripod hung over the fire. But the oddest thing was that this gent had been shaving at the seep. He had a narrow black beard, an elaborate mustache, thick black hair, liquid dark eyes, and sideburns, except that one had been scraped away with a straight-edged razor, and the other had been lathered up and was destined for the same fate.

"Put that cannon away, boy. You make me nervous. As you can see, I'm on foot, I need water, and all I've got is on my bent back."

"Speak slow, sir, so I get the drift."

Gladstone ignored him. He uncapped Bitter's canteen, poked it under the dribble of the seep, and let the alkaline water slither into it. Water was everything in the barrens of Nevada. It was more important than bullets. He drank thirstily, and then refilled the canteen.

"What are you shaving for?" he asked.

The man shrugged, not liking the question.

"You need a beard in the desert, fella. Beards shelter from the sun and wind, keep you cool in heat, and warm in cold. Cut your hair off and you blister your mug. Don't be so dumb."

The young man bristled. "It is not your business."

15

"Everything around here is my business. Where you headed? Why are you here?"

The younger man seemed reluctant. "I am adventuring. I am going across the desert. Maybe to Tonopah. There. You know more about me than I do about you. Is that how it goes in America?"

"What's taking you there?"

The Alsatian sighed. "Take your water and go away . . . *bon soir, ami.*"

"What's in them panniers, fella?"

"Whatever you think, *mon ami.*"

That seemed an odd answer. But it would be greenhorn stuff—flour, blankets, a pickaxe and mining items, the usual junk for those who planned to locate a bonanza in gold or silver in the middle of nowhere.

"Fella, you need to vamoose. Go back where you came from because this here country kills people like you. That stuff in there, it won't help you. You break an ankle somewhere fifty miles from water or a hundred from help, and then what? Go back to France, if that's the place. What did you say your name is?"

The young man drew himself up quietly, a certain iciness in him. "I am Albert Gumz."

"Go ahead and shave. I'll start some flapjacks."

"I have not invited you to stay, my friend."

"I've invited myself," Gladstone said. He was interested in the mule, which was big and strong and probably young, and was making a meal out

16

of desert brush. That mule could solve all his problems. The mule would put Brass back in business. With the mule, he could go back to Bowler after a few days, when he was nothing but bones, collect his mining gear, the cask, and anything left of Bowler's and take off. And let this dreamer make his own fate minus a mule.

The young man plainly didn't know what to do, so he returned to his shaving. He had a small mirror set in the cliff next to the seep, and now was scraping off his other sideburn. The beard followed, and then the black mustache. When the Frenchy was done, he'd shed a dozen years, or so it seemed. He was a neatly combed, dark-haired virgin.

"You'll regret it," Gladstone said. "You'll blister and you'll hate the day you did this."

"It is springtime, is it not? And if it's spring, then I will not burn or freeze."

"You're hoping to find a bonanza. Sonny boy, there ain't any bonanzas. I know a few pockets, a few ledges, where a fella can gouge out a little quartz and trade it for a box of shells or a new pick, but, fella, this is mean country, and it kills everyone that gets cocky, and it's a mysterious country, too. It fools a man. He sees things marching across the sky, like flowing springs, or whole cities, and he heads for them, and they're nothing, just the devil playing tricks on some poor mortal. Now that you got your beard shaved

17

off, there's exactly one thing to do, and that is get out before you croak. Go back to Eureka. This ain't country for a fool like you, and it don't matter what gear you got in there, it'll kill you before you know it."

"It didn't kill you, my friend."

"It was no smarts that kept me alive, boy. It was luck and cunning and caution. And tomorrow my luck could run out."

The Alsatian smiled. "I think I'll stay."

"Don't talk to strangers like me, fella. You don't know what I'm up to. I might steal your mule and let you rot here until you're another pile of bones."

Gladstone found himself staring into the bore of that shining revolver. The young man grinned, baring even white teeth, and returned the weapon to its sheath at his waist.

"Maybe I'm a bank robber," Gumz said. "How do you know what I am? How do I know who you are, my friend?"

That sure amused Gladstone. "You'll figure me out, and I'll figure you out. This country, it bares all secrets. Men come in here with a secret, and first thing they know, they ain't got a secret any more. You can't hide in here. You can't hide who you are or what you do or how you feel or whether you're the Second Coming."

"This is a very good land to hide," Gumz said. "I can see all day and into tomorrow. In my pack is a spyglass. I see farther than a man can ride in a day."

"No one rides around here, fella. There ain't but a little grass. This is foot country. This is burro country. That mule, you better have grain for him because he ain't gonna last long on brush. He'll gaunt up. There's nothing but hot rock and gulches that run off a rare rain, and a little cactus and sagebrush. The rock tears hoofs, and you're a hundred miles from a farrier. So, fella, set your notion aside and vamoose. This is no place to hide, and no place to make your fortune."

"You sound like you're the owner of the state of Nevada, my friend."

"No one owns this country, no one can, including the government. This is no-man's land. It's big. It's bigger than wherever you came from. It's bigger than I can cross in a month, and there's only one person here, and that's me. You know what happens to a man in here? The rock is cruel, and it rips open a man's heart and soul, and leaves him with nothing. But you'll figure all that out if you stick around here for long. Do you know what happens to people who wander in here? They're all piles of white bones. The vultures eat everything. They can spot a meal ten miles away."

"You have your water now, am I correct? You are thinking of leaving? You thinking about stealing my mule, my friend?"

"Pushing me out, Gumz? I already thought about it, and I'd 'a' done it if I wanted to do it."

The foreigner cleaned his straight razor and slid it into a small bag. He seemed formidable, as if there were more to him than Brass had imagined. And he had been swift on the draw, much more familiar with a handgun than Gladstone Brass had realized at first.

The foreigner stowed away his gear and approached Brass.

"We seem to have problems, friend. You've persuaded me that I shouldn't venture into this country alone. On the other hand, here you are, many leagues from help, with only a gallon canteen and a few odds and ends. And you are heading for Eureka, are you not?"

"Where I'm headed ain't your business."

Gumz smiled. "Ah! The desert keeps its secrets, at least for the moment. And if you reach Eureka, you'll still be in a bad way. You need to get a new outfit, am I not right, friend?"

"You calling me friend gets on my nerves, Gumz. You sound like an insurance salesman."

"You read me well. I've been thinking, *mon ami*. You're in a bad way. Something has happened to you, which so far you have declined to tell me. But it leaves you afoot and dangerously dry. As for myself, friend, I wish to pass through this empty land to Tonopah and arrive at Tonopah one week hence. I may want to invest in a mine there. Maybe we could combine forces. You know this country. I have a mule and food. If you will take me there over the next week or ten days, I will pay you for it. You can outfit there, I suppose."

"Somehow, Gumz, that don't make a bit of sense."

"No sense? Please tell me what does make sense, friend?"

"There're roads to Tonopah. But you're cutting south from Eureka, through the emptiest land in the country. Why? And don't friend me."

"It's just a lark, sir."

"See ya," Gladstone said, and lifted his provisions.

"There's some gruel in that kettle. Join me, *ami*."

Gladstone settled his provisions on the dirt, and let the young man dish him some oatmeal. Any food would taste fine, he thought. Then Gumz served himself.

"You interest me," Gumz said. "Here you are. What do you get from it? From this life in this naked rock?"

"Nothing."

"Why are you here?"

"So I don't have to deal with people like you."

"Why not a home? A wife? Children? An income? Friends?"

"I don't want any of it."

"You're a loner, then. But for what?"

21

"It's not what I am wanting, it's what I'm against," Gladstone said, surprised at himself.

"You don't want people around?"

"I drive people as far from me as I can. Even this country is filling up. I couldn't stand one day with you, and I won't even think about a week, heading for Tonopah."

"What would happen if we were thrown together?"

"I'd probably kill you."

The gruel tasted good. He hadn't eaten oatmeal for years. He'd lived on cornmeal or flour and whatever he could scrounge.

"You left someone to die?"

"He shot Tía María . . . my burro. He's got a broken ankle, or twisted, I don't know. So he can die."

"What's his name?"

"Bitter Bowler."

"I heard he's the king of this country."

"He may think so, Gumz, but he won't be king for long."

The younger man stared into the flames. "I will try you again. Take me to Tonopah. Near that town, I will give you my mule and packsaddle, and leave you. I will take with me only a small sack of personal things, and give the rest to you."

"Mules are not prime around here," Gladstone said. "But if you insist, I'll lift it off you."

"Let us go, then, my friend," the Alsatian said. "I move best at night."

Chapter Three

Bitter Bowler wasted no time after Brass left. Those vultures feeding on two carcasses were reminder enough of the hourglass. He drank some more, putting enough water into himself to revive his body. His ankle howled at him. He had to move, had to find a staff or crutch. Had to get to water. There was, at most, a gallon and a half in Brass's wooden cask. It would last him two days.

He reloaded his revolver, angry that he had wasted a shot on the burro instead of killing Gladstone Brass straight off. But it was too late to change that. The contents of Brass's pack lay strewn about, including some britches. He crawled over to the britches and cut them into a strip, which he wound around his ankle, stiffening it. The pain thundered up his leg and into his gut, but it didn't matter.

He needed a staff, a crutch, and there was nothing that would do, except maybe Brass's pickaxe. He crawled over, chasing vultures away, and picked it up. It weighed heavily in his grip, its massive head able to bust open native rock. But the head was loose on the long oaken handle, and maybe it could be removed. Bitter dug at the wedges holding the head in place, worked them free, and gradually worked the head free. He had a staff of oak, but only three feet long. It would have to do. He stood, tried resting his weight on the short staff, found it possible but enormously hard.

He made a sling for the cask, collected whatever he could manage to carry, which wasn't much, and eyed the hazy valley below him that stretched to some infinity. There would not be a mortal in all that rocky world. And no place to sip water. And not an animal to kill, except on occasion a desert hare, or a lizard. The country shimmered in the midday heat. He would head upslope. Behind him lay a towering ridge, mostly covered with scrub juniper or mountain mahogany, and in some high pockets there would be bristle-cone pines, ancient survivors of a harsh world, with wood so hard and resinous that the trees stood for centuries after they had died. Somewhere among them would be a tough stick suitable for a crutch. And then he would walk until he could walk no more.

The vultures flapped away when he moved, but crowded back the moment he left them. That was fine with him. He liked the vultures. They cleaned up the rotten world. He gauged the slope before him, knowing he would have a desperate time of it. The gradient grew steeper as it gained altitude. But if he was to survive, he must climb upward. There might even be water up there; certainly there would be none down in the barren, rocky, weed-choked desolation below. He learned to put his weight on the pickaxe handle, which meant putting his weight on his straightened arm, taking the load in his shoulder. It was a grim business. His only solace was the revolver, which would put him out of his misery. But slowly he ascended. He guessed he needed to limb three thousand feet and cover three miles, a daunting distance for a man with a shattered ankle that howled whenever he accidentally let his weight settle on that leg.

There seemed to be a natural trail up an ancient watercourse that was littered with loose rock, making his progress even more treacherous. But he persevered, resting now and then, and once permitting himself some water.

He was in his forties, younger by far than Gladstone Brass, who was gray-haired and whipcord thin. They had wrestled one another for this country for years. The only thing they had in common was a wish to be left alone. They were at peace only when no other mortal was in sight. But beyond that, they differed in every way. Brass was a miner, always on the prowl for minerals, locating ledges with gold quartz, or strata with dark carbonate silver, or sometimes copper or zinc. Brass would swing his pickaxe, bag the ore, and support himself with it. Bitter Bowler scorned that, and lacked the curiosity that might lead him to a new outcrop. Instead, Bowler feasted on

Brass's ledges, pocketing ore from Brass's pockets, and enjoying Brass's rage at the piracy.

He climbed a while, and rested, and climbed some more, unused to the exertion. Bitter Bowler had devoted his life to doing as little as possible. He had been raised in comfortable circumstances. His father, Clarence Bowler, was the founder of the Kansas City Secretarial College, which annually churned out scores of young ladies skilled with the new typing machines, and excellent at filing, stenography, and all those allied arts. Bitter, then called Junior, was a lackluster student until he reached high school, and then was gripped by darkness and began to fail courses right and left. He failed rhetoric, English, Spenserian script, algebra, history, woodworking, ethical science, and biology. Nothing helped. The admonishments of his mother, in particular, only irritated him, and his father's warning that he would come to no good and have a miserable life only amused him. He finally was booted out of school and home, and set adrift. He clerked in groceries, was a messenger boy, but mostly he was a thief, having mastered the art of pilfering food from grocers and shirts from dry-goods stores. And all the while, loathing everyone around him more and more.

He loathed women most of all, because they reminded him of his mother, but next on the list was Gladstone Brass, who he despised beyond description. And now he was mortified that Brass had saved his life.

He climbed uphill, over boulders, across gulches, with unusual determination. He had never been a determined man. The hand that clutched the axe handle became bruised and then openly bled, but he continued. The slopes changed. Now there were patches of dried grass, juniper, sage, and chill breezes. He reached the lowest of the bristle-cone pines, but they were stunted and had shed little wood. But higher up he could see a field of them, each well apart from its neighbors, and that field was littered with downed wood. So, he would find his crutch. He gloated. Gladstone Brass be damned.

The sight of twisted wood lying everywhere inspired Bitter, and he hobbled his way upward the last hundred yards with renewed energy. Here was a bonanza, and in little time he found the perfect crutch, which even bent at a right angle at shoulder height, and would slide nicely under his armpit and carry his weight. He hobbled about a bit, satisfied, and cast aside the oaken handle.

He could retreat the way he came, and reach Angel Cliff seep about the time his water ran out—or he could follow the cool ridge, and gamble. He gambled. A long way off lay Eureka, and he needed to get there to re-supply and heal, so he set off northward, master of a hazy empire that spread as far as he could see or imagine. And then luck pounced again. For in a rocky dell he discovered a snow-melt pool, not yet blasted away by summer sun. And the still water was fresh, too, not laden with crawlies and bugs. A few birds flapped away as he descended, but soon enough he lowered his cask to the ground and began filling it with cool water, using his mess plate to scoop it up and pour it. The cask would be heavy, but he could endure that so long as he could drink.

Of food he had very little, mostly cornmeal taken from Gladstone, but he had starved before and he could starve now. Water was the thing, and he now had it. He decided to descend in that unfamiliar gulch, and make his way to Angel Cliff, when he spotted something else: a streak of mineralized red rock, with seams of white running through.

That was worth a look, so he worked his way laterally, examined the find, which looked promising, and wished he had some mining tools to sample what he saw. But there was plenty of scree below, including loose pieces of quartz, so he pocketed a few, made careful note of where he was—he'd lost half a dozen finds, and so had everyone else in this confused wilderness—and slowly made his way toward the silent basin ahead. At his next rest break, he pulled out the quartz, found it flecked with native gold, licked it for a closer look, and supposed he might be rich, and soon able to drive that rotter Gladstone Brass clear out of Nevada.

He was delighted with himself. He had turned disaster into triumph. He proceeded carefully down the rock-littered gulch, which had channeled an occasional wash off the peaks, but otherwise showed no sign of life or moisture. By the end of that day he had reached the stupefying emptiness of the basin, and settled in a rock crevice for the night. His leg hurt, and there was no help for it but to rub it gently, and try to push the pain aside. It wasn't just the ache in his ankle, either; his shoulder screamed at him, and he was still fifty or sixty miles from Eureka.

He struggled through the next day, a hot one, planning to rest a couple of days at Angel Cliff. But when he finally dragged in, he discovered a saddle horse, a pack horse, and a man. That was perfect. He had his revolver, and it would buy him a ride on the saddle horse, clear to town. And whatever lay in the pack that had been on the pack horse would help, too. He studied the camp, noting that the two picketed horses were staring at him, and decided that the best course would be to walk in and see how things stood.

"Hey, the camp!" he said.

The man rose slowly and peered into the twilight. Even in the low light Bitter could see the sidearm the man was wearing. But that was nothing to worry about. Only idiots would bring horses into a place like this where even a burro would have trouble making a living.

"Come in slowly," the man said quietly.

"Don't mind if I do," Bitter said. "I'm plumb tired out."

The man watched as Bitter hobbled in, leaning heavily on his makeshift crutch, his back bent under the weight of Gladstone's five-gallon cask.

"You're in trouble," the man said.

"Broke a leg," Bitter said, looking the man over.

"Well, let's hear about it," the man said. "You are?"

But Bitter was not enjoying the moment. The man wore a black vest, and a bright star glinted from that vest.

"Ben Bates," Bitter said.

"You're used up. Here, let me help," the law-man said. He helped Bitter ease the cask to the ground, all the while looking over Bitter's leg and sheathed revolver and knife and the small sack of possibles.

"On my way to Eureka," Bitter said. "But it's getting harder every day."

"Broke the ankle, did you?"

"Tripped in some scree and landed hard, and next I knew, I was in trouble. I shot my burro for the blood, and lived with vultures, and finally found a way to get out."

"I admire it. Most men, they'd be a pile of white

bones by now," the lawman said. "I'm Beef Story, and Eureka's my county."

"You here for something?"

"A wanted man."

"Who you looking for?"

"A bank robber. Young man, black-haired, sideburns, mustache, small tufted beard, maybe an accent. Foreigner probably. You see him?"

"No one like that, sir."

"He worked it out, all right. Smart son-of-a-gun. Waited for Wells, Fargo to deliver to the bank, and then slid in the back door of the bank and lifted the pouch before the tellers knew what happened, and he was out of there. Eight thousand in new greenbacks. We know he came this way. That's all we know."

"And you're on the hunt?"

The sheriff eyed Bitter. "The man's moving south. We've wired Tonopah, and they're waiting. He may be laying low back here. But it's no place for people who don't know what's what."

"Well, ain't that something," Bitter said. "I sure wouldn't mind spending it."

The lawman eyed Bitter. "You're in bad shape. You likely can't get to where you're going. Maybe I can help. I'll leave some rations and you can rest up here. I'll be gone a week, ten days at the most, less if I succeed. When I return, I'll lend you the pack horse. I'm carrying grain going out."

Bitter weighed that. He wasn't used to kindness. It made him itch.

"Maybe you could help me," the lawman said. "Tell me about water holes, Tonopah routes. No one goes anywhere in this country except by water holes."

"I don't share water with anyone," Bitter said. "I know a few, no one else does, and no one else is gonna know where they are."

Beef Story sighed and nodded. He had plainly dealt with old-timers like this one. "I know some," he said. "Enough to make my way. If you're here and wanting help when I return, I'll help you."

"I'll think on it," Bitter said.

Chapter Four

Gladstone Brass tried to hurry the young man along, but the foreigner was intent on sightseeing and wanted to know about every ridge. Gladstone wanted nothing more than to hustle the Alsatian down to Tonopah, the new silver camp, and get out with the mule and outfit.

Gumz was placidly leading his mule along, gawking at every hill and every juniper bush. Brass hated Tonopah. It was too close. Some prospector down there had picked up a rock to throw at his mule, found it was heavy, took a closer look, and found it was rich silver ore. And that brought another invasion. A man could hardly live in peace with swarms of bonanza-hunters flooding in. There were prospectors chipping rock in every gulch for miles around.

"Why are you going down there?" Brass asked.

"To invest. There are great mines, and I wish to buy shares."

"From Eureka?"

"From anywhere. I'm new here. I wish to see the country. I might grubstake . . . that's the word, isn't it? . . . someone. This country is mineralized. There might be fortunes sleeping under our feet."

"You got the bug, like all the rest. You'll go away broke."

"I wish to live a life of ease. I was born despising toil. My friend, shall I spend the rest of my life cleaning chamber pots? Shall I devote my one lifetime to selling handkerchiefs? Shall I hoe rich women's rose gardens? Shall I bake pastries for shoe factory workers? The easiest way to live a life of leisure is to strike it rich in a place like this."

Brass grunted. Where had he heard that before? Mostly knocking around in his own skull. But that was before he knew how well the country suited him.

"Now, *ami*, what is that range to the right?"

"The Park Range. It's full of juniper, but water's scarce. It's plenty high, and there's pools after

33

it rains. But it's a cheat. What looks like water country dries a man out and kills him."

"So where's the next water, friend?"

"Portuguese Peak, off on the east. Just the opposite. All rock, not much green, but there's a good well and it waters a long gulch year round. It's a little off the trail to where you're going, but it's good water and it's the place to stop. We should get there around dusk."

"I was wise to hire you. I never would have known."

"I've been around, fella. I know where to get a drink."

"How did you find it?"

"You get smart, and if you don't, you die fast. You read the rat tracks, the birds, the paw prints. You watch the skies."

"You live alone. Is that your pleasure?"

"I don't want any other way, fella."

"You don't like people?"

"I just get the itch is all. I get the itch talking to you."

"What do you do? Your life is running by."

"I look for mineral. I can spot mineral miles off. The color changes. The rock's brighter. There's reds or blacks or yellows. Sometimes whites, sometimes glint, or shine."

"And what have you found?"

"You think I'd tell you, do you? Listen up, fella. You keep your nose outta my life, or there's big trouble here. I'd ditch you in two seconds, and let you find your own water."

They hiked in silence down a long valley crowded by towering ranges that were mostly naked rock. The ridges looked black, not green, but there would be nothing but resinous sharp-needled brush there. The whole country was deceptive and bound to disappoint. Which suited Brass fine. It kept people out. They found a patch of tan grass, somehow standing long after it perished, and Gumz let the mule feed while Brass scratched where he itched.

"It is not like Metz," the foreigner said. "I like it better than Metz. There are too many people there, and they never know from year to year whether they are to be ruled by France or Germany. Now it is Germany. Tomorrow, who can say, eh? Here a mortal can fashion a life as he sees fit."

"You must have a chunk of money."

"My family, *ami*, is not poor. Maybe I am looking out with a sharp eye, and maybe there will be some companies that will interest us."

"Well, you'll go back there and tell them how backward we are. And that's just how it is. We ain't Europeans."

"I am embarrassed, *ami*. You penetrate my very thoughts."

"It don't make a bit of sense, you going from Eureka clear down to Tonopah."

"Silver, *ami*. It is more attractive than gold.

35

Eureka lies on a silver bonanza. But it is old. So does Tonopah, but it is just an infant."

Brass shut up. It still didn't make sense to him.

They nooned under a gray cliff that briefly hid the sun, and rested for a while. Gumz seemed well supplied with simple fare, including hardtack.

Later that chill day, with the bulk of Portuguese Peak rising sharply on the left, Brass stopped, studied the creases in that vast pile of rock, and chose a path up a sandy gulch. Some birds floated in the distance, black dots that suggested water.

"This is not the way to Tonopah, yes?"

"It's the way to water."

"I have enough for now."

"The next well is thirty-five rocky miles, and uncertain. There is a law here, Gumz. Water when you can."

The Alsatian smiled. "I will take the risk."

"Then you'll take it alone."

"But that peak, it is miles east, and we are going south."

"Do whatever you want."

Brass watched the struggle pass through the Alsatian's face. And then the man shrugged. "I am not in a hurry. Who knows what I'll see? You are my guide."

"I want that mule alive and well when you give it to me."

Brass hated agreements. One party or the other

would always try to weasel out, or change the terms. That was one good reason to live as he did. He didn't have agreements with anyone, and did exactly as he pleased. Here was the Alsatian, weaseling on him one long day out. And there were four more days to go.

The gulch narrowed and sliced deep into the mountainside, and brush began to choke the narrow trail upward. The trail was well used; Brass had climbed it many times, along with all sorts of two- and four-footed creatures. Gumz's mule climbed easily, its muscles rippling in the sunlight.

They topped a crest and entered a tiny plateau, scarcely an acre, and blocking the way was a rough fence of twisted wood, with a gate consisting of a single straight pole. And next to the gate was a crudely painted sign:

Drinks 50¢ man, $1 beasts.

Somebody's joke, maybe. Brass pushed the pole aside and headed toward the tiny pool that caught the dribble from a fissure in the tan cliff, and Gumz with his mule followed.

"Stop right there," the woman said.

Brass found himself facing a gray-haired female, armed with a sawed-off double-barreled shotgun, both bores pointed straight at him and his party. The shotgun never wavered. Beyond, he could see something new—a rock cabin, a fresh garden, and a pen with a mule in it.

"You drink, you pay," she said. "Up front, in my pocket before you take one sip."

"Woman, put that piece down," Brass said.

"After both barrels end up in your hide," she said.

"Madam, we don't have a nickel between us. And if we must return to the desert, we might perish."

"Then croak. It will do you good," she said.

"But, madam, you have no right. This is public land."

"I took it, and it's mine, and any son-of-a-bitch tries to lift it from me, he's wolf bait."

Those twelve-gauge bores made formidable black holes in the scenery. Indeed, they seemed larger than anything else in sight. Larger by far than the holstered popgun that Gumz wore at his waist.

"You gonna pay or leave?"

"You would send us to our doom, madam? The gentle sex would do that to us?"

"I'm a widow, and I have no truck with the ungentle sex, of which my late husband was a prime example, and good riddance, the lazy lout."

"Madam," Gumz said, "we shall toil for our water. Let us help you for an hour, and we shall partake of your water and leave."

"Toil, is it? There's no living male in this country knows a thing about work. You all come here to dodge work. You couldn't put in an honest day's work to save your life. Two dollars of water is two days' work, and by then your bill would go up by four more dollars."

"Your arithmetic is wrong, madam. There are two of us. We could put in a little time, and succor our bodies, and the innocent mule, and be off."

"My arithmetic is this, foreigner. There are sixteen double-aught buckshot in each barrel, thirty-two balls aimed at your lazy hides, and they speak far better than I do."

"We'll cut wood."

"Between the two of you, I wouldn't get a half hour of honest labor. Are we done here?"

Brass eyed the little flat with amazement. Someone had put hundreds of hours into that cabin, and more into the garden and pen. There was even a small haystack. Was she alone?

"You have a man here, madam?" he asked.

"I wouldn't have one on the place."

"You have done an amazing amount of work."

"You wouldn't know the meaning of the word."

"That masonry, the way you laid up the cabin walls, that's something to see."

"I learn by working, which is more than you've ever learned."

"How long have you been here?"

"A while," she said. "And I accomplished more in a few months than you have in a lifetime. I laid up every wall, built every fence, dug and planted that garden."

Brass ignored that. "That is a fine garden. I see squash and potatoes and tomatoes coming along."

"If the grasshoppers don't get it, I'll feed myself with it."

Gumz was growing restless. He was a long way from the trail that would take him to Tonopah, and he was getting itchy, eyeing the surrounding cliffs as if he expected bad news to tumble off the rims.

"Madam, I might have a little cash in my pack. I'll look and see. Two dollars is it? I'm not sure I can make change."

"On the barrelhead. I don't make change. Some gold dust will do if you haven't bills."

Gumz led his mule some distance from Brass, which seemed odd. But then he unbuckled one of the panniers, and pawed around inside, apparently loosening some other bag, and began some sort of digging and examining and rejecting, until at last he settled on some bill or other, and buckled it all up, glancing furtively to his side.

"Can you change a five-dollar bill, madam?"

"What do you think I'm made of . . . gold?"

"Well, I will give you the five dollars, and ask for a receipt for three dollars, which I can apply to my next watering here."

"I don't have a paper and pen, but I'll remember you. I can write a little. Next time you come in, tell me about the five dollars and I'll let you drink up."

That seemed to resolve the matter. She eyed the crisp new fiver and tucked it into her apron, and lowered her cannon. Brass, Gumz, and the mule headed for the little pool, took their fill, and loaded their canteen and cask.

"I didn't catch your name," Brass said to her.

"Agnes," she said. "That will suffice. I have disowned my late husband's name. "Call me Wet Agnes."

"I will call you a beautiful woman with a great heart and a gift of kindness," Brass said.

"Kindness hell," she said. "But I have a soft spot for lazy sons-of-bitches."

Chapter Five

The foreigner seemed to draw into himself more and more as they approached Tonopah, and that suited Gladstone Brass fine. He didn't know anything about Gumz, but Gumz didn't know anything about him, and several days of travel together hadn't changed that.

They traveled from well to well, seeing no one. Then, not far from Tonopah, that changed. Spicer's Spring lay at the end of a *cul-de-sac* and was widely known and reliable. Someone was there. As Brass and Gumz headed up the narrowing gulch, they spotted a man with two mules, who was observing them coming.

Even from a distance, Brass could see that the

man was well equipped. The mules were big, the rigging on them new and smart, and had the whiff of money.

"This man up there, is he an officer of the law?" Gumz asked.

"No, he's dressed too smart for that," Brass said. "He's worse. He's got cash in his britches."

The man was eyeing them carefully, although he didn't appear to be armed. He stank of money. He was wearing one of those flat-brimmed hats with four dents in the crown, a khaki shirt, some of those jodhpurs that flapped out at the thigh, God knows why, and high-top, lace-up boots much favored by sportsmen and big-game hunters. The rigs on his mules were new and clean. A rage boiled through Brass even before meeting the man. This one was a company man, sent out by some mining outfit to locate new claims. They were coming into Nevada like flies arrived at manure, and set off a rage in Brass every time he spotted one.

On closer look, Brass discovered wire-rimmed round spectacles on the man, the sort worn by Teddy Roosevelt, which were all the rage.

"Gentlemen, good afternoon," the man said courteously.

"It's not the weather we're interested in," Brass said. "We're here for water, and you won't slow us down."

"It's good water, sirs. I've just refreshed my

mules and filled my canteens. It's maybe a bit alkaline. I did a quick test, and it's quite potable, and won't affect the bowels."

"You exploring, are you? What's the company?"

"Nevada Minerals, sir. We've started location work in the whole area."

"Well, there ain't any. Prospectors here've been over every ledge for a hundred miles. Waste of your time."

The man smiled. "We have means . . . I'm carrying a small laboratory . . . that may help us find what eluded others."

Gumz listened carefully, an odd caution in him, and then led his mule to the spring, which tumbled into a small pocket and disappeared somewhere under stone.

"I'm Davis Whitecastle, and you, sirs?"

"I'm just no one at all, and this here fellow, he's from somewhere I never heard of," Brass said.

Whitecastle smiled. "I've heard that's how it is in the desert. Very well, then. I'll leave you my card. The thing is, we pay handsomely for leads. Show me some mineral, a ledge, a bit of quartz, and you will be rewarded, believe me, even if the find doesn't pan out. We're open to any and all signs of color, and it needn't be silver or gold. Salts of copper, tin, lead. There are lots of ores that we would find worthwhile and would like to develop. We pay top dollar."

"A man can't hardly get around any more without bumping into people," Brass said.

Gumz was slowly relaxing. At first he had shielded himself behind his mule, but now he was letting the mule head for a drink, and approaching this apostle of corporate power.

"*Monsieur*, I am from France, except that Kaiser Wilhelm has temporarily made it a part of Germany, and I am myself looking for opportunities in the mining field. The name is Gumz, my friend, Albert Gumz, of Gumz et Fils, in Metz, Alsace, and I should like to learn about your company."

"My pleasure, Mister Gumz. Nevada Minerals was recently incorporated in Carson City, and is capitalized at ten thousand shares with a par value of ten dollars. We are always looking for investors interested in exploiting what we believe to be the greatest untouched mineral reserves in the continental United States. Nevada, my good man, is the mineral capital of Nature. Virginia City! Austin! Ely! And now Tonopah. Wherever you turn, there's riches beyond imagining, and the company has evolved the means and technology to develop them."

Brass was getting as itchy as hell, and wanted to get out. Either that or get Whitecastle out. He could hardly stand being even ten feet away from the man with all his educated airs and shiny equipment. The country was going to the dogs.

Next thing Brass knew, Whitecastle was pulling minerals from one of the panniers on his mules, and showing them to Gumz.

"Now this is one we're interested in," Whitecastle was saying. "Copper's the thing. The world is wiring its cities. It's malachite and azurite, from Arizona Territory, and we're looking for that throughout the Southwest. The copper mines at Jerome, Arizona, are among the most lucrative in the world. So, you chaps, you spot these green or blue colors on any ledges around here, be swift to contact me, Box Forty-Four, Tonopah, and we'll be ready to deal on pleasant terms for all parties."

"I don't have all day," Brass snapped. "You coming with me or not?"

Reluctantly Gumz abandoned the geologist and followed Brass out of the gulch. Brass was so upset his stomach was roiled up. What was his world coming to?

They struck corrugated country, dry and monotonous, but with giant ridges making landmarks to measure their progress. The day was hot; Brass sucked on his canteen, itching to unload Gumz and get back to his own cliffs and gulches, as far from Whitecastle and his ilk as he could get.

But it was not to be. They topped a rise and ran smack into another exploration party, this one with half a dozen burros packing small loads and water, and three bearded prospectors.

"Well, har-de-doo," said one. "Dry as dust around here."

Brass eyed them malevolently, but Gumz did all the howdying he could manage.

"Good to meetcha. You know where Spicer's Wells is?" one of them asked.

"It's gyp water, no good," Brass said.

"Just came from there," Gumz said. In no time, he gave the three detailed instructions.

"We've hired on for Golconda Metals," one said. "They grubstaked us."

"You and a hundred others," muttered Brass.

"You got something against them, old-timer?" one asked.

"Yep, people with half-baked ideas get suckers to back them."

It was intended as an insult, but the man just laughed. "Beats sitting at a desk," he said.

The others in the party looked itchy; their beards were bobbing. "See ya," the talkative one said, and away they went, three more scouting every ridge for hundreds of miles for signs of color. If they had any brains, they'd look for color and only color. That was the key. Reds, greens, ambers, whites, sometimes blacks and deep browns. Find colors like that and they would keep assayers happy.

Gumz watched them hasten north.

"What are their chances?" he asked.

"It's hardly been explored around here, and usually by half-wits," Brass said. "But likely they'll die of thirst. I've seen some who find color, start digging, and run out of water, the mineral more to their liking than breathing in and out and seeing the blue sky. Seen some bones around a little color. Once they see a little quartz with a few flecks of gold, they won't eat or drink. Just dig until it's too late to get to water. Serves 'em right, I'd say."

"I hardly know where to go in Tonopah to invest," Gumz said.

"You'll get took. The smoother they talk, the worse their deal. They start talking butter and sugar and blue skies, watch out."

They pushed south again, bending around spurs of ridges, wrestling with heat now. The cool days were about gone, and next would be the summer inferno.

Brass saw several more parties, cutting through the valleys, all of them spreading out from Tonopah, and it graveled him so badly he could hardly stand it. He itched to shoot out their canteens and casks, and give them a taste of a place where water was worth more than twenty-four carat gold.

Late in the day they topped a dry ridge and Tonopah lay before them, a few miles distant, flanked by brooding blue mountains.

"All right," Brass said, suddenly uncertain about what might come next.

"That's it?"

"Hour's walk. You gonna deal with me now?"

Albert Gumz stared at the dusty little burg, small and unimportant and rudely thrown up, a camp rather than a town. Brass watched him closely. If the man was crooked, now was when it would all come out.

"Well, are you gonna make good?"

Brass was watching the hand nearest the revolver, but Gumz didn't dive for it. He seemed undecided about something, looked at the surrounding rocky slopes, and again at the little settlement far off.

"I need to empty my pack," he said. "Not much in it, what's left of the feed."

"I'll take the feed with the mule."

Gumz shrugged.

It was an odd moment, and Brass half expected the man to want to be taken the rest of the way to town, which wasn't in the deal.

Gumz seemed to come to some sort of decision, unbuckled the left pannier, and pulled a gray canvas sack out of it, and then added another duffel bag full of whatever he was carrying, along with a small trench shovel. "A lot to carry," he said.

"Not so much, leaving me the oats."

The mule shifted and sighed under the lighter load.

"You got a bill of sale for me?" Brass said.

"No."

"Write one."

"Just take him. He's yours. I haven't got a pen. Or paper."

"I got what'll do," Brass said. He dug into his pocket, found a couple of stray bullets, and extracted one. He set his bag on the ground and spread it out.

"Write it here," he said, pointing to the pack-saddle on the mule, and handed Gumz the cartridge. It was plain that the foreigner had never written anything with the lead in a bullet.

"What's the date?" he asked.

"Don't know. Just make it May First."

Slowly Gumz scraped the lead tip over the duck cloth, leaving a faint inscription on it.

May 1, 1902, sold to Gladstone Brass, one gray mule, Albert Gramma.

Then he handed the cartridge back, smiled faintly, and handed Brass the lead line to the mule.

"The name don't matter at all," Brass said. "I got about six. Have yourself a fine time in the place. And watch your back. You'll likely have those bags lifted the moment you leave them somewhere."

Gumz shouldered his burdens, nodded, and headed for town. Brass stood stockstill, waiting for some fool move, but it didn't happen. Gumz

49

trudged slowly over the rocky crest of a rise, and vanished from sight. The light was lowering.

But Brass wasn't through. He retreated to the last ridge, reached the top, and watched Gumz diminish along the road to Tonopah. And somewhere far down there, the man turned into a gulch and disappeared. Brass waited patiently, but the man had pulled into some side gully out of sight, and was gone from view. The twilight was making it difficult to see the fellow.

Brass sat down, while the mule tugged restlessly on its line. A long time later, Gumz reappeared, a shadow in the settling evening, and started for Tonopah. The foreigner was too far ahead for Brass to know what he was or wasn't carrying. But if he had to guess at it, he'd guess that the foreigner left something in the side gulch, well hidden from the world. That was a fool's game. Not one man in a hundred could remember where he had hidden something in the vast and anony-mous wastelands of Nevada.

Chapter Six

The lawman studied Bitter Bowler for a moment, and came to a decision.

"You're in a bad way," he said. "I'm going to leave you some rolled oats, good for man or beast, and be on my way. One way or another, I'll be through here in a few days, and, if you need help, you'll have it."

He pulled a pasteboard box of the oats from one of his panniers, and handed it to Bitter, who accepted it with a nod. Bitter wished he had shot the lawman when it would have been easy, and commandeered two fine horses, sacks of food, and all the gear a man might need to survive in this arid landscape of rock. But something had stayed him. Most likely it was because the lawman was well aware of that possibility and was ready for it. The lawman's own revolver was well cared for and ready at the man's belt.

"Well, if you find the bank robber, share the wealth," Bitter said.

Beef Story stared, nodded, and mounted his saddle horse, always facing Bitter. The man was no fool. Bitter watched him and his fine horses retreat, ride around a bend, and disappear. Bitter was alone at Angel Cliff, surrounded by a heavy silence, with a wrecked ankle, a little food, some gyp water dribbling out of a seam, and no way to travel.

He had no way to boil up some gruel, but he had water and oatmeal, and he mixed them together in his mess bowl and let the stuff work. He unwrapped the rags pinning his right ankle, and studied it. The area was swollen and hot, and hurt badly. He could wiggle his toes and move his foot, but at some cost in pain. Lousy luck. He didn't know how long it would take to heal up so he could walk. He didn't know whether the ankle would heal straight and true. He didn't know how to splint the break to make it come together properly. He didn't even know if it was a break at all. Maybe it was just a bad sprain.

He washed the rags clean and wrapped them, wet, around his calf and ankle, and wondered if he could find something to use as a splint to hold his bones together. There was brush back a ways, living on the dripping water. But the thought of cutting something and fitting it to his wound deterred him. That would require effort. So he gently finished wrapping the ankle with what little he had, and it would have to do.

Rotten luck. He could wait here for the sheriff to return and help him go to Eureka, but he didn't really want to ride a few days with a lawman. There might be a few dodgers out on him, and the sheriff would no doubt plow through every one that came to him. He didn't know what in hell to do. He thought of waiting right there for the next traveler, and killing him for his mule and goods, but he didn't like it. Beef Story would know exactly who did it. He thought of sliding out of sight when someone showed up, and snatching the mule—it had to be something he could ride—and getting out of there with the stolen mule and whatever he could snatch. But again, even if the parties at the seep never saw him, Beef Story would know who did it, and keep an eye out for him.

There weren't very many options. But the more he pondered it, the more he realized maybe he could make it all work if the right people drifted in. Some greedy greenhorns looking for a bonanza would do fine. Experienced prospectors or geologists would not bite on his bait.

Meanwhile, he needed to gain some ground. He spent the next days gaining strength, washing his duds, scrubbing himself clean, exercising lightly using his makeshift cane, and eyeing the trail, waiting for the right men to come up the gulch for water. After three days, he was presentable, stronger, and rested. But the oatmeal was boring, and the seep had become his prison, never mind that he was sitting in the middle of a vast wilderness without a fence. Water was king of the arid country. It governed everything he did, and everything done by anyone else traversing this bony spine of the state of Nevada.

The next afternoon a burly, full-bearded old-timer named Hairless Pete—no one had ever heard any other name for him—wandered in, studied Bitter Bowler, and smiled.

"You bought the package," he said. "It'll be a story to tell if you get out."

"I can get a ride out when I want it," Bitter said.

But Hairless Pete just continued to smile, filled up several dented canteens and jugs, and led his sorrowful mottled burro down the trail. Bitter was tempted to empty his revolver at the retreating man, but there was no point in it. He settled back to see who would come next, and a day later he was rewarded.

The pair who showed up that afternoon was exactly what Bitter Bowler was looking for. They found him at once, and approached easily, ready for some convivial talk.

"Well, old boy, looks like you're in a fix," said the older one, the one with melancholy eyes and a frame so skeletal Bitter wondered if the man were ill.

"It's a fix, all right," Bowler said. "Ankle's so swollen up, I'm thinking it's busted. But who can say? Looks like you gents got here just in time."

"You out of chow?"

"Burro's dead. Limped here on a stick, everything on my back."

"Yes-siree, you had bad luck," the skinny one said. "Nick of time, that's when we came. This here is empty country. We haven't seen a live one in days."

Bitter looked the pair over. These two were not greenhorns. Each led a mule with a heavy pack, including some picks and shovels and some mineral testing kits. The tall, skinny one was a weathered chestnut; the stocky one was pale, the sort who spent a lot of time deep underground.

"I'm Billy Bob," Bitter said. "Looks like you could help me a little. That is, if it don't weigh too much on you. Where'd you say you come from?"

"'Round and about," said Skinny. "Lew here, he's been a mucker in Jerome and Bisbee, and also up to Virginia City. He got tired of seeing dark. Me, I'm a top man, moving ore cars to the chutes, pushing the tailings cars to the dumps. Mostly in Jerome. We know ores, silver and copper, and we've seen some quartz, too, and when the Tonopah strike cut loose, we did, too. I'm Deacon, by the way."

"I guess you got an eye for ore," Bitter said.

"We thought we did, but so far we're finding we got a lot to learn. Hunting down color just isn't the same deal as working in a mine."

"I got a little oatmeal here, boys," Bitter said. "Sit down, and we'll fill up."

"Billy Bob, I hate to eat the last of your chow, you in a fix like this."

"Well, gents, oatmeal isn't much, but if we don't eat it, those mules sure will, and I think we got first choice."

"I never did spend time with food," skinny Deacon said. "It don't do nothing but keep me going. So sure, dish up that gruel."

This was going just as Bitter hoped. The two visitors watered their mules, filled their cask and canteens, staked the mules in the brush, where they could gnaw on twigs and leaves, and then settled beside Bitter's austere camp.

"This water, it's a little alkali, ain't it?" Lew asked.

"Gyp water, but mild enough. You won't get the trots from it. Some water around here, it's gonna cramp your bowels," Bitter said. "The more you live here, the easier it gets. I can drink stuff that would cramp up a greenhorn for a week, and hardly notice."

"You been out here long?"

"I've been here since I was knee high, sonny. I've roamed this country from one end to the other. I've emptied out a dozen ledges and pockets, and know of a dozen more."

"You know of more ledges?" Deacon asked, spooning up the gruel.

"Hell, yes. You never know about them. You find some color, and it tests good, and you've got a little ore going, and you start to dig it, and sometimes it's nothing but a little pocket, and in a few weeks it's gone, and you've got a lot of quartz to haul to the nearest town and try to peddle for some grub. That's how it mostly is. There's color all over, but only a few outcrops lead back into the rock, a good seam that shows no sign of pinching out. I know of a mess of them, but it takes work, and sweat, and if you've got something, you've got to keep it secret or go file on it, one way or the other, and if you file, everyone's swarming in and likely someone'll steal your ledge from you."

"That's how it is around Tonopah," Deacon

said. "The country around there's got prospectors every hundred feet, it seems, and we decided to move ourselves out of there where there's not so many buzzing horseflies."

"Smart, boy," said Bitter. "If I wasn't laid up, I'd steer you to one or two of those ledges. You could dig in and see if you got a pocket you'd clean out in a week, or something worth looking into."

"You'd do that?"

"Well, I figure you fellows won't leave me here to croak, and I'd be owing you something. A lot. For keeping me alive. I was thinking just this morning, time's running out. I'm fifty, seventy miles from help, and I've bought the farm."

"Yeah, we'd help you," Lew said. "But how you gonna move?"

"Ride a mule. Walk with my stick. See that stick? That's bristle-cone pine, and it's bent like a handy crutch. I walked maybe twenty miles on it, getting here. Hardest thing I ever did."

"I never saw wood like it," Deacon said.

"Well, anyway, finish off the gruel. I'm in your hands, gents."

"Billy Bob, you need to get somewhere? Any chance you could just ride along with us? Like maybe to one of those ledges you know about?"

"I could manage that for certain. Couple days ago, I thought I was done for, but I got to water, and now I'm halfway getting ahead."

Dusk was settling over the cliff and seep, and

the three men sprawled on the hard gravel below it. The darkness of the cold world lowered upon them and had a way of drawing them together. Sometimes animals showed up at the seep and took their fill silently. But in the rocky wastes, they were rare, and this evening there was none.

"You fellas, you seem to be up and up," Bitter said. "That means a little to me. I've got a few ledges, and seems to me I could pay you back for taking care of me while my leg heals up. I could be sharing some good gold quartz, that's one ledge, and two silver carbonate ledges I know about. Pretty much like the stuff outcropped around Tonopah, if you didn't mind hauling me around with you for a few weeks, until these bones get back together."

The two stared at him.

"That's an offer?" Deacon asked.

"I guess it is," Bitter said. "A third each . . . we divide whatever we get three ways. I can't do much digging, not with this ankle, but you can, and you can dig it out and get it assayed, and drill in to see if it's a mine or a pocket, and see if the ore gets better the farther in you go. Some are like that, you know. The surface ore's been weathered, but the ore is rich once you get past what sun and air and wind's done to it."

"That sounds mighty fine," Lew said. "Billy Bob, the three of us might just hit a real pay streak. Turns out we came along at the right time, and turns out you had something to trade."

"I'm game," Bitter said. "We can work out the details as we go along. Nothing ever works out the way you plan. It costs a lot of time and effort to bag up the ore and get it to a market, and you never know what someone's gonna pay. You walk in there, thinking you've got a mess of silver, and they offer you a few dimes, and you walk out of there thinking there's no justice in the world."

"Well, you'll teach us the ins and outs," Deacon said.

"I'm planning on it," Bitter said.

Chapter Seven

Lew hoisted Bitter Bowler onto the bony back of a mule, and not even a saddle blanket eased the pain. Bitter's ankle hurt all the more, dangling off the mule. But it beat leaning on a stick with every step.

He steered the prospectors east, down a grade into a vast flat stained gray with sagebrush. The two carried improvised backpacks, now that Bowler had commandeered the mule, but they weren't complaining. A seasoned desert rat was leading them to ore, and that was a fountain of happiness in them.

The dawn was chill and silent. The vast flat oppressed all conversation, but Bowler knew that when they hit the foothills of the towering range to the east, they would turn gabby, and spill their life secrets. There were *playas*, sinks, in the basin, where the rare rains collected and evaporated, having no place to go.

The mule wasn't happy with its human load, but Lew tugged it along and didn't let it entertain any notions about pitching Bitter into the dry and dusty dirt. All in all, Bitter was content. He would try to find that ledge he had spotted when he had fled to the seep, leaving behind dead burros and a heap of tools and gear. He didn't know whether he could find that ledge; the sameness of the ridges and peaks could confuse a man trying to remember a place, or locate a treasure. The desert was full of lost mines and hidden bonanzas, stuff hidden by deluded prospectors who were sure they could locate the hiding place easily. It just wasn't like that. The land was so vast it swallowed direction; it swallowed miles and yards and feet. It multiplied gulches, magnified ridges, and offered different vistas as the sun moved, shadowing some, revealing others, obscuring still others.

One way to retrace was to look for old prints in the floor of the desert, undisturbed in the perpetual dry, but he saw nothing, and his mind could focus only on his leg, which hurt with every step the mule took. But he'd find that ledge; he wasn't some tyro piercing the lonely wastes the first time. He'd survived, prospered, made his way for years, and a map of the whole area was burned into his brain.

By midday they were all weary, and Deacon halted the party in a sagebrush field. They set down their packs, sucked warm canteen water, ate a piece of hardtack to hold off hunger, and let the mules gnaw at the few blades of brown grass tucked under the umbrella of the sagebrush.

"I marvel that you know where you're going, old-timer," Deacon said.

"We're heading straight toward a new ledge I spotted," Bitter said, privately less sure than his confident utterance.

Late that boring day, they pierced foothills, gentle grades with gulches dividing them, and just as Bitter knew they would, they began to talk.

"That was about the loneliest piece of real estate I ever hiked," Lew said.

"I did it leaning on a stick," Bitter said. "We're not far, now, four or five hours."

"You know which of these gulches it's in?" Deacon asked.

"Down to one or two," Bitter said. Three or four or five, anyway. "And much higher. We'll climb two or three thousand feet to find it."

"Any water?"

"None as has been located, but no one's hardly been here," Bitter said.

"I'd hate to locate mineral and it's so dry we

can't dig it out," Lew said. "I promised my woman I'd be back in six months, rich or poor. That's what I gave myself. She didn't mind. She worried herself sick every day I went into the pits and didn't see sunlight for ten hours. She said she'd get by doing laundry, and she and the girl would make their way while I give this a whirl."

"You'll likely do fine," Bitter said. "Real fine."

"He's got a woman and I've got a Latin grammar I'm studying to keep me warm," Deacon said. "I got it packed, and also Caesar's *Commentaries*, got that, too, and I'm getting halfway good at Latin, but I don't know what it's good for. Maybe I'll teach someday, or start a school if we hit some pay dirt."

Bitter thought he'd keep the books; the pages could be ripped out and put to good use. He steered them confidently toward the looming range to the east, which now caught the late afternoon sun and began to glow the color of gold. It was as if the whole craggy range, which was strung north and south for as far as the eye could see, were twenty-four carats, with a few diamonds sprinkled up high. The upper reaches had a faint dark skin, juniper mostly.

He congratulated himself. He'd find the ledge and put the two to work, hard work, gouging out the quartz. He had an ankle to mend, so he didn't need to worry about getting up a sweat. If it was a pocket, they'd empty it; if it was better, he'd have the start of a mine to file on once he took over. But there was no point in taking over until he got his leg working again. What could be a better deal? All he had to do was sit around and wait, while they hammered rock.

They reached some steep grades, and Bitter turned crosswise, sending them north along the massive front. He was looking for boot prints, his own, left there a few days earlier. Or at least one left-footed print, and some dimples where his stick had pushed into gritty sand. But nothing caught his eyes.

"Best go the other way, then," he said, so Deacon, Lew, and the mules retraced their steps and headed south along the façade. Bitter didn't see much there, either, and finally decided to head up toward the scree where he and Brass had fought it out. From there, he could find his way down to the brownish ledge. He was sure it was brown quartz. It glinted in the gloom of the cañon. Quartz came in all sorts of tints, and a good geologist or prospector knew what the colors meant. But that had always eluded Bitter.

He finally settled on a likely gulch that rose steeply beside a smooth ridge.

"We'll take this ridge up," he said. "There's a flat up there, with some stuff on it, tools we can collect."

"That's welcome," Deacon said. "All I do is bust tools."

They climbed through late light, penetrating thick juniper groves, and as the light faded, Bitter knew he was lost. At least for the moment. It wasn't something to admit, though.

"We got a little way to go tomorrow, and meanwhile we got a ton of sticks around here for a hot supper," he said.

"Hard to find, eh?" Lew said.

"I know exactly where I am. What do you think I am, anyway?"

Deacon was looking amused. Bitter's hand got itchy for the cold comfort of a revolver, but he let the moment pass. He'd use it soon enough, after he got some hard work out of this pair of dudes.

"Head for that gully. We'll settle in there, but back from the wash. Hide the fire. Never build a fire on an open mountainside for anyone to see," Bitter said.

"I'm glad we've got you to steer us," Lew said.

The miners were soon gathering juniper wood, which lay everywhere, and fixing to boil some beans with a little side pork, which surprised Bitter.

"I've been around the bend a few times," he said. "Hid for a week from some Paiutes looking for me. I found a fault in some rock just big enough to get into, and they passed right by. Woke up once with a lion crouched three feet away, thinking I'd be supper. I jumped straight at him, got my paws around his neck, but he sprang loose and away. I've found so much mineral I can't remember it all. Got some mines stole from me, but I kept on going. Now I've busted an ankle, and keep on going. That's how I live. Keep on, don't quit. And pretty quick now, we'll all be rolling in cash."

"Mabel would sure like that, Billy Bob," Lew said. "And my girl, Daisy, she'd get a new outfit the day I got back to Jerome. I've been trapped once three thousand feet down, and it took two days for them to dig us out, and we were half dead for lack of air, but they reached us, and that air coming in, it sure was sweeter than anything ever came my way. Six of us, and we all got out, but Schultz was sick for a month and never went below grass again. Once you've seen that, you hate the pits, hate them, and want to get away. That's why I'm here, earning nothing, instead of down there, earning two-fifty a day and paying union dues. Here I am, topside, stars above me, clean air, nothing going to fall on my head or trap me. I'm thinking I could get used to this in a hurry, even if we don't hit a big pocket."

"Lots could go wrong, fella." Bitter said. "And if it can, it will."

A wall of cold rolled down from the high country, and that made the fire welcome. Bitter pulled a saddle blanket over him, undid his belt and revolver and tucked them close to his head, and fell into an easy sleep. He awoke before dawn, sensing some movement in camp, and discerned the shadow of one of the miners above him, but then the man moved away. Bitter clutched his revolver and waited, but nothing more happened, as a faint glow built along the high ridges to the east.

The altitude brought mean cold; it had probably frozen hard just above. But the three boiled up some java, waited for more light, grained and watered the mules, and finally set out, this time to the north, but two hours' travel did not yield the ledge, or even the scree area where Bitter and Gladstone had fought it out.

"Tell us square, Billy Bob, have you lost it?" Deacon asked.

"I've lost things worse than this. We'll keep looking," Bitter said.

They eyed him skeptically. This country was so big it ate memories.

"I'll find it, dammit," Bitter added.

He took a moment to orient himself. Across the vast flat below, the reef where the seep bled gyp water into the gravel was visible. He could beeline that way, but that didn't help him here.

"It probably was nothing," he said. They stared. He had bragged that he knew of half a dozen good pockets or ledges, and now they were plainly thinking about his brag. "We'll climb, and then work south," he said.

They gained a few hundred feet of altitude, and then he had them turn. They were close to the scree fields. In an hour he hit the place where he and Brass had fought. The vultures were gone; nothing but bones remained of the burros. There wasn't much left except the tools. Rats and raptors had made off with the rest.

Silently Deacon and Lew collected a hammer, a pickaxe, a shovel, and a pry bar.

"All right, now I know," Bitter said. He led them steadily downslope, chose the right gulch, and halted them a while later at the brown quartz ledge.

They eyed it silently. It ran maybe fifty feet, a couple feet wide at one point, but pinching out at both ends. It was little more than a pocket, and the quartz wasn't exactly glinting with gold.

They helped him off the mule. The gulch was narrow, maybe twenty yards across at that point, and choked with brush. Some of the ledge ran well above the height of a man, and they would need to make a ladder to work it.

"All right, collect some samples and bring them to me," he said. "Up there, middle, down there."

The miners headed out with their picks, ready to pry loose a fortune if one lay in that pocket.

It all was working out fine, Bitter thought. *Let them dig it out. I'll enjoy it.*

They returned, each with half a dozen samples. He eyed them, licked them, noted the visible gold flecks, the wire gold threading one, and smiled. In a month he'd be on his feet, the ledge cleaned out of the surface quartz, and he would be the sole owner of the gold mine.

Chapter Eight

Gladstone Brass was happy with his new mule. It was tractable, unlike some. It had a gentle eye. It was healthy, had good hoofs, and was more or less obedient, which was rare. Mules were twice as smart as horses, which is why they had a will of their own. Brass now possessed the new pack frame with panniers, too, and miscellaneous mess and camping gear in it, even a folding camp stove and a bedroll. Albert Gumz had abandoned most of it, seemed glad to get rid of it upon entering Tonopah. Brass calculated the time it would take to recover his pickaxe, shovel, and hammers, strewn in the scree of the mountain where he had met Bitter Bowler. Brass didn't have his gear together, not yet, but he would soon, and the mule might well be a better beast than his dead burro. He needed a water cask, his mining gear, and food.

The Alsatian puzzled him. The man was secretive, hiding something, changing his identity, but seemed pleasant enough. Well, that was that. Brass retreated from the Tonopah area as fast as his legs could carry him. It was swarming with crazy fortune-seekers and amateur mineral hunters who didn't deserve to be called prospectors. Brass's privacy was being threatened as it never had been for decades, and if he had his druthers, he'd drive all these invaders out of the whole country.

His passage through to where he'd left Bitter Bowler was mostly from well to well, so it took him again to Wet Agnes's new redoubt in the Portuguese Peak area. He should be able to water there; the Alsatian had a credit of $3, and Gladstone could use it up on water and any food she had for sale. There were hoofprints in the dusty trail running up the gulch, which suggested that Wet Agnes was doing some trade.

Sure enough, she was ready. When he reached the pole gate, she leveled her shotgun.

"You got one and a half?" she asked.

"Agnes, you're looking cuter than ever," he said.

She pulled the trigger. The explosion rocked her back. A load of buckshot whistled over his head.

"The other barrel's aimed at your pants," she said.

Gladstone instinctively covered his crotch. "Agnes, you're not only beautiful, you're the most intelligent woman I've ever met."

The second charge echoed through the gulch, and scraped up dirt a little to Gladstone's left. The smell of burned powder laced Gladstone's nostrils.

She calmly broke the scatter-gun, ejected the spent shells, dug into an apron pocket, reloaded, and aimed the piece squarely at his heart.

"My heart is broken that you don't love me," he said. "You're the queen of Nevada."

"Fifty cents for men, dollar for beasts," she said, "or git."

"We have a three-dollar credit. That was what you said. I witnessed it."

"It's his credit. I dealt with him, not you."

"I now own his mule. The credit comes with the outfit."

"Beat it," she said. "The next charge turns you into a soprano."

"This mule is thirsty. We can't make it to the next well," he said.

"Then croak."

"Could I perform some labor in exchange?"

"Prospectors never heard of honest toil."

"I see you have a woodpile in need of chopping. I'll split wood for an hour, and then water myself and my mule."

"What did you say your name is?"

"Gladstone Brass, wandering troubadour, emperor of no-man's land."

"Go chop wood," she said. She swung the pole wide, and he and his fancy new mule entered. The mule headed straight for the little pool, nosed the water, and refused to drink it. Brass eyed the beast, wondering whether he'd come out ahead after all.

A man was sitting on a bench in front of the rock-walled cabin. He startled Brass. They stared.

Brass discovered a man in sturdy trail clothing, with a black vest and a star pinned to it.

"Good afternoon, Mister Brass," the lawman said.

This took some getting used to. Gladstone squinted, discovered a six-gun at the man's belt, saw some dust-caked boots, noticed a straw hat, and under it a pair of assessing eyes that were surveying him piecemeal—his scraggly beard, his grimy shirt, his soiled britches, his broken and bruised hands, victims of a thousand hammer blows, his missing teeth, and his alarming blue eyes.

"You'll do," the sheriff said. "I'm looking for a bank robber, and you're not him."

"This is Sheriff Beef Story, from up north. He forced himself on me. I don't know your name, but it's not worth knowing," she said.

"But I just introduced myself, madam."

"Well, I forgot it." She turned to the lawman. "This one came here a few days ago with the criminal."

Gladstone Brass found himself sucking air. "I came with a man who hired me to take him through this dry country safely. He paid me with this noble mule. I was well paid."

"Was he dark-haired, foreign, with a narrow beard, mustache, and long sideburns?"

"Those vanished at the first well he could reach," Gladstone said.

The lawman chewed on that a little. "I should

71

have guessed," he said. "And what was your arrangement?"

"Tonopah, sir. If I'd take him safely there, I'd have the mule. Since I was in dire straits, having lost my burro, I accepted. It was an ordeal, leading that criminal about for days."

"How did you lose your burro?"

"Bitter Bowler shot it, sir, even as I was trying to help him. It was an act of pure perversity. He had broken an ankle and the vultures were circling his burro."

"And did Bowler shoot his own burro?" Story asked.

"You would have to ask Bitter that question," Gladstone replied. "It is beyond fathoming. I am a prospector, a sole proprietor, choosing a solitary life by choice, and living out my days in honor. I cannot say the same for Bitter Bowler. The criminal had no cash, and so I wanted to turn him down, because nothing is free in the world, especially my services."

"How did the criminal pay you, Agnes?" the lawman asked.

"He led this mule away from both of us, this mule right here, dug into one of the bags, and pulled out a five-dollar silver certificate."

That awakened the sheriff's interest. "I will take it," he said. "Silver notes. That happens to be what the foreigner stole from the bank. Fives, tens, twenties, new Treasury notes."

"You won't have it," Wet Agnes said.

"I will have it. The law requires it. It's stolen property."

"You won't. Not unless you plan to violate my honor and modesty and virtue."

Wet Agnes won the argument.

"What was this foreigner's name, or didn't he say?" Story asked Brass.

"Well, Sheriff, he started out as Albert Gumz, and then deviated a little along the way."

"And what nationality?"

"He didn't know."

Beef Story frowned. "Let's try that again."

"Alsace-Lorraine, which changes color like a chameleon. French, maybe."

"And what were his plans?"

"Tonopah. He was looking to invest in a mine. That's what he said, anyway."

Story smiled. It was the first hint of happiness to cross his face. "We've got him," he said. "Now then, this Bitter Bowler. A broken ankle? A rough customer with shifty eyes?"

"That's him. He's probably vulture meat now. He couldn't walk twenty steps."

"Afraid not, sir. He was at a seep a few days ago, and I gave him some chow."

"You didn't do the world a favor, sir."

The lawman stared. "A man in trouble . . . ?"

"Deserves it," Gladstone said. "You're interfering with justice." He figured he wasn't getting along with the lawman. Maybe the lawman should try to get along with him.

A faint smile built along Story's mouth. "You want to file some complaints?"

"I solve my own problems. All I want is my privacy. The world's going to hell, all these people coming in here thinking they own this place."

"Who does own it, Mister Brass?"

Gladstone declined to answer that one. "Time for me to move out."

"You owe me some chopped wood," Wet Agnes said. There was menace in her voice.

"You're so beautiful I dream of chopping a whole cord of it for you," Brass said.

"Why didn't I shoot you in the crotch, you goat?"

Brass turned to the lawman. "Was there ever a more sublime and beautiful woman?"

"Oh, yah, there's Chicago Pauline, who runs the house of joy in Eureka. Now there's a double-barreled shotgun of a lady for you."

"She's not half as sturdy and handsome as Agnes, here," Gladstone said. "I wouldn't trade Agnes for ten Paulines."

"Well, it'll cost you fifty cents a man and a dollar a beast," she said.

"Where's your axe, Agnes?" he asked. "I'll whack away at your woodpile."

"You've never done a day's work in your life, so don't start now," she said.

"Time for me to get out," Beef Story said. "He's in Tonopah? Albert Gumz?"

"Yes. And he headed up a gulch north of town and hid something."

"You watched him?"

"I have my ways. If you don't find the bank-notes, I will. Better bust your butt."

"What gulch? Can you describe it?"

"They all look alike. They're dry and rocky and there's not a landmark in sight."

Gladstone was losing his patience. He collected his mule, tipped his ancient plug hat toward his hostess, and started out. He had his water, the mule had his drink, and soon he would return to his solitary ways. The whole trouble with civilization was the people.

They watched him go. He was soon deep in the brushy gulch, and back in the empty world he favored. The whole country was filling up. But that would pass. That's what he liked about this place. It drove everyone out sooner or later. They couldn't take it.

At the foot of Portuguese Peak he swung north. He had just enough water for a quick visit to the slope where Bitter Bowler ruined his leg in the scree. Gladstone wanted to see with his own eyes what had happened. If Bowler was on the loose, he would be something to watch out for. And he wanted to see what was left of his kit. There should be his packsaddle and maybe some gear, especially his pickaxe, shovel, and hammers. Given the amount of water he was carrying, he would need to hurry.

The trip took him across empty gray flats, with nothing but half-parched sagebrush covering the gravel. The mule nipped at on occasional brown blade of grass tucked under a plant. That pleased Gladstone. This mule could make a living in the middle of Nevada. But it was too bad it was a mule, not a jenny. It would be hard to converse with a mule. He had never had trouble talking to the various lady burros—"burras" he called them—over the years. He confessed his darkest secrets to his girlfriend burros. They would always listen attentively, as true companions should. But talking to a mule would be a different matter. Gents rarely confided in other gents. This was going to take some getting used to.

He began debating what to name this mule that tagged along so cheerfully. Maybe Sylvester. That was a fine, noble name. The mule did seem like a Sylvester, but maybe there was something better. It would take concentration. There weren't a lot of names that came to mind. This mule would not be any Tom, Dick, or Harry. Not even a Joe, Jack, or Paul. And certainly not a Mark or Luke or Matthew or John, given Gladstone's icy scorn of the New Testament. No, none of those. This mule would be named for something admirable.

Maybe the mule's name should not be humanized at all. Maybe the mule should be named Lightning, or Thunder, or Sunrise, or Dust Devil. Or maybe Thorn or Scorpion. The choices were making Gladstone irritable.

There were no vultures up in the scree ahead.

Chapter Nine

Nothing. Some whitened burro bones, but none of his tools. Everything in Gladstone Brass's kit had been taken, even his packsaddle. And nothing of Bitter Bowler's stuff lay around, either. Somehow the old desert rat had gotten back here and collected, busted ankle and all.

That meant he had someone with him and a ride. Now Gladstone would have to track down the thief and get his tools back. He couldn't make a living without a pickaxe and shovel and a hammer or two. And he would need his mortar and pestle and scale and mercury and a few chemicals he used to see what was in the ore. All gone, but not for long. He would find out where Bowler was hiding and there'd be a reckoning.

Gladstone Brass studied the subalpine slope, looking for clues. A hoofprint, a glove, anything that might lead him to Bowler. This place was too remote and dry to be found by some wayfarer wandering the Nevada backcountry. And the scree was hard to traverse. No one would work through the sharp-edged rubble that had tumbled down from the high country.

Bowler must have fashioned a crutch from something and dragged himself out. He must have headed for the nearest water, which was the seep at Angel Cliff. So that was where Gladstone would go, and keep a sharp eye out, too. It was daunting. The land was so vast that it could hide armies, and Gladstone could well spend the rest of his life in the area without ever seeing Bitter Bowler again. But Bowler was a desert rat, and would hang around, because that's all he knew.

Sylvester followed gladly. Mules knew when they were headed for a drink. Gladstone had not yet lived with Sylvester long enough to call him a friend, but things were looking up.

"You like gyp water? You'll get some and be glad of it," Gladstone said.

The mule slobbered.

"I can cook and eat you if I have to," Gladstone said.

The mule butted him.

"So that's how it is, you bonehead?"

The mule slid his yellow teeth around Gladstone's arm and hung on.

"You happy with Sylvester? You want to be called Thunder or Dimwit or Dolce Vita?"

Sylvester clamped his grimy teeth down.

"All right, you're Sylvester."

The mule stole his hat and began chewing on the brim. Gladstone retrieved it with a violent tug. Maybe he'd trade off the mule.

He hoped to discover Bitter Bowler at Chalk Spring, and edged into the area with elaborate caution, but in fact there was no one in sight. He turned Sylvester loose in the brush below the seep, and dug into his kit for food. There wasn't much. A few oats. He couldn't live on nothing; game was scarce in the big dry, and found only on the ridge tops, unless there had been a lot of rain. He would have liked simply to camp at the seep; sooner or later Bitter Bowler would show up and meet his fate. But that wasn't possible unless Gladstone ate Sylvester.

He considered his options and surrendered to the one he hated most. He would go to Eureka to re-supply. He had no cash or ore. He needed food and tools. He needed a pickaxe, shovel, maul, chisels, and some prospecting chemicals, like a bottle of mercury.

If there was one place he loathed, it was Eureka. There was a saloon there, The Miner's Rest, where he would drink up the entire wad of cash he would get for Sylvester. Eureka, the remotest burg in Nevada, existed as a depot to supply the surrounding mines. It had plenty of hardware, canned food, bulk grains, mule and ox shoes, and the worst evil Gladstone Brass had ever heard of—barbed wire. He had come across barbed wire around mines, and made a point of severing it not once, but ferociously every few yards. Let the owners learn a lesson.

There were women in Eureka, but Gladstone was suspicious of them. They would take everything in his pants. An assayer operated there, and usually bought up whatever ore the prospectors brought in. Eureka existed to satiate male needs, hardware, booze, and women. It was one of the most isolated places in the country, sixty or seventy miles from anywhere else. That gave it a certain brio; it was a haven for outlaws, desert rats, serial killers, con men, wife killers, and anyone who planned to be invisible for a while.

It was two hard days north, about fifty miles, with only an intermittent seep for water, and nothing to sustain Sylvester. But in this country there sometimes weren't choices. Gladstone sliced as much brush as he could stuff onto Sylvester's back, filled his canteen with the gyp water, and took off. The days were getting hot, and night travel kept man and beast from perishing from thirst. The south-facing rocky slopes radiated heat, but the valleys cooled quickly. Gladstone set a comfortable pace. He knew the country. He knew the stars. He knew the ridges. He knew the way to Eureka. What he hadn't counted on was a boot giving out, and when he felt the flap of a loose sole, he cussed the stars and the ridges and especially Bitter Bowler. If his gear hadn't been stolen, he would have spare moccasins. Well, let it flap. He had a knife; he could turn a bad boot, or several other items, into a sandal if he had to.

By dawn he reached the intermittent seep, and found it dry. He scraped around with a stick, but found no wet below it, either. He poured a quart from his own supply into his hat and let Sylvester slurp it up; he limited himself to a few sips. Sylvester gnawed on the brush for a while, and then Gladstone was off. The eastern heaven was bluing, except for a rosy line along the ridge that hid the rising sun. He had come a great distance with only a few rests, but by evening he should be walking into that nefarious town.

The boot quit him midmorning. He cut the sole loose, cleaned out some holes, and strung some thong through them, fashioning a crude sandal that would slow down the insults of the desert. He pushed on through midday heat, not yet an inferno, but that would come in a few weeks. By evening he raised Eureka. He could see it ahead, at the base of a long slope, its few lamps wavering in the dry air.

He descended a long grade even as his thirst ascended, and what he longed for was higher proof than water. The more he thought about The Miner's Rest, the more an itch rose in him, an itch that required immediate scratching. He passed the red brick opera house, and the ornate Jackson House, a hotel for swells unlike himself, and continued through darkness toward the light puddled on the dirt street in front of the saloon.

He hated civilization, and would make quick work of a drink or two, and then figure out what needed doing.

"Sylvester, I lack a plugged nickel," he said. "Maybe I'll sell you."

Sylvester was paying no attention to Gladstone, but a lot of attention to the various horses tied to hitch rails along the way.

By then Gladstone knew what to do. There was a box of .44 caliber shells in his outfit that might buy a few drinks. That was a popular caliber. He would have no trouble. He eyed the soft glow of a red lantern off a side street, and resolutely ignored it. There were more important things to achieve, such as bliss in The Miner's Rest.

Eureka had been a lively silver- and lead-mining town in its heyday, but now the miners were fewer and the lode had been dug up and carried away. The town was quieter, which suited Gladstone perfectly. He reached the lamp-lit saloon, and dug into the fancy new pannier to extract the box of cartridges that had belonged to Gumz. Maybe he could trade two for a drink, which would give him twenty-five drinks, which would be about right.

"Sylvester, you're on your own," he said. "I will be looking for you at dawn."

The mule nipped at Gladstone and trotted away. Sylvester was familiar with Eureka, and knew where to find a water trough, and maybe where to cop some feed from a hapless horse or two. Mules weren't dumb.

Gladstone was getting twitchy, so he hastened through the double doors into the dimly-lit pleasure palace. The proprietor wasn't wasting any lamp oil on a week night. At least Gladstone thought it was a week night. He barely remembered what year it was. This was no rough plank bar; the backbar was mahogany as was the long bar itself. All of it hauled by ox team some vast distance from a railroad. A half dozen yawning males sipped quietly, none talking to anyone.

The barkeep wore an apron, a sleeve garter, and oiled hair parted exactly in the middle. "What'll it be, old-timer?"

"You run a tab, do you? I won't have some coin until I do some dealing tomorrow."

"No tab, pal, but we take dust. I'll pour for a pinch."

Gladstone sighed. He eyed the bottle of Old Foggy bourbon with a yearning that could never be requited. He could almost feel the initial sharp jolt, and then the smoothing out as it sailed past his tonsils and into the pit. "I have been a year and ten days out in the desert, my friend. Have pity on an old desert rat, momentarily waiting for his luck to change."

"We want your patronage, fella, and if you'll clean the spittoons and sweep up after we close and wipe down the chairs and tables, and fill the lamps with oil, and trim the wicks, I'll pour you a double."

That was an admonition to descend the staircase into perdition. Gladstone groaned, licked his sun-blasted lips, and dug into a pocket.

"Here is your damned profit," he said, laying the box of cartridges on the mahogany.

The barkeep lifted the cover and saw fifty shells in marching order.

"A drink for two shells," Gladstone said.

"That would be a piss-poor deal, old-timer. What did you say your name is?"

"There's no need for you to know. There's no warrant on me, and no reward listed in a dodger."

"I'll give you one for the box."

"That's no deal, absolutely no deal, I never will, and you can just forget I ever walked through your door." He started to pick up his box of shells, sighed, and nodded. "Make it a triple and it's yours."

The barkeep did even better. He plucked up a bottle of some infernal amber spirits called Cherry Orchard from some rotten distiller, and poured a generous dose into a tall glass, and handed it to the desert rat.

Gladstone snapped it up, sucked some of the awful stuff into his mouth, gasped, resisted the urge to spit the whole load into the barkeep's mug, and swallowed it. The stuff went down like lava. He sipped another, and another, until he began to buzz. He always knew he was about to have a fine time when his old body started buzzing. Some might call it a tremble, but it was a buzz, like the buzz of a wasp, while the rotgut went to work and improved his outlook. He watched the barkeep examine a few shells, stuff them back, and move the prize to the backbar, out of reach of greedy customers.

Oh my, the world began to improve rapidly. After a half hour of determined sipping, he got social and wanted to hello all those fine fellows, but most had fled into the quiet night. After another half hour, Gladstone wanted to pick a fight with any son-of-a-bitch who might be standing at the rail, giving offense. Since he could see none, he picked on the barkeep.

"You crook, you cheated me out of a box of shells," he said.

The bartender lifted a club he had resting under the bar, and that was about the last thing that Brass remembered.

Chapter Ten

Gladstone Brass was aware that his head hurt before he knew where he was. He awakened to a throb just above his forehead, where his wiry gray hair sprouted. He lifted a calloused hand and discovered a small goose egg there, which had risen mysteriously. Last evening he did not have that goose egg. Now he did. That was odd, and painful.

His arms worked, his toes wiggled, his fingers flexed. His stomach roiled, and that was the clue he needed. His stomach was behaving exactly as it always did following a feverish reunion with John Barleycorn, his lord and master. He sighed. He felt a wave of nausea crawl like a swarm of beetles over him, and resisted the temptation to sit up and deposit what was left in his stomach all over the floor.

Which raised the odd question: what floor? Whose floor? He was not on it, but on a bench above the floor, with a wall on one side and a drop off to planks on the other. Some soiled daylight made its way through a grimy window some distance away, signaling a new day, or maybe not so new. He was a vast distance from the time he carried a Waltham pocket watch. He hadn't paid attention to time for three decades. Time was immaterial where he lived through each day. In the backcountry, time as measured by the tick of clocks didn't exist.

An outhouse was summoning him. If not that, then any convenient spittoon. If not that, then the stoop of any rear door. He eyed the place dizzily. It was a saloon, and he had spent some while residing at its rear, upon this bench, apparently placed there by someone, for he had no recollection of settling there by his own powers of muscle and navigation.

There was not a soul present. It presented opportunity. For there, on top of the mahogany backbar, were scores of bottles, all of them containing ardent spirits. For the moment, he was rich; he could sample as he chose. Except that his stomach was vetoing the proposition, and nothing could override that veto. He sat up, feeling nausea wash through him. He stood, rubbed his goose egg, and decided a brass spittoon would answer his most urgent need. When that chore was accomplished, he looked for water, and found a white enameled pail of it behind the bar. A dipper gave him drink. The water was not making him any more comfortable, but it improved his spirits.

This was The Miner's Rest. He had arrived in Eureka. He had traded a box of cartridges for something, most likely a generous dose of rotgut, which had evoked cheer that had evoked the goose egg that now cracked his brain.

He could use some java. Whether he could down breakfast was another matter. He needed to trade something for some cash, and proceed. He peered into the sunlit street, seeing little traffic. No doubt Sylvester would be waiting patiently out there. The double doors of the saloon were locked, and after rattling them a time or two, he retreated to the rear door, which opened on an alley, and let himself into the bright day, which hurt his eyes. He rounded the shiplap-sheathed structure but did not discover Sylvester. That proved worrisome. He peered up and down, seeing a buggy as it passed the emporium, and a slab-sided wagon drawn by a dray. But no mule. He thought Sylvester might be at the opera house, since he liked singing, or at the offices of the *Sentinel*, since he liked asinine opinion. But Sylvester, with the pack frame, was nowhere in sight. His entire wealth on earth had disappeared.

That meant Sylvester was engaging in truancy, and would require tracking down. He was used to tracking in the middle of the trackless basin and range country, but not in towns. Tracking an errant beast in Eureka meant patrolling the streets and cross streets, and studying yards and alleys. Eureka was a considerable burg, having once contained ten thousand souls, though that number had diminished along with the lead and silver ore that brought them.

There was a problem in all this: Gladstone Brass was not fit to walk. Part of that was age and hard living, a life in the wilds on sprung knees, lame hips, and a bad back. Still, he heaved himself up the main drag, looking for the wayward mule, and then back again, thinking the beast had deserted town and returned to the nearest well.

That's when he spotted the sign in gilded letters over the door of a brick structure. EUREKA COUNTY SHERIFF, it said. He would report the stolen mule. Or at any rate, maybe the officers of the law might have some idea about the missing beast. He did not go lightly into the offices of any lawman, having counted them his natural enemies from childhood onward. He was not a criminal, though he often thought he should count himself one, since there was hardly any law on the books that he didn't oppose. But now an emergency propelled him into the office. His entire fortune, other than the rank clothes he wore, had absconded.

Within the interior, brightly lit by morning sun, he beheld a young, muscular man with fair hair, bold blue eyes, and an unblinking stare that took in the desert rat, head to toe.

"You are missing a mule, perhaps?" the man asked.

"You are a daisy," Brass replied. "Tell me where."

"I will do that in due course. Describe the mule, if you will."

"Sylvester is gray, a gentleman, a good listener, and devoted to his pack frame, which contained all my worldly goods."

"And you are?"

"Gladstone, and just don't call me Glad."

"Surname?"

"Oh, I'm just another prospector, making my lonely way in the silver state."

"Brass," the lawman said. "I'm Deputy Olson, Ole, currently the law in Eureka county, while the sheriff reels in a bandit."

"Ah, indeed, I gave your man the information he needed. The robber is named Albert Gumz, and he was *en route* to Tonopah, carrying a mysterious load in a gray sack, which, I understand, was a Wells, Fargo money bag. I performed the service of telling the sheriff where the gent was headed, and how he had altered his appearance."

Deputy Olson weighed that briefly. "Your mule was wandering the streets, robbing feedbags, poking his snout into the livery barn yard, nipping hay. His owner was unknown, and my efforts to find an owner went unanswered. So I did what was needful, Gladstone, and led him to the Bjorn Brothers Livery Barn, on Sixth, where he now resides with a full belly and ample fresh water and numerous four-footed companions. You can redeem him any time."

"You did not have my permission to pen him. He was a free mule, living freely, according to the wishes of his owner, sir. Now you can come with me and bail him out, at no charge to me."

"He was also a public nuisance, Gladstone, and I preferred this remedy to any other, such as bringing a charge against you. You can thank me for it."

The goose egg on Gladstone's skull inspired meekness, so he accepted what the deputy had done, and nodded his gratitude.

"They want a dollar a day to feed, grain, and board a beast," Olson said.

"But I don't have it."

"Then you'll have to work for it," Olson replied. "There's no lack of employment here if you're willing to wash dishes or saw wood or weed gardens."

The thought of working for a living sent a chill through Brass. He hadn't worked for three decades; neither had anyone in the back country. The reason he was living out his life in the lonely mountains and basins was to avoid toil. He might have been an accountant, or a blacksmith, or a store clerk, or a gravedigger, but such a thing rankled his very soul. Work was bad. Working for someone was worse. Working for a man who peered over your shoulder, who criticized and carped, who made you redo what was done, who paid peanuts and was never satisfied, that was he hell that Gladstone Brass had fled long before. He would rather croak than work. He had been fired from every job he'd held. He'd started a fight with every employer who'd hired him. He wasn't meant to work. He was different. He was unique. Work was for the unwashed, not for him. But there were no other options. Thus whatever lay before him in Eureka, Nevada, was dark and desolating.

Maybe he could steal his mule and get out in the dead of night. Yes, he'd find a way to slip away. Which meant casing Bjorn Brothers and studying the landscape, so to speak. He sighed, remembered to thank the deputy, and headed into brain-blasting sunlight.

The livery barn proved to be on the north side of Eureka, surrounded by mining supply warehouses. A whitewashed wood fence encased a pen, and a squat whitewashed barn sat astride the only egress to the interior. Gladstone shuffled clear around the outfit, looking for a rear exit, and finding none. The Bjorns knew how to keep their bread buttered, but the arrangement would be disastrous in the event of a fire. Brass headed for the barn, rehearsing what he intended to say once he determined that Sylvester was within.

He was met at once by a black-bearded man with bold blue eyes.

"You own the mule," the man said. "That's one dollar. Feed, water, board, one day."

"I've come for my kit," Brass said. "I want to fetch it, and I'll pay you later."

"That packsaddle stays here. I'm holding it for a surety against board."

"But you have the mule itself for that. I want my property."

Bjorn smiled, and flexed his muscles. He was built like a brick funeral parlor, with enormous arms, thick hands with fingers the size of bear claws, a bull neck that supported a massive head that sprouted jet hair in all directions.

"Call me Gladstone."

"I'm Black Bjorn," the liveryman said. "You don't seem glad."

"I had a run of bad luck, lost my burro, but won Sylvester in there. I need to hock things to pay you."

Black Bjorn grinned. He lacked two or three incisors. "Tough luck, eh? Maybe I get to keep the mule, you can't pay the feed. A few days, I'll own the mule."

"OK, I'll take my pack frame and hock it."

"Hey, fella, you ain't hocking nothing in there. You bring me some greenbacks, you get your mule back. Good mule, eh? I sold him to a foreigner a while ago, now I got him back. You rob a bank or something?"

Gladstone saw how it would go, and didn't reply. The liveryman grinned, his eyes greedy.

"Hey, desert rat, now you gotta work. You work for a dollar a day, give me the money, and maybe you get the mule back someday."

"I'll shovel your manure for the afternoon, clean up your stalls, and I'll take the mule and my kit this eve."

Bjorn laughed. "You're a card, desert rat. Naw, you gotta work. Real work. Hard work. You gotta earn money faster than I charge for boarding the mule. Only you don't work. No desert rat works. That's why all of you go out there, so you can wander around, make a living by chipping a little ore now and then. Tough luck, Gladstone."

Brass felt the rage rise in him, felt his goose egg hurt, felt his stomach roil up again, saw that this massive brute barred him from Sylvester, saw that the civilized world that he had escaped long before was as cruel now as when he had fled it as a young man.

"I'll be back with some cash soon as I have a grubstake," he said.

Bjorn just grinned.

Let the man think what he wanted to. Tonight there would be a mule heist.

Gladstone walked off with only the clothes on his back, uncertain what to do. If he could steal an axe or saw, he might be able to cut through the rear fence at night. But if the Bjorns bedded in their livery, as many liverymen did, he'd be discovered.

He needed a grubstake. Someone who would outfit him for half of any mineral discovery he came up with. But those were hard to find, especially when he didn't even have a few dimes to pay for a meal, or buy him a drink.

He sure didn't know what to do.

Chapter Eleven

Beef Story raised Tonopah late in the day, which suited him. If the old prospector's account was right, that was about the time of day the bank robber, probably Albert Gumz, cut Gladstone Brass loose, gave him the mule, and walked toward town with a heavy sack over his shoulder. At about the same time Brass had watched him turn abruptly, head into a gulch, and vanish from sight.

Story eyed the raw camp below him at the foot of Mount Oddie, only a couple of years old. This was high desert country, with naked rock mountains and naked basins. Not much of it was level land. Story debated what to do, and the decision leaped at him. He'd have a quick look at the gulches before heading in. Gumz had no shovel, probably not even a trowel, and if the sack was lying about, it would be tucked under some sagebrush, or something like it.

His horses were restless, sensing water ahead, but Story was in no hurry. He had worked southward through a land of vast silences, a land where he scarcely saw a bird. The nights had been harsh and cold, the days fiercely hot. The wells, as they were called, didn't fail him. He had gotten a good education in the ways one traveled through the most hostile country a man could penetrate. The shoes on his horses had actually been ground down by the shards of rock, and he might have to have them shoed again if he could find a farrier in town. He studied the layout, seeing what probably was the Mizpah Mine, the biggest silver producer around, but there were head frames and shafts everywhere, some vertical, some horizontal boring into slopes. He wiped away sweat, swallowed some tepid water from his canteen, and chose a likely gulch that cut right half a mile ahead, and a mile or so out of town.

There was movement in town, distant traffic, but even here, not far away, he worked through a world of utter isolation, without another mortal in sight. He reached the gulch in a few minutes, found it rising sharply into the wall of a high naked mountain, and turned up it. The sagebrush thinned and quit about three hundred yards ahead; the Wells, Fargo sack would be closer, if Story had calculated right. Gumz was a clever crook, but not familiar with the country, and the bag would not be far off the bottom of the gulch.

Story rode through the sagebrush, studying each clump for a telltale mass of solid gray tucked under it. It was slow work, and sometimes the sagebrush deceived him. But he was a patient man, and certain that this was the best first step to take. He could catch up with Gumz later, after he had the missing $8,000 in silver certificates on his pack horse. Another quarter mile took him to a sharp, shallow bend in which he could see naked rock on either side of the sagebrush-choked gully.

He spotted the bag easily. Its gray color was oddly brighter than the muted hues surrounding it. He eyed the surrounding slopes, looking for observers, found none, dismounted, tugged the bag out from under a massive clump of silvery green sage, and carried it to his pack horse. He unbuckled it, discovered the missing bills, nearly all of them in Treasury packets. A packet of fives had been broken, which confirmed the old prospector's account. Beef Story fanned a few other packets of bills, satisfying himself that they had not been tampered with, and then collected the loose fives and counted them. There were thirty-nine. Wet Agnes had the fortieth. So the fellow had not taken any into town. That was wise of him. Story buckled the satchel, slipped it into one of the panniers on his pack horse, and headed down the gulch.

It had been easy. Catching Gumz would probably be easy, too. This little journey had worked out well, so far.

This wasn't his county, so that complicated things. He could report to the Nye County sheriff, or at least the local constables, as a courtesy. They would need to make the arrest because his own powers halted at the county line somewhere behind him. Then again, he could simply nab his quarry in a way that avoided attention, and be out of Tonopah with no one the wiser. He chose that course. The best protocol was the quietest.

He rode into town just when the day was settling into long, low light. The place was being thrown up fast, most of it with imported lumber, brought some vast distance. A narrow-gauge rail line was pushing toward Tonopah; the mines needed coal for their boilers, and the rail company saw the opportunity. But for now, the town was fed and supplied by giant freight wagons, which Story saw at every hand, some of them with twenty-mule teams. He rode quietly through the town, wondering what the safest way to store the banknotes might be. A hotel room would do it, as long as he preferred not to make his presence known.

The rutted gravelly street was not crowded, but the saloons would be at the end of a hard day. He might have trouble finding a room in a boomtown, and that would present some serious problems. He tried two hotels and a boardinghouse, but they were jammed, most of the rooms double-rented on twelve-hour shifts. He headed for the livery barn, asked if he could sleep in the loft, and got turned down.

"Got more drifters up there than there are bedbugs," the wizened proprietor said.

All right. He'd camp out of town. He had employed his bedroll for four days, and he could do it again. He wondered why he bothered. He had recovered the cash. His quarry was a shadowy young man with a slight accent, dark-haired, name unknown, like a hundred others in Tonopah. He was weighing all this when he spotted a Wells, Fargo northbound coach in front of a solidly built, mortared rock Wells, Fargo office.

He headed for the office, found a skinny clerk, and posed a question.

"How do I send a bundle to Eureka?"

The dark-haired man was quick with a reply. "Coach to Carson City, rail to Reno, rail to Elko, coach to Eureka, sir."

"There's no direct route?"

The youth shook his head.

Story didn't like it. Too many hands shuffling $8,000 around. "What about eastbound?"

"There is no eastbound, sir. Tonopah's supplied by California."

That decided it. Beef Story was going to deliver the goods to the bank at Eureka by himself, and deliver the robber, one Albert Gumz, to his own jail in his own town, without any help from anyone. He nodded, abandoned Wells, Fargo, and began to lay plans. He could camp out of town, or in town. Or at a mine. He mounted his saddle horse, collected his pack horse, and headed up the sharp slope toward the Mizpah, the largest of the silver mines in the boomtown. Along the way he pinned his star back on. This would be an official call.

He tied his horses to a rail; they both were blowing after an arduous climb to the mine. There he found an unmarked office, or so it seemed, still lit by lamps. Not a spare nickel was wasted on the building. Within, two-by-fours stood exposed. There was little more within than a battered desk and chair, and a battered safe, plus a mustached man in a sleeve garter.

The gent eyed Story, the badge, and bag. "I'm Paternoster, the shifter," he said. He saw the confusion in Story's face. "Second shift boss."

"Beef Story, Eureka County. I need a safe place to store some cash."

"I don't think . . ."

"Bank robbery. It was hidden but I got it. I need to stow it while I go after the robber. He's here somewhere."

"How long?"

"Don't know. I'll want a receipt. There's eight thousand, minus five dollars."

Paternoster eyed the small safe, normally used for payroll. "My shift ends at two. I can't let it stay over."

The deal was done. Paternoster drafted a receipt, quickly counted the packets of bills, and dialed the safe open. The bag barely fit.

"I'll come for it by midnight. With or without my man," Story said.

"What's his name?"

"Albert Gumz. That's the most likely name. There are others."

The shift boss studied his personnel ledgers. "Not here."

"He's not the type to dirty his hands."

"A swell, then. The town's swells collect at the Tonopah Club on Main, and also the Nye House. Stock traders, salesmen, bank clerks go to the Nye House. On Mizpah Road."

"That's a help. Thanks," Story said. "Mind if I leave my horses here?"

"Put them in the hay pen." He saw that Story was once again uncertain. "Mules pull the ore cars. We keep feed for them above ground."

"I'll pay you," Story said.

"Midnight," Paternoster said.

Story stowed the horses, which would enjoy a bonanza of hay, and headed downslope into Tonopah, not at all sure he could snare his man. He had no photograph and only a vague description. How many young men would there be who were black-haired, of medium height and build, clean-shaven now, and spoke with only the slightest accent?

Story spotted the Tonopah Club at once. It was well built of stone, large, long, and seemed well patronized. Lamplight spilled onto Main Street. He cased the place, discovering a rear door and double outhouse behind in an alley. The outhouse stank. He tried the club's rear door. It opened at once, but he did not go in. He circled around to the solid front door and entered.

The place was not crowded. A dozen young men lounged about, their pale faces lit by a wagon-wheel chandelier. A consumptive tinhorn with fevered eyes operated a faro game and a fat cardsharp commanded a green baize poker table at the rear. Neither had a game going. A well-built and well-stocked bar ran down one side, patronized by gents in checkered suits and elaborate sideburns.

The barkeep, bald and wearing a clean apron, waited to serve Story.

"Looking for a fellow named Gumz, Albert Gumz, about some mining shares," Story said. "I'm ready to deal."

"Don't think I know him. What'll it be, sir?"

"Old Orchard and ditch. Would you mind asking?"

The barkeep didn't hesitate. "There's a gent here wants to see Albert Gumz. Is Albert Gumz here?" He raised his voice. "Albert Gumz around?"

The yawning collection of males stared. None responded. Half of them could have been Gumz. Story shrugged, sipped the cheap booze, coughed, studied faces, and decided that this wasn't the place. He left the glass half full and retreated into a night that was rapidly getting chill.

That left Nye House. He patrolled the street, not finding it, and tried a side street that led toward the mines. Mizpah Road. There was an imposing two-story building with a small, unlit marquee with the name Story wanted. Once again he circled the structure. This one had indoor plumbing. There was a rear door, dark and locked.

Story headed for the front door, black enamel with small diamond windows. He entered upon a wave of warmth, and discovered a dimly lit and handsome interior, an imported walnut bar and backbar, and various males in suits and cravats. Not a place for working stiffs, Story thought. He studied the layout. This one had gambling, too, but in a separate rear room, well-lit and mostly empty, though some patrons were collected around a silent poker table.

"What'll it be?" the barkeep asked.

"Bourbon and ditch," Story said, "and a favor. I'm looking for a gent I've never met. Albert Gumz. You know him?"

The barkeep pointed. At the far end of the bar sat a smooth young man with black hair, medium build, well shaved, and alone.

"That him?"

"Investor, he says. He's looking for properties. You want me to let him know?"

"No, I'll get over there in a minute."

Pure luck.

Gumz was sipping red wine. That was rare enough. He wore a black suit with a vest and cravat, and the suit coat could accommodate a lethal weapon. Story studied the coat, looking for the bulge of a weapon, and realized he couldn't say for sure what was in there.

Story carried his drink over to Gumz and set it on the bar.

"You're Albert Gumz, sir?"

"Ah, indeed, *mon ami*, and whom do I have the pleasure of meeting?"

"Beef Story, sheriff of Eureka County, sir. Would you care to walk in front of me toward the door? Leave your drink on the bar, sir. You won't be needing it."

Chapter Twelve

Idiots. That's what Lew and Deacon were. Lazy louts. Bitter Bowler fumed. He sat helplessly, waiting for the two virgins, as he called them, to start gouging out some quartz. The stuff was threaded with visible gold. Wires of gold ran through the brownish quartz. It would fetch plenty in Eureka.

But Lew and Deacon did everything but dig. They sat and smoked pipes. They studied the ledge, measuring the exposed quartz. They plucked up quartz that had weathered away from the ledge, examining it for gold. But they didn't work. They didn't smash and pry and lever the quartz away from its matrix, a heavy layer of gray rock that overlay the ledge.

Lazy, that's what. These two were just another pair of lazy bums looking for a fortune in Nevada's no-man's land. That was bad enough. Worse, Bitter was dependent on them. It was their mule that carried him, their food and water that sustained him. He was weeks away from the time he could walk. Weeks away from the time he could dig out ore, carry it to an assayer, sell it, buy food, buy tools, buy clothing, buy dynamite and caps and fuse.

Three men and two mules consumed feed and water fast, but Lew and Deacon seemed unaware of the mounting danger of running out. They had hardly dug ten pounds of quartz, not enough to fill a small sack, not rich enough to buy what was needed in Eureka to support three men.

At the nooning, Bitter tried once again. "We're out of water, almost. And a day's walk from the seep. We're low on food. The mules are starved. They can't live on sagebrush. And you two don't work."

Deacon replied: "That ore, it don't pull out easily. I'm thinking, you've got a lot more ledges, and maybe there's some easier ore. We're all partners now, so you should be showing us what you've got, and we'll take you around on the mule and feed you up."

Bitter suppressed an impulse to start yelling at them. He didn't have any ledges, but he knew of half a dozen worked-out pockets, mostly left behind by Gladstone Brass. They wouldn't yield much. Maybe a few pieces of ore Brass had overlooked.

"This is the best I've got," he said. "You dig, and we'll do fine."

"Nah, this here ore takes dynamite."

"And where will you get that if you won't dig enough out of here to buy it?"

"Your other ledges, old man. You're stuck, ain'tcha? Bad leg. Show us what you got, or we'll leave you here for the rats."

There it was. Some partners. They wanted to know where his other mines were before they killed him. But he wanted to get to water while he could. Get him to a seep and he would have a chance. Leave him here and he'd be dead soon enough. He'd connected with two bums.

He swallowed his rage. "All right. We'll water at the seep, and then I'll take you to another pocket, and you'll see what I've got."

They smiled at him and began packing up. The whole episode had yielded a few pounds of quartz with maybe enough gold to buy some cornmeal or some grain for the mules. Lew had an anticipatory look about him; he was plainly itching to get a gander of every ledge and pocket that Bitter knew about. That was it. These gents weren't planning on doing a lick of work. They would sell what they knew of without working their muscles at all. Their game was to stake every pocket of ore they could learn about and then sell them off. Why prospect, why work, when an old-timer could do all that for you?

Except that Bitter still had the revolver strapped to his waist.

"You got a few more, eh?" Lew said.

"I got four, five, six even, some of them I've hardly dug into. Could be bonanza ore, only I got no partners to help me get at it," Bitter said. "I got so much ore hid away it'd take me two lifetimes to get it all assayed." *Life insurance,* Bitter thought. *Put their greed to work.* "Yep, and not all gold, either. I've got a couple of silver lodes, and some more that are mixed. Got a silver-lead one, and a couple of copper showing up, bright blue and green, azurite and all that. And that's not the end of her, either. I think I've got a tungsten deposit, but I need assay chemicals to test it out, and I can't afford 'em. Hope to buy the stuff in town when we get there."

They sure were listening as they stuffed gear into their mule packs.

"And there's some so high up they're in snow most of the time. It's where no one goes, because they freeze up. But I got some samples off a cliff there, way up, that I haven't had assayed yet, but it's likely platinum mixed with a few more I'm not sure of. So you bet, I got so much stuff located that I can't hardly figure what to do next. Maybe I'll show it to you, maybe not. Depends."

Lew continued to break camp, but Deacon walked downslope a little, turned and looked upward, and began to gather some loose rock, scree that had tumbled a long way from its source. First he collected a few dozen tan rocks, and then he built a small cairn. These two were no fools.

They knew a thing or two about losing a ledge, losing a pocket of ore in country like this. Not that that rinky-dink cairn would help them much. An old hand knew the land, knew it better than he knew his own hands, knew it because he roamed it, climbed it, descended it, heard the wind whistle through it, saw the distant ridges from the one he stood on, knew what the distant patches of green or gray meant. But these two didn't have that instinct. So they would build little cairns, that might wash away during the first storm to cross these wastes.

That suited Bitter fine. He was getting to know this pair, and he already knew enough to know they'd never be partners, never do a three-way deal in which they worked equally and shared the wealth equally, and each had a say in how they would dig and sell.

He managed to climb onto the mule they had lent him, and Lew handed him the sack with the few pounds of quartz in it. The rest would go on the overburdened second mule. The animals were hungry, but there would be brush to gnaw on at the seep.

All the rest of that day they descended to the anonymous sage-choked floor, and then climbed a well-used trail and reached the seep at dusk. They watered the mules and turned them loose, and settled down to an evening of telling tales while the beans boiled.

Bitter Bowler had a few more in mind, and he considered each one of them a form of life insurance.

"Few days ago, I was sitting right here along with the sheriff of Eureka County," Bowler began. "I don't have much truck with lawmen, but he had business, so I listened in. Seems someone robbed the bank up there, and then came into this country. Lotta money, greenbacks being delivered by Wells, Fargo. The man slipped into the bank right after the delivery, took the bag, walked out, and rode this way. The sheriff . . . Story's his name . . . was wondering if I'd seen him, but I hadn't. He offered to help me get to town and left me some cornmeal to cook into hotcakes, and that's what I've been living on until you two helped me out."

"How much got took?" Lew said.

"He didn't rightly say, but it was a mess of silver certificates, Treasury notes based on silver metal. You see anyone handing out brand-new greenbacks of that sort, you have got your eyes on the man that took the bag. He's around here, hiding out, so keep an eye open for him."

"What's he look like?"

"Dark-haired, medium, with some sort of foreign accent."

"Lot of those around," said Deacon. "I imagine if we find him around here, he's outta luck."

"You can't rightly spend those brand new

bills, serial numbers all marked," Bowler said.

"Well, you can if you're smart about it, a few here, a few there, and crumpled up some."

"The sheriff didn't do anything for your ankle?" Deacon wondered.

"He said he'd be back soon, and he'd put me on his spare horse . . . he was taking horses into here, with grain . . . and take me out."

"He likely to come through here?"

"Said he would, right about now."

Lew and Deacon glanced at each other. "I got nothing against me," Lew said.

But somehow that changed the evening. They doled out the beans before they were well done, and Bowler chomped down on some tough mouthfuls of tough food. It didn't matter; it was food, and he was getting past a busted ankle. But after they had cleaned up the beans, Deacon made a proposal.

"Nice night to hike, not too hot. What say you take us to the other ledge you were telling us about?"

"Pretty nice right here, fire and all," Bowler said.

"Well, we're going."

"Stay here . . . maybe that bank robber'll float in. This country, it's all about wells. You go from one well to another most of the time. He's around here somewhere, and he's got a lot of money."

Lew and Deacon were listening, and unhappy.

"Maybe the sheriff, he'll ride in. He's got some food. He went out with plenty, a loaded pack horse. We're down to a few beans, and we're two, three days from Eureka. He gave me some feed, and he'll do it again. How you gonna feed three men and two mules with what you got there, less than a pound of beans? If you ask me, we should head for Eureka and sell that quartz to an assayer and get us a grubstake even if it isn't much."

"Old-timer, you worry too much about eats," Deacon said. "We run out of food, we kill a mule, and eat just fine for a week. Nothing like good mule to fill the belly, right, Lew?"

"I grew up on mule," Lew said. "I'm half mule, I ate so much of it."

That alarmed Bitter Bowler more than anything else that eve. It was as if they were announcing their plan to kill him, and enjoying doing it. He thought he should dig for his revolver and shoot both of them, except that they were waiting for something like that, and the odds weren't exactly in his favor.

He wanted to get out. These two were fixing to kill him. He couldn't walk so he needed a mule to carry him. They were eying him with the same wariness he was showing them. They were armed; he was armed. It sure was a puzzle. He didn't know what to do but keep on talking. He had sunk into cold fear, and scarcely knew how he would sleep that night. In fact, he wouldn't. He'd lie on the dirt, his revolver in hand.

"Well, you shoot the mule that carries me, you'll lose out on the biggest one of all, the one I'm going to file on and then live on Easy Street. You know Butte, Montana? It started as a silver town, but the farther down they got, the more they found copper. More copper than anyone had ever seen before. Silver, gold, that was a by-product. Copper everywhere, just when they started needing it for electricity. My big one's the reverse. There's copper on top, all sorts of green and blue ore, stuff no one cares about. But I found an outcrop lower down that's pure silver, and I spent some time working out the geology . . . you fellers know your geology, don't you? . . . and it all pointed in one direction. The copper was on top, and the richest silver was under there a thousand feet or so, which means a swayback old prospector like me, I can't do it. It'll take capital and men and machines and shafts and head frames and all the rest to make it all work out. But I got it figured, and I tested it by looking in the right places for float. Know what float is, Deacon? It's stuff that gets weathered out of a high rock formation and gets pushed down, sometimes miles away, by sun and wind and gully washers and all that. I found this copper float where it should be, but I also found the silver float right where it should be. I been sitting on that deal, wanting to raise enough to mine it myself, and not let some money men steal it from me. So far, I haven't figured how. But it's there, east of here, and I'll file on it when the time is ripe."

"So where is it?" Deacon asked, plainly skeptical.

"You think I'd say?" Bowler replied. "It's east of here. It's all mine. I won't take you there."

"I think you will, old-timer," said Deacon.

"That one lives with me and dies with me, boy. I showed you a good pocket. That's pay enough for helping me. The rest, they stay with me."

"You'll howl soon enough," Deacon said. "You'll howl and we'll be listening."

Chapter Thirteen

Skunked. Gladstone Brass knew what he would have to do, and hated it. He had spent three decades not asking anything from anyone, but now he needed a favor, and the one person who could do that was Deputy Ole Olson. Nothing could be more humiliating. Getting help from a lawman was like getting help from a rattler.

He climbed two steps and entered, but the deputy did not seem to be around. He peered into the jail at the rear, but no one was in there. But then the deputy appeared, surveyed Brass, and offered a hand.

"Somehow I knew you'd be back," he said.

Gladstone Brass spilled his story while the deputy listened. Then, at last, there was silence, while Olson frowned.

"All I want is my pack. Then I can hock something, pay him off, and get some grub."

"That's Bjorn for you," Olson said. "Come with me."

Gladstone, a little gimpy, could not keep up with Olson, who sailed ahead with all the bodily assets of youth.

Black Bjorn met them at the door with a scowl.

"You have this man's property," Olson said.

"He'll get it back soon as he pays me for the mule."

"I said you have this man's property. Give it to him."

"I won't."

"Then you'll come with me. The charge is theft. One packsaddle and contents."

Black Bjorn reconsidered.

The deputy loomed over him, suddenly a lot more formidable than he had been.

"People run out on me all the time," Bjorn said. "Sticking me for feed."

Brass collected his stuff, and within the hour he traded Gumz's bedroll and camp stove for a pick and shovel, bags of beans and cornmeal, a few oats, and a woman's straw hat bedecked with pink silk roses. That left him with $1.09, which he was tempted to spend on a parting shot or three, but in a fit of virtue he headed for Bjorn's livery barn to pay up. Black Bjorn affected not to be present, and made Brass wait an hour, but finally collected the dollar and let Brass collect his mule, load up, and walk away.

Gladstone Brass was back in the prospecting business, minus a few chemicals that would help him test promising ores, but nonetheless in business. He was feeling so perky he forgot to limp, and hustled away from Eureka before its temptations ruined him again. He would not forget Black Bjorn, and would exact some sort of justice when he could. Once he had gained the top of the hill south of town, he turned back to examine Eureka, the nest of vipers, the congregation of rats, the lair of greedy villains, including every grocer, hardware man, saloonkeeper, assayer, and liveryman in the whole place.

Ahead lay a thousand square miles of nothingness. A land so little used and abused that it would never change. A land innocent of greed. With every step he felt better, as if his spirit was coming home, as if he had been destined some eternity ago to live out his days in great contentment in the basins and ranges of Nevada, lord of all he surveyed.

The pick and shovel were a comfort. They would sustain him. He would use them as little as possible, but in moments of need the pick would free ore from the vein, and the shovel would lift it into his pack. That was everything a mortal required except for female servants. He wouldn't mind having someone do the work.

"I didn't have to eat you," he said to Sylvester.

Sylvester anchored Gladstone's arm between yellow teeth and sampled the shirt.

"Don't eat that. I've some oats for you."

But Sylvester hung on, a lovelorn mule stuck with the likes of Gladstone Brass.

"You'd better get used to it," Gladstone said.

He reached Sulphur Springs the first evening, and drank sparingly because the water was famous for the trots. But Sylvester drank heartily, and began chewing on brush.

"You'll be sorry, and I'll show no mercy," Gladstone said.

The next morning he wished he had imbibed more of the elixir of Sulphur Springs, but that was how life in Nevada played out.

The next evening they were at Chalk Spring, and Gladstone fried up some johnnycakes and fed one to Sylvester. Now they were deep in no-man's land, enveloped by silence, with little company but a few lizards and some distant birds, and he was a happy man.

He veered east, setting a course straight toward Portuguese Peak, and spent a hot day traversing a brushy basin and wishing there were less sun roasting him. He was low on water but intended to refill soon. He pierced the narrow cañon late in the afternoon, making his way up the worn trail through dense brush, and finally topped out at the pole gate.

Wet Agnes had raised her prices. One dollar, man or beast, the sign said. Don't ask.

He didn't see her, so he slid the pole off its cradle, and entered, only to hear the mighty crack of her twelve-gauge, and feel the hot air stir as double ought buckshot seared by.

"Next one turns you into a soprano," Agnes said.

"Wet, my beautiful dreamboat, it's your old friend and slave, Gladstone Brass," he said.

She appeared from behind a boulder, the blue steel of her weapon gleaming in the late light. She reminded him of a longhorn bull, big and tall, snorting and pawing the earth, lord of his dominion.

"You, is it? Two dollars . . . I should charge extra, since it's you."

"Madam, you are the most glorious expression of womanhood in a ten-mile radius," he said.

"Two dollars or beat it."

"In a twenty-mile radius," he said.

"Beat it."

"In a thousand mile radius," he said.

"Horse puck," she said. "That would include San Francisco."

"You are an improvement on any woman residing there," he said.

"You want to drink without paying. And you're too lazy to work for one."

"I have brought you a gift, beautiful lady."

"Bribe, you mean. Remove your lazy butt from my land."

Instead, he unbuckled one of Sylvester's panniers, and extracted the straw hat with pink roses. He snapped a dent back, rotated it, and approached.

"Set it down right there," she said, the bores of the shotgun lowering toward his groin. That was the last place he wanted the barrel to point.

He slowly lowered the straw hat and set it on the ground, where breezes plucked at it.

"There's no way on earth I would wear that thing," she said.

"It'd look real fetching on your mule. Cut some ear holes and put it on."

"Why would I do that? Put it on your mule."

"Agnes, you take that hat and hang it on the wall."

"Why would I do that?"

"To remind you your top half is real pretty."

"All lazy men do is connive to find ways to avoid work. Like now. You want me to take care of you and you never lift a finger. That's what the hat's about."

"Agnes, you are a rare and handsome woman, both top and bottom."

"I see straight through you, Gladstone Brass."

"You can hardly wait."

"For what?"

"For when you can wait on me hand and foot. That's your mission in life."

"You can't bribe me."

He led Sylvester toward the little pool, and she did not interfere, even though the bores of the shotgun followed him. He filled his canteen, let Sylvester slurp up water, which was more valuable than gold in this country.

The moment had arrived. He turned to her and bowed.

"Madam," he said, "it would be my honor to be your dinner guest. I see that your garden is fairly bursting with victuals. I particularly admire those potatoes, which look about ready to dig up. Madam, I have not enjoyed a potato in years. This is not the country for them, and I marvel that you have such big and healthy plants growing there. Do you suppose it's time to dig one up and see what treasures lie under the soil?"

"I am proud of my potatoes," she said. "It took some skill to bring them along." She eyed the half dozen plants. "It's just because I'm curious," she said.

"I will shovel them up."

"No you won't," she said. "I don't allow lazy men in my garden. This is just because I'm curious," she said. "I've been meaning to open up a hill."

She plucked up her spade, shiny edged from hard use, and gently slid it under the plant, and lifted, baring a fine collection of big spuds. She collected a dozen or so, and a few dwarfs, too.

"I will wash them for you," he said.

"No you won't. You don't know how."

"Of course I know how, woman."

"You don't know how to wash anything. Your feet stink."

"It's a hard country, Agnes."

"Don't Agnes me. We're not up to first names yet."

"I confess, madam, I'm not an expert in the scrubbing of my toes. They tend to take care of themselves without much water, and there's no soap to be found."

"There's amole, a yucca root, which makes a good soap."

"I would be obliged if you'd show me how to use it, madam."

"No, you're too lazy. Even if I showed you, you wouldn't profit from it."

She washed the new potatoes and built a small fire in the stove and started them boiling.

"I have very little salt," she said. "Potatoes and salt dance together, but we will not have that luxury."

"I know where there's salt, whole *playa* full of it," he said. "Just scoop it up."

"I knew you were good for something," she

said. "The potatoes will take a while. There's no heat in this cottonwood. Not like pine, which burns handsomely and cooks food fast."

"Yucca root," he reminded her.

She sighed, entered her rock-walled cabin, and returned with some black roots of some sort, which she sliced open and dropped into a bowl of water.

"Off with them," she said.

"Madam, I'm no good at undoing knots."

"Men are helpless," she said, and kneeled before his ancient boots, slowly unraveling the cords that bound them on his withered feet.

"Sir, your feet are rancid," she said. "You are in need of instruction."

She slowly worked the ancient boots off, releasing a new cloud of toxic gas, and then she examined his extremities, which were less soiled than he supposed they might be. Mostly they were bluish white, having been hidden from the sun for a generation or two.

"The root needs mushing around in the water to bring up some suds," she said, working the root around the bowl. Sure enough, some soapy suds began to appear, and when they sufficed for her purposes, she washed his lower appendages fiercely, not bothering to spare him pain. Then, with the grimy water, she washed the inside of his venerable boots as well, and turned them upside down to drain.

"You don't know how to do anything," she said, and turned to the potatoes, which were bobbing about in boiling water, waiting to be snatched up and devoured.

His feet felt rebuked, but at least the cool desert air was repairing the damage. He must remember that. Each evening, he could undo his boots and let his poor feet enjoy the desert air. He hadn't thought about his feet except to curse them when a thorn pierced them or a rock fell on them. But this woman had in the space of a small visit brought his feet to his attention, and showed him how he could improve their happiness. Happy feet equaled a happy prospector. If he kept his feet happy, he would be ahead of all his rivals in the mineral-hunting business.

"Have some potatoes, sir," she said, handing him a tin mess plate with two big ones rolling about. "And don't call me Agnes."

Chapter Fourteen

Beef Story had done it all in a few hours. He had his man and the stolen money. He relieved Gumz of a pocket pistol and a knife strapped to his calf; he returned to the Mizpah Mine and collected the bills in the safe; he saddled his horse and pack horse and put his manacled prisoner on the saddle horse and took the lead lines. He would walk.

It had all gone so smoothly he had surprised himself. But now came the hard part. He had to take Gumz through a wilderness that took five days and four nights to cross. He either had to stay awake four nights or bind the prisoner in some way. In addition, he had to feed and water the prisoner, himself, and his two horses. There would be no one to help him. The back country was some of the loneliest in the world. There were rocky desert areas where not even a respectable bird tried to live.

Gumz watched him, obviously amused. The foreigner was clever and alert and, worse, enjoying it. He smiled when Story extracted the five-shot pocket revolver, smiled again when Story discovered the knife sheathed in the man's britches. The prisoner wore a suit of clothes that spoke of money and privilege and class. Even though the prisoner said not a word, he somehow conveyed the idea that this trip would be a contest of wills, and there was no assurance that Story would deliver the Treasury bills or the prisoner to the court in Eureka.

Story didn't know how he would manage. But he knew the country and Gumz didn't. He knew about watering holes, and Gumz didn't. He knew that a man needed good boots in the sort of country they would be traversing. Bare feet in the Nevada desert were a death sentence.

He took them out of town and north into the

vast unknown, with only the North Star and Big Dipper to guide him. A crescent moon softened the blackness just enough for him to stay oriented. He took them across the giant basin north of Tonopah, with ridges east and west.

The prisoner said not a word. Around midnight, by Story's reckoning, they were five or six miles north of Tonopah, and caught in a vast rocky barrens. The moon had cut east.

"You can walk if you want," Story said.

"I would like that, sir. The irons hurt."

"The irons stay on, behind your back."

Story carefully helped the prisoner down. The man stretched, and then they proceeded.

"I suppose we're on the honor system, Gumz. You'll pledge upon your honor to escape, and I'll pledge to stop you by any means."

Gumz thought that was amusing.

"This back country is my friend," Story said. "I can find my way. I know where the wells are. The deeper we go, the less chance you have of getting out. Right now, if you were to escape, you might make it back to Tonopah . . . with luck. Tomorrow is a different deal."

"Why do you tempt me, Sheriff?"

"This is dangerous country. You should know what you face."

"Dangerous, yes, Sheriff. But it is not hard to know south from north. I can read the stars and follow the sun as well as you."

"You're working your hands free. That's an old manacle, not worth a damn. It's too big. And when you've freed one hand, you'll swing all that iron at me. But you'll be leaking blood before that iron comes my way."

"Thank you for the warning."

"You could grab the rein of that saddle horse and make a run for it."

"Something tells me, Sheriff, you'd like to see me try."

"You're an observant man, Gumz."

"You found the Treasury notes, I believe."

"Minus the five dollars you gave to a certain woman."

"The gentleman who took me through here must have seen me hide the bag."

"He watched you turn up the gulch, yes. All I had to do was look."

"I wasn't sure I'd ever find the bag again, in spite of my best efforts. Careless of me, yes? I am a stranger in a strange land."

"This country is like that. Why'd you rob that bank?"

"I don't believe I know what you are talking about, Sheriff."

They laughed. The night was chill, and the endless walking made Story's legs ache. He preferred a saddle or a buggy ride if he could manage it. At first light Story lined up a few distant peaks as best he could, and turned right, crossing the sage-choked flats and entering a long draw that led steadily uphill.

"I have a photographic memory," Gumz said. "But I don't recollect this area."

"I'm not taking you back the way you came south, Gumz. I'm taking you through country you've never seen. Your memory won't do you much good in the maze we're going to work through, with a lot of low hogbacks and angling gulches, and gravel underfoot, so you won't find a trail. There aren't many wells here, either, and we might not make it if I miss one. But if I can't find a well, you'll do worse. Get me?"

"You have all the advantages, Sheriff."

Indeed, it was corrugated country, with gulches leading into *playas*, or dry lakes, so there was no certain drainage that might lead anywhere. Off on the horizon was Portuguese Peak, but Gumz wouldn't know that. Soon the sun would blast down on them, wring water out of them and the horses, parch their throats. And there would be no shade. That's the way Story wanted it. Gumz was smart; he would know that the man he was with was his only ticket out.

They did find some shade at midday under an overhang that sheltered a wash.

"I'll unlock the irons and give you a drink," Story said. "Turn around."

One of the manacles hung loose.

Gumz smiled.

126

"Lie down on your stomach," Story said.

Gumz did. Story unlocked the remaining hand iron, pulled the manacle away, and threw it out. It was more dangerous hanging loose than out of sight. He let Gumz sit up, and handed him a canteen. Gumz drank deeply, and wanted more, but Story pulled it away, and drank some himself. He poured a little into his felt hat and let each horse swallow a few licks.

The midday heat baked the desolate countryside, and seemed to impose walls of silence upon it. Story was worn down after a night and most of a day without sleep. Gumz, lighter of build, seemed better off.

"I'm going to have a *siesta*," Story said. "If you think you can bust outta here, now's your chance. When it cools down, I'll move out."

Story settled against the shaded rock wall and let himself relax. Gumz stared, obviously tempted. Then Gumz struggled up the rocky cleft to look out upon the heat-baked maze, now wavering and dancing in the brutal sun. The horses found the shade, and stood quietly, heads down, and waited.

Story dozed, not really getting the rest he craved. He was indifferent to Gumz's fate; if Gumz fled, what did it matter? Someone would find his bones somewhere. But Albert Gumz was no fool, and after a while he retreated to the shade and dozed himself, about ten feet distant, which suited Story fine. Story fell into a nap, and when he awoke with a start, the sun was low and lighting up distant bluffs. The temperature hadn't dropped and wouldn't until late in the evening.

Story gazed at the young man, who slept quietly, and wondered what possible chain of events had brought this man from northern France to here, and why he had engineered this desperate robbery. Gumz knew nothing about the desert or its cruelties and that had been his undoing. The foreigner had been forced to hire a guide to take him across this empty, dry land, and that had \been his undoing.

Story rested a little longer. The sun had found its way around the ledge, and now its rays bored in upon the men and animals. It was time to go.

He shook Gumz awake, and nodded. Gumz stared about him, absorbing this strange world, and stood.

"Water?" he asked.

"One canteen, and we'll be wanting it later."

"I need it now."

"So do the horses, and they are more important."

Story tightened the girth straps on the horses and wordlessly started north, straight over corrugated country, his sole bearing the top of Portuguese Peak, miles ahead, with its famous well. The horses followed without being tugged along, and Gumz struggled beside his captor. After an hour or so, it became plain where they were heading.

"There is water?" Gumz asked. His voice was raspy.

"We'll know when we get there," Story said. It would be Wet Agnes's water, and if she made a fuss, the bank would donate another silver certificate to her bosom.

Night fell, and with it some relief from the heat, but not from the howl of their bodies and throats for water. It was slow going, up and down, no discernible trail, which is why Story had brought them there. They struggled onward, weakening until Gumz stumbled. Story paused on a ridge top, poured a little of the warm water into a mess bowl, and handed it to the foreigner. It wasn't enough. He gave himself an equal amount. It wasn't enough. He gave a larger portion to each horse. It wasn't enough. He kept a quart or so back. He had cut this closer than he had realized, and they might not make it.

But the night began to help. Cool air eddying down the mountainside caught them, holding out promise. The horses perked up. They reached the foothills of the peak, and Story turned west, working his way around to the gulch that would lead to Wet Agnes's oasis.

"We are going to the woman," Gumz said.

"Agnes, yes. A mile or two more."

"The thought of it makes me strong."

"Then help me find the right gulch. If we miss it, we're in trouble."

"By night it is hard."

They passed a gulch an hour later that might be the right one, and then the horses quit. They yanked free, and headed straight up the brushy gulch, hell-bent for a drink.

"Trust a horse," Story said.

They followed a path through the brushy narrows, the horses far ahead by then.

Story paused. "Have a drink," he said.

Gumz swallowed, and somehow willed himself to leave some for Story, who drank it.

Now the canteen was empty. They were out.

"How come you to rob the bank, Gumz?"

"It is a sad story, Officer. My family, they are investment bankers, Gumz et Fils, and we have succeeded by keeping a keen eye for promising properties. It reached us that the silver mines at Tonopah might hold far more promise than was being made public, and I was sent by my family to investigate, and if I was satisfied with the honesty of the management, to purchase shares for my people. Well, sir, this West of yours, it has its ways unknown to some Frenchman from the city of Metz."

"Gambling?"

"That, and drinking, and, ah, all the distractions. Soon enough, sir, I was relieved of every *centime* entrusted to me, and, well, sir, you can imagine the rest."

"I suppose I can," Story said.

"It all was fine in the abstract, sir, but this land, it exacts its own toll, and I was innocent of any knowledge of it, and still am. You knew that, and went to sleep knowing I would do nothing but entrust my safety to you, sir."

"That was the general idea, all right."

"I am a foolish man, sir, and now I will pay the price."

Story didn't argue with that. They rounded a bend, and there was Wet Agnes, her shotgun leveled, her white Mother Hubbard gown covering every inch of her but her face and hands.

"I couldn't stop those nags, but I can stop you," she said. "Four dollars, men and beasts."

"I'm Beef Story, official business, madam."

She squeezed, and a terrific blast rent the night, and a load of buckshot sailed just over Story's head.

"If it's official, I charge double," she said.

Chapter Fifteen

She fed them oat gruel, which was devoid of taste but nourishing and comforting. From the moment she admitted them to her oasis, she bustled about with an energy Beef Story had rarely seen.

She had converted the little shelf half way up

131

the mountain into a garden of Eden, every inch of it growing something of value. And she had done this so swiftly that not even the prospectors roaming that naked country got wind of it until it was there.

"That'll be five dollars in all, stolen bank money," she said. "Men and beasts and breakfasts."

Story dug into a pannier on a pack horse and extracted the bill, which she promptly tucked into safe quarters midway between her ample breasts.

"Safer than a bank," she said, clearing away chipped bowls.

The prisoner ate slowly, masticating the oatmeal, peering out upon the vast gardens that supported her. "You stay busy, madam," he said.

"Busy! You wouldn't know the meaning of the word," she said. "I don't know your story, but you're lazy. Lazy people rob banks. Busy people don't need to. Lazy people carry guns around, wanting to take wealth from others. Busy people don't need to take a thing from any other human being. Men are lazy, women less so. My husband was lazy, and produced nothing. I am not lazy, and produce everything."

"That's a hard verdict, ma'am," Story said.

"Hard is it? You know why I came here? Because prospectors are lazy. They wander around all day doing nothing. They could be

132

earning a living, working in a trade, but instead they run away from honest toil and spend their entire lives wandering around, hoping for a bonanza. I make good money selling them water."

"You shame me, madam," Gumz said. "My laziness was my undoing. If I had been more industrious, I would not have gambled away a large sum, wanting to double my money without effort. And I would not have resorted to desperate means to repair my fortune."

"Well, fella, you belong here. Your nature won't change. Once lazy, always lazy, I say, and this empty land is where the laziest men collect. But even at that, you're not half as lazy as this sheriff here. What do lawmen do all day? Nothing."

"Madam, I work hard at my profession," Story said.

"Hard, do you? All right, do the dishes. There they are, there's the pan."

"That's not my profession, ma'am. I keep the peace."

"Ha, that's what you call it. Lawmen are laziest of all. What do you build? What do you buy or sell? What do you construct? Do you sow and reap? Do you cut hay? Do you write, or ship, or spin? Nothing."

"Keeping the peace is a productive task in itself, madam. It allows others to go about their business."

"Ha! You sit at your desk and chew Bull

Durham. You wander about, rattling locked doors. You collect your pay for sitting in restaurants, sucking a coffee cup."

"I walk in harm's way, madam."

"You don't even walk half the time. You're glued to a chair. There's nothing lazier than a lawman. Look at that gut on you. You should quit and start prospecting. At least a prospector digs ore once in a while, but you don't even do that. Now wash the dishes."

"Dishes? I lack the skill, Agnes. That's woman's work."

"You said it, buster. Even this bank robber could wash dishes better than a sheriff."

"My skill is shooting, madam. I am deadly. That's what makes the world safe."

"The only skill you've got is passing gas from both ends of you, Beef Story."

"I seem not to own your esteem."

"This bank robber is worth more than you. He had enterprise."

"Madam," said Gumz, "he is right. His office is to protect the world from bank robbers, and I am a witness to his success."

"Then you wash the dishes."

"Madam, I grew up in privileged circumstances, and am innocent of the knowledge that would permit me to wash dishes faultlessly."

"Ah, so you wish to return to that life. You'll have it. You'll be sent to Carson City, and there you will be housed and fed and clothed for free, and you won't have to lift a finger, and others will cook for you, sew your clothing, clean your cell, and even make all your decisions for you. It'll be a life of leisure for you, five to seven years, with time off for good behavior, which consists of doing no labor."

"You have me there, madam," Gumz said. He turned to Story. "I think we should both abandon our lazy lives and live a life of liberty and leisure here in the middle of nowhere."

"It's a temptation," said Story. "Work can be seductive. I once dreamed of making furniture. But I succumbed to an easier life."

"We even have enough to buy some mules and picks and shovels . . . those seem to be the badges of honor in this country. What's more, Sheriff, all we need to do is disappear. You went after me and were never seen again. I was a fugitive and was never seen again. This is the place. There's a thousand mysterious cañons never seen by mortals. What do you think? The press will have a field day for a week, and then it will all be lost from memory."

Sheriff Story yawned. "Prospecting back here is too much work," he said. "I make good money just to wander around Eureka, rattling locked doors. The only heavy lifting I do is carrying drunks to the jailhouse. She's right, you know. It's time for me to face up to reality."

Agnes finished the dishes, polishing them with a cloth, and then evicted them. "I wish to get into my bib overalls. I am tired of serving breakfast in my nightclothes."

She pushed them out the door of the rock cabin, and shut the door hard, as a sign that her privacy should be respected. The new day was well along. The little plateau remained in shadow, but the vaulting rock walls caught the sun and brightened the valley. In one corner was a cornfield, each stalk pushing upward, not yet tasseled. Another patch was devoted to wheat, green and verdant at this stage, just forming its head. Another to oats. A small pasture of rolling slopes contained her mule. A garden bursting with oncoming tomatoes, potatoes, carrots, cabbages, a few ready to harvest, filled a large space near the cabin. Most of it was directly watered from the spring.

"A lot of work," Story said. "Just pulling caterpillars off, and keeping birds out, and cutting all that wheat. Lotta work. Have you ever dealt with box elder bugs? They keep coming and coming."

"She's got herself a pretty little corner," Gumz said. "But I prefer stately homes with drawing rooms and damask curtains and Brussels carpets. And grand parties, with caviar and champagne."

"Yeah, but Carson City's got plainer rooms, I think. No carpets on those floors."

"Very true, sir, and you can retire to your barren offices in Eureka, and consult the feed store calendar on the wall as the hours and days and weeks slip by."

"I guess we'd better pack up and go, Gumz. We're still three days and two nights from Eureka."

They bridled the horses in the small pen, brushed and saddled them, and led them to water. Both animals drank well, as if they knew they would not enjoy another drink for a long time. Story anchored the panniers to the packsaddle, made sure the two canteens were brimful, and walked to the cabin to tell her they were off.

But she met him at the door. She wore bib overalls, a white blouse, and straw hat.

"We're off, Agnes."

"Not yet," she said. She hiked to the garden and returned with two giant zucchinis.

"Spare canteens," she said. "Good for man or beast. They grow faster than I can eat them. Full of water."

"A valuable gift, Agnes."

"Call me madam. Strangers who use my first name aren't to be trusted."

She collected her shotgun and followed them to the pole gate, saw them through it, and slid the pole in place behind them.

Story lifted his hat to her.

They worked down the brushy gulch in the building heat.

"That place takes a lot of work," Gumz said. "I grow weary just thinking about it."

"She won't last long. Lonely in there," Story said. "I like to be with people."

"She was right about me. I've never even made my bed," Gumz said.

"You're about to learn how, Gumz. Every day."

"I wouldn't mind a life of leisure, Sheriff. It's my station in life."

"I had no station in life. I was born on a farm, didn't like wrestling a two-bottom plow, ran away at fourteen, and never looked back," Story said.

"And sitting at a sheriff desk's as far as you could get from plowing, am I not right?"

Story didn't reply for a moment. They were threading their way toward the vast basin between towering ranges. "She's right, Gumz. I'm in the laziest profession there is. I mostly sit on my butt and get paid for it. I haven't done a lick of work in years. Real work, like digging or sawing or hammering or shoveling or even clerking."

"We would fit right in around here, Sheriff."

After a while they emerged from the gulch and beheld a vast, sagebrush-dotted wasteland that shimmered in the heat. The blue sky seemed brassy. The distant mountains were veiled in heat haze.

"The reason prospectors don't work, Gumz, is that there's nothing to do. As far as we can see, there is nothing that requires work. The land's too dry to plow. There's no reason to build a house or a barn. The only thing that requires work, as far as we can see, is minerals. Finding gold and digging it, that takes work."

"Right now, the zucchini looks more attractive," Gumz said.

"Zucchinis take lots of work, Gumz. She's watering and weeding and harvesting and drying them, or whatever she does, from dawn to dusk. Now that's work. What's not work is owning a little ledge of gold, and digging some now and then, and just enjoying life in between. There's a little work in it, but not much. Not as much as I do in office. Each eve I make the rounds, check the saloons, and that tires me out. I must walk a mile a day just rattling locked doors. And there's no let-up. I got to do it every day, and there's no time off. Now a prospector, he's got time off. He's always got company, too. If he's lonely, he just talks to his mule. He takes no sass from a mule."

"You married?" Gumz asked.

"No plans for it, long as Sally's place is open for business."

"I'm not, either. It's work, being married."

"You said a mouthful, Gumz."

Story turned them north once they were clear of the spiny ridges at the base of the mountain. There were no landmarks to fasten on, other than Portuguese Peak, but he knew the general direction they were heading to reach Chalk

Spring, the next seep, and a mean one with gyp water that would give a man the trots. But that was how life was lived in the back country. It beat puttering around in a town somewhere. You could see distant gulches that maybe never saw a mortal, and climb up there where no man had ever been, and check it out for whatever secrets it possessed. And there were enough of those distant cañons and crevices and peaks to keep a man exploring for a couple of lifetimes. Imagine standing on top of one of those peaks and thinking that you owned it all, everything for a hundred miles, hardly another human being in the entire place. All yours, and so lonely no one else would ever penetrate it. Now that would be something.

"How far to the next water?"

"I'm not going to tell you, Gumz. Your life depends on me. If you knew the way, and knew how to live out here, you'd desert me, and then there'd be a manhunt, and you'd find that I haven't been a lawman for nothing."

Chapter Sixteen

Bitter Bowler gloated. The rubes had fallen for the oldest con in the book. He had a secret. He knew where a fortune lay hidden. He knew where the rainbow's end was. He knew where the pot of gold waited. He knew where the lost mine lay, the treasure of the Sierra Madre was buried, where a king's ransom rested.

But not for long. Lew and Deacon would get restless with each passing day, and would soon unload him if he didn't take them straight to it. He needed time, needed to walk again. Needed food and water. Until he could have that, he was at their mercy. If they had any mercy.

"Well, I been thinking," he said. "I'd take you to it, but only if it's a three-way split, fair and square, and you swear to it."

"Nah, I'm not swearing to nothing," Lew said.

But Deacon shut him up. "Yeah, me and Lew, we're in just like you say, old-timer. Ain't we, Lew?"

"He shows us the place, I'm in."

"Don't know whether I will," Bitter said. "It's my retirement, my life on easy street after wearing my fingers to the bone all my life. I'd hate to get took."

"Maybe we're the ones getting took," Lew said.

"That settles it. You'll never see it," Bitter said. "My mouth's so buttoned up you'll never get a word outta me."

Deacon had no luck smoothing things over. They were far from succor, with three men and two mules to feed and water. "We got other things to think about," he said. "Like eats."

"We could have eats the rest of our lives if this old coot would join up with us," Lew said.

"But he won't. He'd be dead if we hadn't come along. So let him croak." He turned to Bitter. "Get off that mule. You're done. You can sit here on a rock and wait for the train to stop at this station."

Wordlessly Bitter climbed off the patient mule. "All right, leave me to croak," he said. He found a rock ledge, hobbled there, and sat on it, first examining it for rattlers. "My secret dies with me."

"Well, sit there, then. I'm taking this quartz to Eureka. We need some feed," Deacon said.

That did it. Bitter clambered aboard his mule. They bickered all the way to Chalk Spring, and then Deacon took off for Eureka with the bag of quartz. He took half the remaining cornmeal, leaving too little to feed Lew and Bitter the four days he'd be gone. If he returned at all.

The spring was barely running, a dribble so weak it took several minutes to fill a canteen, and the remaining mule licked up most of the dribble as it leaked from strata in a rock face. It was lousy water, too, with a bad taste, and a lot of iron in it. Bitter didn't look forward to four days with Lew, and not enough food, and no food for the mule, and Lew armed better than he was. The mule, freed of its burden, made its way to some brush and dined on it, drifting farther away, which worried Bitter, who had no way of catching the beast. Bitter eyed Lew, who was keeping the cornmeal to himself, and wondered who would shoot first. He guessed Lew would try it at night, coward that he was. They fell into dead silence, Lew circling around the place while Bitter sat, immobilized by his bad leg. Bitter believed that the only thing keeping him alive was the story about the mountain of silver.

Late in the day, Lew built a small fire and made some batter from the cornmeal and fried two johnnycakes—and then ate both, enjoying his theater, and even flashing a triumphant grin at Bitter.

But Bitter had known hunger intimately now and then, knew how to subdue the howl of his empty gut, and waited. He didn't wait for night, or wait for the next palaver. He waited until Lew's back was turned momentarily, drew his old revolver, and fired it at Lew's back. The ball hit the spine, threw Lew forward and onto his belly, and Lew thrashed around, his arm diving for his own weapon. Bitter's second ball quieted Lew after a few moments.

Bitter was in possession of a mule if he could catch it, a handful of cornmeal, a few pieces of gear, including a pick and shovel, a canteen, and a bedroll. He had also acquired an enemy; Deacon would come after him.

Bitter eyed the silent warm body. Lew looked almost boyish, sprawled on gravel. Bitter collected the man's revolver, but there wasn't anything else worth taking. The mule would have to carry

Bitter's weight plus all the gear, which would likely produce a mule rebellion. Overburdened mules were famous for not budging.

Bitter felt bad. He didn't regret shooting Lew, and he had done what he had to do, but that didn't comfort him. He stared at the body in the gravel, the vomit rising in his throat, but he swallowed it down, and that was that. If he had any brains, he'd stay a couple of days and dine on Lew. But a terror of Deacon filled him and he decided to move on as fast as he could.

But the mule was in no hurry to return to the seep, and was far afield, gnawing at anything he could subdue with his yellow teeth. Which meant that Bitter had to wait, and wait, and wait a few feet from the man he had killed.

"You worthless thing, you come in here or I'll kill you and eat you for a week!" he yelled.

The mule's ears perked up, he whiffed, and trotted straight in.

"That's better. You was owned by some desert rat like me," Bitter said. "Man learns how to talk mule, and then a mule listens."

Bitter took care to clean off the débris from the mule's back, blanket it, and saddle it. He put what he could into a duffel bag that would sit in his lap, and boarded the beast. Then he lifted the duffel, and the mule snorted.

"Let's go," Bitter said, and slapped the mule's rump.

But the mule wouldn't budge. It stood lock-kneed and no force that Bitter could muster could move it. Sadly Bitter jettisoned the pick and shovel, but that did not do it. Finally everything but the paltry little bag of cornmeal, a tin bowl, and two canteens. That did the job, and the mule sagged slightly, his back less arched.

"You're too smart for your own good," Bitter said. "You'll be turned into mule meat just as soon as I feel up to it."

The mule had a rough walk that sawed at Bitter's crotch, but the rider endured, and the mule moved away from the carnage at Chalk Spring into the limitless night, the heavens sprinkled with sparks. Bitter didn't know where to go, just anywhere but Eureka. So he cut southward, thinking maybe he could make Tonopah, sell the beast, and somehow start over. It was a vast distance away. But Bitter had been in tougher binds, and he felt he had a good chance.

He crossed a vast basin so dry it didn't even support sagebrush, and struck some low hills that soon vaulted into the crevices of the next range west. He didn't know just where he was; the night played its tricks. But he chose to head straight up and over. To hell with the wells and seeps he knew about; he'd find new ones, where he'd never been, anything to put distance between himself and the stinking body at Chalk Spring.

He was traversing naked rock, the range so arid that it didn't support vegetation. No wonder it was all unfamiliar and forbidding. No creature dared enter country like this, remote and deadly. But some recklessness drove him on; he wanted to distance himself from the body of that person once known as Lew, from that mother's son left to die in a lonely desert spot scarcely visited by anyone. Dawn caught him in a rocky defile that stretched upward to nowhere. The mule didn't like it. Animals have a sense about water, and resist places like this. Bitter knew that he could not get down and lead the mule, not with a broken ankle. That made this ascent even more perilous. But somehow the mule didn't rebel, and Bitter arrived in a tawny cañon, and he could see that up a mile or so the rock changed color to red and gray, but it was just as naked of vegetation as it was below.

Midday he topped the range, and discovered a vast panorama westward and southward, with distant ranges disappearing in haze. It was hot. He watered the mule from the canteen, using his tin bowl, and sipped sparingly. Then to his surprise he discovered a dark crease dropping southwest, and headed for it. The crease brimmed with brush, plus a few junipers and mountain cedars. But he found no water. A damp spot poked grass into the sky, and he let the mule eat. He dismounted, picked up his tin bowl, hobbled to a likely hollow, and began scraping away the damp soil, but not two feet of patient scraping yielded water. He rested, disappointed, but after a few minutes he discovered an inch or so of fresh, clear water seeping in. He exulted. He filled his canteens, and then let the mule sink on its knees, its head deep into the little pit, to lap the water. Bitter had found a watering hole unknown to the world. The brushy defile tumbling away before him was too choked for travel, but he resolved to keep it in sight when he descended. There might be more water and grass below.

That afternoon he and his mule wrestled their way down the treacherous slope, laden with scree, boulders, loose rock that often blocked passage. The mule scraped a fetlock on sharp rock and began to limp. Alarmed, Bitter dismounted, bound the laceration with a piece of shirt, and worried his way downslope again. And then he saw the rainbow strata, a jolt of color in a gray stone world. Blue, green, red, a thin line of mineral as bright as a circus wagon. And he had no way to reach it. He could not climb. But as any prospector knew, there are ways and there are ways. He studied the heaped and scattered rock underfoot, and soon found what he wanted— rich salts of copper, green and blue, sometimes with native copper gleaming at him. He felt exultant. He didn't know where he was. He didn't even know the name of this range. He didn't know what he would eat, or where he could get help. But he knew he had struck mineral, copper, maybe mixed with other metals, and in a place well hidden from prying eyes. All his. And he was in grave danger. He studied the horizons, and could not discern any landmark he knew anything about or had ever seen.

"Well, Mister Mule, what'll we do?" he asked.

The mule clearly wanted to head back to that watering hole near the top. Grass and water were more precious than anything else in his mule life.

"All right, we'll spend some time there. I've eaten grass, and I'll eat it again if I gotta."

The mule tugged hard, his head twisted around, itching to return to the ridgeline.

"We got all the time in the world, jackass," Bitter said.

He let the lamed mule work its way back half a mile to the gulch that sliced down the slope, invisible until you were almost on top of it. The little pit was half full now, so Bitter let his mule suck it up, drink and drink, and then wander about, snapping at every blade of grass in the defile. Bitter lay there, studying his blue rocks, licking them, bashing them apart to see what lay inside, calculating if only with wild guesses how rich the ore might be.

It would be cold up there at night, but he had the saddle blanket, and that would do. He watched the sun plummet toward distant ridges, and drop behind them and throw his world into swift twilight. But here and there the sun still lit western flanks and then withered away.

What a day. It had started with a fight about food and a death, but now his life was filled with promise and wild hope. But only if a one-legged man on an injured mule could make it out, memorize the place, and find some way to return. The oddest thing of all was that he was lonelier than he had ever been in his life.

Chapter Seventeen

Bitter Bowler had a bad night. His ankle ached. He was cold. The ground was as hard as a skillet. And his stomach was complaining. Dawn found him chilled and miserable. The mule was nowhere in sight. He had only a handful of cornmeal and no way to cook it into mush or johnnycakes. He mixed some with water, hoping to make an edible gruel, but water didn't improve it, and he was forced to down the miserable stuff a bit at a time.

The eastern heavens glowed, and the eastern slopes brightened, and surrounding peaks and ridges cast long blue shadows westward. As arid as this place was, it had an odd grandeur that quieted him. The world was mysterious and beautiful. He eyed the stratum of mineralized rock, seeing a bonanza in it. He examined his pieces of float, ore that had tumbled from the mother lode above. The sight of it, high up above him, heartened him. He could live a life of leisure in some tony place the rest of his days.

The mule was somewhere down the narrow gulch, but would return for a drink at the seemingly magical well, which now had a foot of clear, sweet water collected in it. Bitter filled his canteens, tucked the mess bowl in the sack, and waited. He badly needed a staff or a crutch, but the low brush did not yield anything usable to hobble around with. He thought maybe to splint his ankle and walk on it, but even that proved impossible. He could find nothing to splint and bind his broken bones.

In time, just when Bitter was finding the wait unbearable, the mule did show up, nosed the water, and drank deeply. Bitter used the moment to slip the bridle over its snout, and then to anchor the blanket and saddle, and tighten the girth. He was ready to move out. He didn't quite know where he was going, but it would be westward to the basin below, where he would look for some familiar landmark.

"All right, dammit, I'm climbing on," he said.

The mule let him, yawned and stretched.

"Git," Bitter said, but the mule didn't.

He swatted the mule's rump, with no effect. He yelled, with no effect. He kicked his boots deep into the mule's ribs, with no effect. The mule had discovered that the human atop him had no means to make him move and could not drag him forward because he could not walk.

Bitter hunted for a stick, a crop, to beat on the mule, but saw none. Nature, all about him, yielded rich copper ore, but no means to make his mule move. The mule had found grass and water, and that was motive enough to park right here.

Bitter cussed the mule, cussed him as masterfully as any muleskinner in the Army, but the mule merely yawned. He tried walking with an arm over the mule's neck to take his weight, but the mule cemented itself to the ground. What had started with hope in the air had turned into disaster. If the mule would not move, Bitter would die right here. He could eat the mule for a few days, and delay his death, but sooner or later he would croak if he could not be carried down the long rocky grade to somewhere, anywhere, where there might be help.

Bitter contemplated all that with irritation. His luck was bad as usual. Why were the heavens shut against him? Everything he had done in his life was merely to survive; he asked so little of the world and its people, just to make his way.

The remaining option was to crawl, tugging the mule behind him. By the time the sun topped the ridges and poured light into the little cañon, Bitter concluded that he had no other choice. And once the mule got away from the water, it probably would permit Bitter to ride him once again.

So Bitter tied the small sack to the saddle, collected the reins, and began to crawl through knife-edged rock that would soon tear his hands and knees to shreds. But there was no other way. He managed a few yards, and was hurting, so he rested. A few more yards yielded a scraped knee with blood oozing from the laceration. Then he hit some clear gravel, and made a little progress, and the mule came along without protest.

Next came some rocky débris, which proved difficult to work around, but he did, and sat on a rock a while to catch his breath. He had crawled a couple of hundred yards. Not so bad, not bad at all. Resting frequently, crawling as long as he could, and standing up now and then, Bitter made his way down the mountainside. At one point he clambered aboard the mule, hoping to move it, but the mule stood stockstill, with its ears flattened back, resisting Bitter. So he crawled some more, growing more and more exhausted.

He cursed Lew and Deacon. He cursed his parents. He cursed the state of Nevada. He cursed the flood of prospectors up from Tonopah. But it did no good, and no one heard him, and there was no one on earth missing him, searching for him, seeking to comfort him or help him to safety. But he was not without mettle, so he kept crawling, resting, crawling, because his life depended on it.

It was during one of the rest periods that he noticed the black rock, débris that had tumbled from a nearby escarpment. He recognized it at once: carbonate of silver, slightly glossy, laid down some infinity ago. He couldn't tell just where it had come from, but he was certain about what it was. Silver! He studied the towering cliffs and cañons, searching for a telltale black band in the gray stone. He couldn't walk anywhere, so he had to sit on the hard earth and study the maze of cliffs and gulches and hope to spot the outcrop, the place where the silver carbonate surfaced, weathered, and broke free.

An odd thought struck him. He had invented a bonanza and used it upon Lew and Deacon. He had let the pair know that he possessed the secret that would open a fortune. And here it was. Copper on top, silver below, exactly as he had imagined it and conned the two greenhorn prospectors with it. That was an invention, but this was real. Could it be? Was he somehow fated to claim a real bonanza exactly like the one he had hoodwinked his two captors with?

He hunted around for more of the silver carbonate ore, but found none. He was certain he would find a pocketful if he could walk. But it was enough. When he reached the safety of a well, or a town, or at least some other prospectors, he would outfit, and he would return, and he would be king of the world the rest of his life.

He slipped the silver carbonate into his bag, along with the copper salts.

But then he eyed the mule, which glared back at him, ready to bolt up the long grade to water and grass. And he knew he would get nowhere, or even survive this lonely place, unless he turned the rebel into an obedient saddle animal. And he knew he didn't have any means, or ny of the special expertise, that would save his life.

He had crawled as far as he could go. His knees were bloody; his hands hurt. A wave of melancholia swept through him. On the day he would die, he had discovered a bonanza. Well, *maybe* a bonanza. A few pieces of float scarcely made a bonanza. But he was done for. He stood, supporting himself by grabbing the mule's mane, and climbed onto the beast. Wherever it went, he would be taken. If it went up to the little water hole, he would die there. He sat the saddle, reins in hand, giving no direction to the animal.

But the beast didn't go uphill. It was far away from that hidden gulch. The mule headed down-slope at a perky gait, intent on reaching the basin ahead. It headed out upon the vast, intimidating flat, boiling in late spring sun, heading straight across to a higher range off in the heat haze to the west.

The mule knew where he was, even if Bitter didn't. The long trek bled sweat out of the animal, and at the far foothills Bitter poured water into his tin bowl and let the mule slobber it up to the last drop. He sipped the last of the canteen's water, and let the mule take its head once again.

By sundown the mule had carried him deep into another range, and was climbing steadily through juniper-dotted slopes, heading somewhere that Bitter could only guess. The beast seemed to know something, and Bitter knew better than to fight the animal. It had probably spent as much time in the Nevada desert as he had. It angled south, sometimes crossing ridges rather than working straight up. All of which left Bitter confused. He couldn't say where he was even if his life depended on it. Which it might.

Just at full dark, the mule burst into a trot, and worked westward across an arid plateau surrounded by ridges north and south, and then raced straight toward a grove of cottonwoods, startling and majestic even in the pale light of the moon. The beast halted at a long pond, actually a pool in a creek, and plunged its head into cool water. Bitter slid off, hurting at every joint, and lifted handfuls of water to his lips, and drank the blessed liquid.

The mule stood at the water's edge until it was sated. And Bitter sat at the edge until he could drink no more. Only then did he look around. The place showed signs of use. Some ashes from fires. But the pale moonlight revealed no other mortal at this nameless place. Bitter thought he should know it, know the range, know where he was, but in truth he hadn't any idea. Why had he never heard of this place?

He slowly undid the girth and removed the saddle and blanket, and then the bridle, and turned the mule loose. It would make a good living this night. Grass lined the creek, even after it disappeared a few yards away. The heavens seemed very large this night; the starry bowl of black sky was as vast as the land he had crossed. He still couldn't walk, but this place was littered with cottonwood débris and he soon found a good stout stick that would do for a staff. Not as useful as a crutch, but he could throw his weight to it and walk. He was mobile for the first time since he had lost his bristle-cone crutch.

He mixed the last of his cornmeal with water in the bowl, and managed to swallow the pasty stuff a bit at a time. That was the end of his food. From now on, he'd starve. But even as he sat near the pond, he thought that the place might have night visitors off the peaks. If his luck held, he might shoot some game.

But he fell into a drugged sleep, and if the pond had night visitors, he didn't see them. He was stiff at dawn. His bloodied knees had scabbed over. His body hurt. But there was clear water, and his mule was stripping cottonwood bark from the stunted silver-leafed trees that dotted this oasis. He wanted food, but there was none. He plucked

up his stout stick and scouted the other camp-
sites, looking for anything edible, but he found
nothing. He eyed the pond for fish, and saw
none. He studied the brush, looking for berries,
or pods, or seed heads, but it was too early in the
year. He would have to go hungry, but his mule
was strong and maybe that counted most.

He gave the mule its head, and it topped this
arid range and descended into another blank gray
basin. The mule headed south again, some
destination in its mind, its gait stronger after a
good feed and ample water. Bitter mostly swayed
along, holding onto the mane, letting this desert-
hardened critter take him to wherever it was
going. He didn't know. Had he crossed the
Monitor Range? The Smoky River Range?

By the end of that hot day, he was fiercely
hungry. The mule cut up a gulch between low,
stone-walled ridges, answered the bleat of another
mule, and Bitter found himself entering a camp
under a cliff where two thin prospectors had
settled. They sprang up, looked Bitter over, and
nodded.

"I'm Bowler, need your help. Any kind of
chow . . . haven't eaten and my belly's pushing my
backbone."

The taller one, hawk-like and mean-looking,
proved to be kinder than his looks.

"Killarney here," the man said, looking Bitter
over. "Seems like you're in a bad way."

"Haven't got much to trade. Tin bowl is all."

Killarney eyed his partner, who was stirring the pot, and came to a conclusion. "We got some beans boiling in there. We'll fix you up. This is Dinwiddie. He's the chief cook and bottle washer."

"That would be a fine thing," Bitter said. "You fellas prospecting?"

"We're geologists, actually. We're heading out to look at some claims. Mizpah Mining Company employs us."

"Claims here? Where am I?"

"You're a little out of Tonopah, fella. Half a day on that mule, I'd say."

"I guess I never heard such good news," Bitter said. "I've been out in country I've never seen, and it looks like I'll live to tell about it."

Chapter Eighteen

Gladstone Brass had a new mission in life, which was to prevent Wet Agnes from washing anyone else's feet. Washed feet were the source of all happiness, he discovered. He hadn't had happy feet since he was in his twenties. He had forgotten what happy feet felt like. He had ignored his unhappy feet for decades, ignored their howling, overriding their pain, expressing scorn for the dirt and grime that caked them.

But then Wet Agnes came along and restored them to their natural beauty, pink and clean and healthy, and with most of the ache scrubbed out of them. All he could think of was having Agnes wash them regularly, before and after his prospecting trips, maybe even once every two or three weeks.

But he didn't know how to achieve this. If she washed his feet and made them happy, she would wash other feet and make them happy, too. He didn't want her washing the feet of Bitter Bowler, who deserved only the most miserable of feet, feet that tormented him with every step. And Bowler was simply at the top of the list. He didn't want her washing anyone's feet except his own, and that only in secret where no one could see her soap up his toes and scrub and polish his toenails.

The task was daunting. All prospectors had unhappy feet. There was not a prospector in Nevada, except for himself, who sprang along on happy feet, in comfortable boots, feet that smelled like roses or lilacs. And there was Agnes, willing to perform this service on them all, or so he imagined. Maybe she was just doing him a favor. Or herself a favor, since his feet were offending her. But now he wanted to post a NO TRESPASSING sign near her watering hole.

He had business to attend to, namely finding ore and selling it to sustain himself. It was a hard life, looking for ore in an arid waste, and no one ever thanked him for sacrificing his life to such a purpose.

"Sylvester, if your feet smelled the way mine did, would Wet Agnes wash them?" he asked. "No, she did it for me alone. She's in love with me. That's it. She scrubbed my feet because she cared about them, and about me."

Sylvester butted him, which was a sure sign of disagreement, if not mockery.

"You are toying with extinction," Gladstone replied.

He reached the foot of Portuguese Peak, and realized he hadn't the faintest idea what to do next. He could not stay at Wet Agnes's another day, because she wanted another dollar for man or beast. So there he was, back in the arid wastes of Nevada again. He stared across the flat basin, and up at distant ridges, and south toward Tonopah, but that didn't help him. His lifelong goal was to avoid work, and since he lacked the proper equipment, thanks to Bitter Bowler, he didn't have to work. So he wouldn't pry ore out of the few little deposits he knew of, and trade it for food. On the other hand, he was devoted to keeping these arid, secret wastes all to himself, and that meant driving out rivals, invaders, interlopers, and adventurers. That took less work, but more skill, and it didn't feed him. On the other hand, if Wet Agnes would feed him, he wouldn't have to work, and wouldn't have to shoo trespassers out of his private world. So the thing to do was persuade Agnes to feed him, but that required that he lay out dollars for himself and Sylvester every time he entered her oasis.

It was a puzzle, all right. Damned if he could figure it out.

The thing to do was find some other prospector, steal his pick and shovel, and get to work digging up some quartz gold. That would have the added advantage of leaving the victim without means of prospecting or making money off of what rightfully was Gladstone Brass's own principality.

That settled, he headed for the Monitor Range, which was rich in minerals and certain to contain a few prospectors, whose tools he would purloin. And he might manage to nab a little cornmeal or flour while he was at it.

"Sylvester, things'll get worse before they get better," he said.

Sylvester clamped yellow teeth on his arm.

All that mean day, the heat lancing in, he led Sylvester across the lonely flat, with not a cloud in the sky to show him any mercy. He rationed his water, and cheated Sylvester out of a full drink, and by late afternoon, under an oppressive sun, he reached the Monitors, and found the trail leading to Poison Springs. The spring did have some toxic metals in it, including cadmium, but the water improved the farther it got from the source, so the trick was to drink it at its lowest point, fifty yards from where it gurgled out in little gushes, with sulphurous gases adding noxious odors to the rocky gulch. It wasn't a spring for tenderfeet.

But tenderfeet is exactly what he found there, five in all, in fancy fresh clothing, shiny boots, flannel shirts, and big straw hats. They were stupid to wear straw in the desert. A true desert rat wanted a felt hat that would hold water in an emergency, or to water his beast.

The sun was sliding under the high ridge to the west, offering instant cool shade there in that gray stone hollow.

They watched him come, most of them standing around a tin cookstove. This was some outfit, all right. Dudes, the whole lot, out to get rich, probably with a few textbooks in their satchels about how to distinguish iron pyrites, fool's gold, from the real stuff.

They were congregated about the spring itself, where it belched from gray strata, so he led Sylvester to the lowest water and let the beast drink. He himself meandered up the slope.

"How-de-do," he said.

They surveyed him suspiciously—his battered clothing, worn boots, and also his face, stained chestnut by years in the sun.

"An old-timer, boys," said one.

"Mind if I sit a spell? Fill my canteens? Let Sylvester have his fill?"

"Not at all. We're the Battle Mountain Company. We organized to hunt down minerals, each of us buying a share, our tools and supplies in common, with Mizpah Mining Company the principal owner. I'm Lester, and this is Horace, and that's Elmer, and over there's Wilbur, and the one with our mules is Magnus."

"I'm Gladstone."

"Well, we're glad, too."

"Gladstone Brass."

"Fellers, this is a true desert rat, Gladstone."

"You fellers geologists and such?"

"Well, we've got a testing kit. We can field-test 'most any rock. We've got a mortar and pestle, mercury, and all the chemicals we need. So we'll cover the country parcel by parcel, bring in every species of rock we find, and test it out for mineral. We're equipped to locate gold, silver, platinum, tin, lead, copper, mercury, and a dozen lesser ones."

"Mighty fine," Gladstone said. "You out for a while?"

"We're supplied for a month, and by the end of a month we'll have examined every rock in a ten-mile square."

"You digging anything or just picking up samples?" Gladstone asked.

"Mostly we're picking up samples, float it's

called, stuff weathered out of mother lodes above. That saves us work, you know. Gravity is our helper."

"Find anything yet?"

"We'd rather not say, sir. We've a lot invested, and want the right outcome."

"Well, I've got a mule does my prospecting for me. Sylvester there. He's got a nose for mineral. He gets a whiff of quartz, and heehaws, and pretty quick he's going right up a slope and gets all excited, and starts licking the vein."

"That so? He's some mule."

"Had him twenty years almost," Gladstone said. "He knows me well as I know him."

"I always heard prospectors name their burros and mules," said Horace. "Why is that?"

"Son, you don't know what solitary is until you've been out here a couple of years. Then you discover you got a friend beside you. Beats having a wife."

"You're a card, Gladstone."

That tin cookstove was burning charcoal and heating up a kettle of savory stuff that had meat in it. Gladstone sure was feeling hungry, having survived on nothing all day. He eyed the camp. This was a luxury outfit, several mules, a tent they wouldn't need, even a couple of folding canvas chairs. Equipment was piled near the mules, and Gladstone spotted a couple of shovels and a pickaxe and a few pick hammers in the heap, along with some fancy testing gear, with bottles and burners.

"You gents mind sharing a bite with me? Had a little tough luck, and I don't want to eat Sylvester," he said.

"Well, we can't disburse unauthorized supplies, Gladstone. We've all purchased a share of this, and that would raise our costs."

Gladstone Brass mulled that a little. It was all familiar to him. The richer the outfit, the worse the tightwads. "All right, fellas," he said. "Mind if I visit? I always enjoy some company, and enjoy hearing good stories. Got a few myself. If you gents want to sit around the stove here, I'd enjoy hearing about your trip so far."

His stomach was grumbling at him, and Sylvester was glaring at him, wanting something to chew on, but this oasis lacked so much as sagebrush. But along about midnight, if he could manage it, he'd depart with a pick and shovel, or maybe a pick hammer, and whatever else he could slide into Sylvester's pack.

"We'll have some tea, Gladstone. We'll spare you some if you'd like."

"Mighty fine, mighty fine," Gladstone said. "It's about the color of good bourbon."

"We teetotal here, Mister Gladstone," Elmer said.

"Mighty fine, mighty fine," Gladstone said. "Mighty fine indeed."

Sylvester edged up, looking for something to steal, but all he could manage was a handkerchief.

"Gladstone, you'll want to put that mule over yonder, with our stock," Lester said.

"Mighty fine, mighty fine," Gladstone said.

He led Sylvester over to the herd, which was hovering close to the equipment pile, and that was all just fine. They were being fed oats from nose bags, which intrigued Sylvester. A few oats littered the rocky ground, and Sylvester made quick work of each oat.

"Say, gents, that tea, did you boil it up with water from that pool there?"

"We sure did."

"Well, I'll not be taking it then. That highest pool, it's got a lot of mineral in there that doesn't do the liver any good. Cadmium, selenium, zinc, maybe a nip of arsenic."

That sure caught their attention.

"Some call this Poison Springs," Gladstone said. "Now that water down at the lower end, it's better. Somewhere along the way here, some fresh water comes in and mixes, and you can drink that stuff down there."

"But it's dirty down there, Gladstone."

He shrugged. "Your choice, fellers."

Lester lifted the teakettle, poured out its contents, and headed down slope to find some fresher water. The rest looked uncomfortable. They had all taken drinks from the higher pool.

"They get real sick, old-timer?"

"Some do," Gladstone said. "Kills a few, especially them that got too thirsty. But most get over it pretty quick. It cramps up the gut some, turns flesh yellow. Makes some men crazy. I seen a few old-timers go plumb mad, all that stuff eating their brains."

"It wasn't labeled on the map," Elmer said. "We're careful about that."

"Nothing's right on any map of around here," Gladstone said. "A man shouldn't come into this here country without a guide saying what's what."

The evening passed uncomfortably; the outfit wasn't happy to have Gladstone on hand, and he was still hungry. Sylvester had profited from the company he was in, after jarring half the animals into spilling feed from their nose bags. At least Sylvester was dining, Gladstone thought.

Night settled. Gladstone retreated to the mule herd and settled under his saddle blanket. The rest climbed into fancy bedrolls. The camp quieted. After a good while, Gladstone arose, softly as a ghost, loaded a pickaxe and spade into Sylvester's pack, added a pick hammer for good measure, and drifted slowly down the rocky gorge and into the emptiness of the sage-dotted flats, leaving not a ghost of his presence behind him.

Chapter Nineteen

Gladstone Brass had solved his most daunting problem, but not his most pressing one. He had the tools he needed to gouge ore out of the rock and to prospect for new lodes. And he had the added joy of scaring away an organized band of prospectors. Poison Springs really wasn't that bad; it merely gave a man the trots. But that crew would spend the next day monitoring their health and imagining dire results. And some might retreat to the safety of Tonopah, done with the dangerous wilds of the desert.

Gladstone felt lucky. His goal was to rid his territory of all interlopers and invaders. He still had to find a way to drive Bitter Bowler out, but he'd find it, and do it, soon enough. But his immediate problem was an empty stomach. It was making him ornery. He hated to eat Sylvester, who was trotting along behind, the most cynical mule in creation. Whenever Gladstone tried out an idea on Sylvester, the mule just heehawed, which made Gladstone mad.

There was, actually, an abundance of food available in central Nevada, but extracting it from Wet Agnes's ramparts posed a problem. Still, borrowing some taters from Agnes sure beat going to Eureka and working as a swamper in a saloon. He knew he would head for Portuguese Peak, and Agnes's copious garden, but beyond that he lacked a plan.

Then he thought he should assault her fortress from the topside, from the peak itself, rather than reach it the usual way, up the long gulch leading to her verdant plateau. Yes, that was it. The peak itself was so formidable, so forbidding, that no prospector had ever explored it properly. There were steep massifs, fields of scree, sudden chasms, trails to nowhere, rocky escarpments that could not be climbed without mountaineering equipment.

Nonetheless, that garden would resolve his entire problem. It could be an ongoing source of good food for himself and Sylvester if he found the means to slide into it now and then, preferably late at night, snatch what was needed, and retreat high up into the aerie of the peak, there to lie back and enjoy life and watch the flight of hawks. If he could manage it, he would have the perfect solution to all his dilemmas. If she was so intent on work, then he deserved the benefit of it.

It was going to take some study. Agnes's green plateau was hemmed by vaulting gray cliffs that defied egress by anything four-footed, or two-footed for that matter. But Gladstone had spent decades in this wild, and he knew that one way or another he'd find a secret passage into that hidden garden, and there he could discreetly pluck up his needs, carefully concealing all that from Agnes, and thus survive month by month without the burden of working. Even prying ore out of a lode somewhere was hard work, something he was so averse to doing that he would rather go hungry.

"Sylvester, I have seen the future, and it works," he said.

Sylvester veered straight at him, and pushed him sideways, almost toppling him. It was an act of ingratitude, especially after Gladstone had taken him into a paradise of spilled oats.

Thus through the remainder of that night he hastened east, and by day he hastened northeast, and by that eve he was near the hidden gulch that would take him to Wet Agnes. Sylvester turned in, but Gladstone rebuked him.

"You're not so smart," Gladstone said. "We're not going to confront that woman and that shotgun. We're going around and up, high above Wet Agnes, and we will find a little pathway down into her garden. Share and share alike, I say."

Sylvester brayed. It so offended Gladstone that he refused to talk to the beast anymore. He was getting mighty hungry, and annoyed, and short-tempered. He chose a ridge half a mile north of Wet Agnes, and proceeded upward. It clawed out from the mountain a great distance, but proved a fine avenue to take him and Sylvester high up the flank. They entered a juniper zone, which was fine. It was heartening to find living things. In many of the basins and *playas* below, little or nothing lived.

Water was becoming a problem. There might be some higher on the peak, but the only sure source was at Wet Agnes's spring and pool. As the evening progressed, it cooled off, and made man and mule more comfortable. Gladstone cut south, crossing some ridges, and feared he had missed the plateau entirely. But then, suddenly, he reached a cliff, and far below was that green garden. He was high up, and as far as he could see, her entire plateau was guarded by similar ramparts on all sides except the one that drained the plateau.

"How are we going to get down there, Sylvester?"

Sylvester didn't know. He stood stockstill and said nothing. This was a serious thing; mules always knew how to get somewhere; that is how mules survive where lesser animals perish. But Sylvester hadn't the faintest idea.

Gladstone's belly was howling at him. He'd gone too long without anything. His water was gone. He had to find a way down there. He began working his way around the cliffs, clambering up grades, down crevices, sometimes reaching the cliff edge, where he could see Agnes's lush garden prospering below. But he saw no way down. Sylvester rebelled at the exertion, as well as the sheer danger that was present in that tumbled world. Gladstone was not just desperate; he was not far from collapse as he stumbled along the lip of the cliffs, risking his neck over and over.

A quarter moon rose, throwing pale whiteness over the landscape. Moonlight caught the peak above, where there was scattered juniper on rocky slopes, but nothing that hinted of water.

Gladstone doubted he even had the strength to return to Agnes's front gate and plead his case to her. He had navigated two-thirds of the cliffs that hemmed her flat when at last he found a gash in the rock, so narrow it looked as though a giant axe had chopped the cliff apart a few yards. It was clogged with rock débris, and some brush, too. It was beyond what a mule could negotiate.

"Supper time, Sylvester," he muttered. He collected his shiny new pick hammer, with its pointy tail useful for steadying himself or knocking a foothold in rock, and started down. He feared he might trigger an avalanche of loose rock, and he also feared he might not be able to return, and Sylvester would wait, lovelorn, high above for his friend. But Gladstone worked his way down the gash in native rock, wary of twisting an ankle or taking a tumble. Desperation gave him a heroic ability to skip and slide, scrape and cling, and a while later he stood, bewildered with joy, in the flat, white moonlight bathing the whole oasis. Far away, and in obscure shade,

Agnes slept in her stone cabin. He tiptoed across the flat, hoping her mule wouldn't bleat, and swiftly filled his canteen. Then he headed for the zucchinis, both food and water for his suffering beast, and found half a dozen giant ones, heavy and succulent. He nabbed a big turnip for himself, and that was all he could hope to carry. It took him a long time even to find that gash in the brutal rock, and the night was nearly expended by the time he began to crawl his way up the harrowing tumble of rock.

But he knew that only patience would see him to the top, patience and care, so he proceeded slowly, even as the moon swung away and left the trail deep in shadow, so he had to feel his way upward. Once he loosened some rock that went tumbling down, making noise, but mostly he clambered step by step, heart hammering, up the cleavage, and eventually burst out on top.

Sylvester clacked his teeth, and Gladstone immediately donated the zucchinis to the patient beast. There wouldn't be much belly salvation in a raw turnip, but he'd learned to make do, and in any case he was elated. With his knife he peeled paper-thin slices of it, and chewed away, relishing the taste of something starchy and vaguely moist. It would do. Sylvester demolished all the zucchini, leaving nothing for Gladstone, so he left no turnip for Sylvester. Fair was fair. Share all or share none.

He was tempted to work his way down the defile for another load, but the night was nearly spent, and he and Sylvester could rest serene in the knowledge that a whole pantry existed below. It had taken Herculean toil to get down there and back up with some eats, but he had done it. He had expended more energy doing that than a month of swamping a saloon in Eureka, but that was toil, and this was living fat off the land. This filled him with joy, like finding another ledge of quartz gold.

He rested there, his heartbeat slowly returning to normal, and then near dawn he started up the flank of the great mountain, looking for a home. What he had in mind was a pleasant grove, maybe in juniper, or something above, where he could settle in, build a nice shanty, harvest firewood easily to cook his booty, and maybe even find a little grass for Sylvester. So even as dawn lit the far side of the humped-up mountain, he slowly toiled upward, looking for a place to settle in for a long time, enjoying Wet Agnes's bounty.

The trouble was, that west face of the mountain was windy. In the winter it would be brutal, and now, in late spring, it was no Eden. Well, he would find something. Mountains were full of secrets and surprises. There was nothing close to Agnes's flat land, but he'd ferret out a spot soon enough.

He found a little grass in the juniper, and turned Sylvester loose while he dozed in the waxing heat of a new day. Dozing is what he did best. He was an expert at dozing. He could doze anywhere, any time he felt like it. But by late afternoon he was famished, and itched to descend to the flat for more vegetables and also to fill the canteens.

As much as he disliked the thought of work, he knew he could make his passage down the cleft much easier with a little bit of labor. There were rocks to move, steps to carve, some brush and old juniper wood to clear. So he left Sylvester up high, to eat his lovelorn heart out on the bit of grass there, and made his way into the cleft with his pick hammer. There he patiently improved the trail, removing obstacles. He reached Agnes's garden at sundown, and waited impatiently for full dark. He didn't doubt that Wet Agnes went to bed early and got up early. When the moon rose, and it was full dark, he slipped out onto the flat and began stuffing his shirt with the goods—carrots, some rhubarb, more turnips, a hill of red potatoes. He had enough to last a couple of days. He had been careful to harvest randomly, so that it looked like nothing more than an occasional failed plant, or maybe the work of an animal. He ascended the cleft easily this time, made his way up to Sylvester, gave him a drink, and settled into a happy evening. This time he could build a fire; it couldn't be seen from the flat. He could roast and boil, and then live in fat comfort except that he pined for some salt.

The next day he discovered a side gulch that was out of the wind. Some strata had been hollowed out, and that left a generous overhang that could easily be turned into a cozy home if he could find the energy to seal up the front with a rubble and mortar wall. He and Sylvester could be protected from winter weather, and enjoy the bounty of the desert. It was a little boring up there, but there was a whole mountain to explore, so he would have something to do.

"Well, Sylvester, I do believe that destiny has brought us to the right place at the right time, and there are happy days ahead."

Sylvester butted him hard, and whirled around to deliver a cruel blow with his rear hoofs.

"Well, it's true I have no ladies for you, Sylvester, but who knows? Maybe we'll catch one to keep you company."

Sylvester whirled again and bit his arm.

"You are ungrateful, Sylvester. Don't forget that I can have you for dinner at any time, so behave. You are a scrawny desert rat, and not a prophet."

The mule sulked away, leaving Gladstone Brass uncomfortable. The mule was trying to tell him something. Probably something ominous. But Gladstone decided to ignore the restless beast. Any man who could look forward to spending the rest of his days doing whatever he felt like doing should ignore the objections of his mule.

Chapter Twenty

Tonopah would be dangerous. Bitter Bowler slid into town expecting trouble. There would be no friends here, only ruthless men ferreting out the secrets of others. Such as his own secrets. For all he knew, he was a wanted man with a price on his head. He hated Tonopah on sight; it was a rough camp, half built up, full of men who'd as soon rob him of his few possessions as let him pass by on the clay street.

Bitter peered darkly at the passing throng, knowing that in the heart of each of those rough males lay a murderous greed. He would trust no one, which is why he slowly perused the main street, looking for signs in windows. In particular, looking for an assayer. He was damned if he would ask where an assayer might be. The minute he asked, half a dozen sharpers would furtively follow him, maybe even knock him on the head and steal his samples.

Not that he could trust assayers, either. Half of them were in league with rich men who wanted immediate word of any rich ore. They'd get him drunk, dope him up, try to ferret out his secret, and then knock him on the head and leave him to his fate in an alley.

Tonopah was sunny and pleasant, actually, but

he ignored that. The men who resided there had their own private tunnels of influence, running this way and that. If the assayer spread the word, and word sneaked out that Bitter had a major strike somewhere, there'd be fifty greedy men shadowing him when he left town, all of them armed with binoculars, watching, watching, as Bowler slid back to his bonanza ridge.

He was as nondescript as any man in town, his clothing so worn it barely clad him; his boots loose at the soles; his mule plainly starved; equipment spare and dented. But maybe that was good. More than half of those bearded males he spotted on the street were newly outfitted with boots that would blister heels, and shirts with all their buttons, and canvas pants so new they hadn't a stain on them.

One tour of the town did not yield an assayer. Another got the same result. He headed for the nearest livery barn with the sign: SILVER KING LIVERY, LIVESTOCK BOUGHT AND SOLD.

"Care for him a day or two?" Bitter asked the red-bearded hostler.

"Fifty cents a day in advance," the man said.

"Don't have it. But I'll give you a lien on the mule."

The liveryman smiled. "I get most of my stock that way. All right, he's mine for two days, and you redeem him for one dollar, by six tomorrow, or he's mine for good."

"I'll have it," Bitter said. "I need to talk to an assay man."

"Only one's up at the Mizpah Mine. He works for them, does independent assaying, too."

"And lets the management know when something interesting comes along."

The liveryman grinned. "You bet. This here livery barn is owned by the mine, too, my friend."

"Should have guessed." Bitter. said. "Say, you got a stick or a cane?"

The liveryman nodded, and pointed. An old cane hung on the wall. Bitter tried it out. He hobbled, then walked, and realized he could make his way now, even with an occasional jolt of pain.

"You got some chow? I'm so hungry I can't hardly stand up."

The red-beard eyed his man. "Well, looks like I'll end up with your mule, so I guess I can stake you to some beans. Pot of them in there."

Bitter found a pot of beans, flavored with side pork, sitting on a woodstove. He helped himself to a mighty bowl of them, wolfed them down, and stepped into the heart of Tonopah with an improved attitude. He edged toward the Mizpah Mine, glancing furtively behind now and then to spot the straggling thug, but there wasn't a soul on his trail. The mine buildings were spare, board and batten structures that would probably last about as long as the silver down below. One appeared to be an office; another contained the boilers to power the lift; another, off a ways, was a powder magazine. And another, unmarked, looked like the laboratory of an assayer.

He clutched his two pieces of float, the gaudy copper one, and the black silver carbonate, and entered. There was no counter here, just a small room with some equipment, including two furnaces, some crushing devices, various beakers and bottles and flasks, and fuel.

The young assayer eyed him from behind wire-rimmed glasses.

"I can't pay for it, but you get to keep what's in the samples," Bitter said.

"That's about the usual, old fella."

"Is it a deal?"

The assayer shrugged. "Let's see the rock, and I'll decide."

"You give the result to me and me alone?"

The man grinned. "My profession has standards, sir."

"So does the bank-robbing profession."

Bitter decided to go ahead. He was itching for news, and he wouldn't get it from palavering with this bought-and-sold employee of the mining company. He dug into his baggy pocket and extracted the two pieces of float and handed them to the gent. The assayer pulled up a magnifying glass, pursed his lips, licked the copper salts, and smiled. Then he examined the silver carbonate and frowned.

"That's silver ore, but I can't tell what's what without an assay. This other, the copper, that's full of copper, and looks like something that would earn me my pay."

"When will you have these for me?"

"Two, three hours. I've got nothing else that's keeping me busy. Where'd this come from?"

Bitter just smiled. Then just to make sure the assayer understood, he shook his head. And then just to put a period on it, he said: "Place so far and so hidden only me's ever gonna find it again."

"They all say that," the man behind the spectacles said. "All right. I'll give you a written report in . . . oh, three hours, maybe more. Have to get the furnaces fired up high. I'm Walt Wacker, by the way. And you?"

Digging again. "I'm George Washington," Bitter said.

"Suits you," Wacker said. "A man who could not tell a lie."

That ticked Bitter off. "I'll be back," he said.

He headed down the slope into town, fevered with the need to steal something. He had a mule to free, and food to buy. But the more he studied on it, the worse his prospects looked. His best bet was simply to panhandle. He'd get his tin bowl and see what sort of coin he could collect. The prospect was so annoying that he almost gave it up. It'd be easier to try any saloon and nip a bottle when the barkeep had his back turned.

Except that he didn't have money to buy a beer and wait for his chance.

He didn't want to call attention to himself. He wanted to slide in and out without a soul knowing it. In the end, he did nothing. He climbed the slope north of town and watched the shadows move across the south hills, and when he deemed the hour right, he walked over to the Mizpah Mine, watched the day-shift miners pour out of the lifts and head into town, carrying their black lunch pails, and thought they were fools, working nine hours a day for $3.50. They vanished in a hurry. Some of the night-shift men were already gathering around the head frame after checking in at the window of a small shack. He decided he would not be noticed, and slipped over to the assayer's lair.

True to his word, Wacker had his assays complete. The room was hot with furnace heat, which vented poorly in summertime.

"Well, Mister Washington, you've got some interesting ores there," Wacker said. "I've written up the reports, percentages, ounces per ton of ore, by-products. It's all on the forms here."

"Well, tell me," Bitter said. "I'm in a hurry."

Wacker grinned, enjoying the suspense. "Fella, you might have something big here. I say might because you brought me just one sample of each ore. A proper assay would include a dozen samples, some from well into the lode, spaced apart along the outcrop. So a single sample isn't any guarantee of anything."

"Dammit, tell me. I don't have all week."

"Well, that copper. There's a lot of it there, plus some silver and zinc and a trace of gold, plus the usual salts. Pretty, isn't it? It's all down there on paper, ounces per ton, but to make short work of it, that sample's about twenty percent copper, and one percent other metals."

"Twenty?"

"Yep. That's as fine a piece of ore as I've laid eyes on. Now, to make a copper mine work, there's gotta be a lot of it. Copper's not a precious metal, but it's in demand, now the country's wiring up. If there's a good deposit that you've got there, you've got a promising claim. But you'll need to do a lot of exploration, a lot of digging around, and going a few feet in to take samples that haven't oxidized. Air does things to ore."

"All right, all right," Bitter said.

Wacker smiled. "Now the other, it's even more interesting. It's all there on paper, ounces of silver per ton, all that, and by-products, lead and zinc mostly, but that piece you brought in, it's running about eight percent silver, and this ore's easy to reduce. Several good ways to take that silver out. Some ores just don't reduce, you know, like telluride gold, things like that. But this silver ore is just about as fine as anything a man could hope for in this life. Of course the same thing is true. You'll need to go back there and get a dozen samples, from wide apart, and fairly deep into your ledge, or outcrop, and bring them in for us to look at."

"Us? Us, Wacker?"

"Mizpah Mine, my employer. I assure you, sir, if this ore is plentiful, and a few more assays hold up, you're sitting on a bonanza such as most men can't even imagine. Mizpah might well buy you out for a price that would let you retire for life, own a mansion in California, or whatever suits, and live as most men dream of."

"You laying it on me?"

"I don't know what you mean, sir."

"You working me for a fool?"

Wacker wheeled over to a table and brought some small dishes to Bitter.

"It's still hot. That button there is silver. I weigh the button against the weight of the rock I started with. This here, as you can see, is copper in this dish. It's still hot. The other minerals have been tested by chemical means, and some mathematics."

Wacker touched the silver gingerly, and lifted it. He dropped it into Bitter's scaly hand. It felt warm and heavy. "That's about two ounces. And this copper's about five ounces."

Bitter knew exactly what to say: "I need a grubstake. I don't have a dime to go back out there and collect the samples you need."

"How big a grubstake?"

"Twenty dollars would put me in grub."

"You willing to give Mizpah a fifty percent stake in the claims, for the grubstake?"

"Nah, not for a good find like that. It's already found. Fifty percent on a sure thing? I ain't that dumb. All I gotta do is more assaying and stake it out."

"You're a good businessman, Mister Washington. You've been around the block, I see. Well, I'll make you a personal offer. I'll stake you to twenty dollars against the first two hundred dollars of ore you bring me. That'll give me a ten to one profit on my investment . . . if the ore is what you say it is."

"Two hundred? I'll do that. Wacker, I'm a millionaire, and two hundred's hardly worth noticing."

"Shake on it," Wacker said.

They did, and Wacker extracted a $20 Treasury note and handed it to the new bonanza king.

Chapter Twenty-One

$20 was a thin grubstake, but what did it matter? Bitter knew he'd be out for only a week or two, collecting assay samples and measuring and staking claims. Then his prospecting days would be over. He could retire to some wicked place like San Francisco and make up for lost time.

He redeemed his mule from the grinning liveryman, and headed into the mercantile district. First stop was the grocery, where he purchased flour and oats and beans, always beans, and sugar and salt and lard.

"Getting outfitted, old fella?" the aproned grocer asked.

"You bet I am, but this is the last time," Bitter said. "I'm about to make a killing. Just one quick trip and I'm fixed for life."

"You got a claim out there?"

"I'm not gonna reveal any secrets, but I know where to go and what I've got," Bitter said.

"Is it near here?"

"Wouldn't you like to know!"

Next stop was the hardware, for another canteen and some mineral testing stuff, including a flask of mercury, quartz pick, sample bag, charcoal block, blowpipe, candle, horn spoon, matrass, and magnifying glass. He'd do his own field tests and not let that crook Wacker give him a song and dance about the ore samples he brought in. He could do his own miniature smelting with a candle and blowpipe. Maybe he could avoid the assayer entirely, and not have to pay the man $200.

"Looks like you're heading out," the hardware man said.

"You bet I am, and for the last time, too. I know right where I'm going, and I'll do a little testing, and claiming, and retire."

"You've already found the lode?"

"Found it and assayed it. I may be sitting on the biggest bonanza ever seen in these parts. Makes Tonopah look like a piker."

"Just needs a little more testing, eh? With all this stuff?"

"Don't you go asking too many questions, because my lips are sealed."

He loaded the goods into his pack. He was outfitted for a couple of weeks, and that was all he would need. The mule eyed him malevolently; the weight brought out the worst in the beast.

Bitter had 45¢ left. The Tonopah Club beckoned. That was a Fancy-Dan joint, and he wore rags, but he'd show them a thing or two. No spirits had wet his lips for a year or two, and 45¢ would buy him two or three good drinks before he headed out.

The place was nearly empty, middle of the day, and the barkeep, in brocade vest, white sleeves with a garter, and black bowtie, eyed him without relish.

"What'll it be, old fella?"

"None of your rotgut. I want the bourbon you got hid under the counter, and make it double."

The keep hesitated. "Forty cents, you know."

"Put it there," Bitter said, laying a quarter and two dimes on the bar.

The barkeep eyed the cash, pulled a bottle of Old Orchard from below, and poured.

"Put in the nickel's worth, too," Bitter said.

The barkeep hesitated, then added a dash, slid the drink to Bitter, and collected the change.

"We're gonna toast me. Toast luck. I'm rich. I'll retire. I'll be up there with Rockefeller," Bitter announced.

The barkeep smiled and that only irritated Bitter.

"You've heard it all, haven't you? Well, I'm telling you here and now, when I head out, I'll be going to a place no man's ever seen but me, right out there in the middle of nowhere, a place only I know about, a mountain of copper and silver, and every bit of it is mine."

"Sounds good, old-timer," the barkeep said, sliding the change into a cash drawer.

"When all your Fancy Dans come in here for a drink, you tell them about me, and tell them they'll get the rest of the story in a few weeks, and that you poured one for the bonanza king of Nevada, dressed so poor you hardly let him in."

The barkeep was grinning.

"This here Old Orchard, it's no good. Few weeks from now, I'll show you what kind of whiskey money can buy."

"Where's this place you're going?" the barkeep asked.

"Wouldn't you like to know! You and all your customers in here, the ones that try to euchre a man out of his fortune."

The more Bitter drank, the more truculent he felt, and by the time he had downed the generous spirits, he was in a glowering mood.

"I'm outta here, and don't you mess with me. You tell anyone about this, and you'll end up in the alley behind here."

The barkeep polished the bar and smiled.

Bitter strode out, untied the line, and led his mule away. The street was mostly empty. No one was paying the slightest attention to a ragged prospector, unkempt, ratty-bearded, wearing boots with soles half loose. Good. He was a millionaire but no one would guess it. Tonopah dozed in the desert sun.

He trotted around the blue mountain guarding Tonopah and headed north, the mule laboring under bags of feed, loaded canteens, and a bunch of stuff to help him analyze ores. He peered behind him now and then to see whether some freebooter or another was pursuing, but of course there was no one. He had kept his secret; not a man in Tonopah had any idea who he was or where he was headed.

Ahead lay the mysterious desert wastes that he knew better than anyone else on earth. He had marked every rock, like a territorial dog; he had wet mountains and gulches, his territorial instinct running deep in him. And now it was all his.

He felt no weariness at all in spite of lacking sleep. He had not stayed over in Tonopah, but had completed his task during daylight. He had hoped to make Poison Springs, where he had treated the rubes to a few lessons, but he knew he couldn't find it in the dark, so he finally turned up a gulch and made a dry camp. There was no wood around, so he had no fire to heat up some beans, but it didn't matter. He shared some canteen water and some oats with the grouchy mule and made a bed for himself by scooping sand and gravel into a depression, and hastened into sleep.

He awakened with a start, certain he was being stalked by unknown criminals, but even as he lay quietly, ancient revolver in hand, the night lay still and windless. No living creature was anywhere close. It was so dry around there that even snakes needed water bags. Slowly his heart quieted. He had let himself be startled by phantasms. But it paid to be alert. He congratulated himself on his wariness. He would let nothing stop him.

Still, he could not sleep, and with the earliest hint of dawn he loaded the mule and struck north, enjoying the cool desert air. He would breakfast at Poison Springs, where there was water, and top his canteens again. As day broke, he studied his back trail, knowing that a fine tracker might have ways to shadow him. A man with a spyglass could do a lot.

Bitter reached the gulch that led to Poison

Springs by midmorning, just as the summer's heat was building, and he trotted in, wary of company. But there was no one present, and the connected series of pools slumbered under brassy skies.

"Drink up, you dunce," he said to the mule. But the animal didn't like that water, nosed around in it, and was slow to fill up. Bitter itched to get ahead, claim his bonanza, but he hadn't been a desert rat for nothing. He boiled up some beans while the mule nosed around in brush, nipping bits and pieces.

While he was waiting for the weak flame to do its work, he patrolled the place. He always studied the ground around springs and wells. You never knew what rubes might leave behind. In this case they had left a broken nose bag, which he snatched up with joy. A nose bag was worth plenty, especially as an emergency pail. He studied the broken strap, resolved to mend it, and then tackled his beans, scalding his tongue on them.

He took his mule north again, knowing he had to cross the anonymous flats on his right, but unsure just where he had crossed earlier. The country lay low, without landmarks, and baked under a sun that sucked him dry. He eyed the horizon to the east, knowing he had to cross that range, and one more range. Or was it two? It didn't matter. He had a nose for a place, and he'd find it.

He wondered whether he was hiking too far north, and spent aching hours trying to remember how and where he had crossed that basin. And then, fearing he would go too far, struck east across a waste so dry it scarcely supported sagebrush. He reached a low blue range naked of vegetation, a range that didn't rise high enough to empty any clouds, and he hunted for the place where he had worked across it, and the place where he had found water. Or had he? Where was the water he'd found on the trip? Hard to say, but not in this range, which was scalding his feet that murderous summer day. It all made him itchy but he wasn't worried. The next range east was majestic, with dark patches high up, which meant either juniper or pine slopes, and water somewhere. Maybe that was the range where his fortune lay, but he was pretty sure it was the range beyond. It was two ranges, or was it three, from Poison Springs? It annoyed him that he hadn't taken note carefully. Everything looked different going this way. The landmarks he had memorized weren't there, which puzzled him. But no matter.

"Getting hot, you varmint? I should trade you in on a barn full of race horses," he said to the mule. "Rich men, we all got some great horseflesh. If you don't have some race horses running, you haven't got there yet."

The mule plowed doggedly ahead, its head low. Bitter watched him, seeing the signs of thirst and exhaustion in the beast. They topped the arid range and descended into worse heat, this time in the late afternoon when they should have been shaded up in a gulch somewhere. But in his eagerness he had pushed out upon a *playa*, a dry lake with only caked and cracked clay underfoot.

There had better be a well ahead. He was sure there was. He had come this way once, hadn't he? But he was having a tough time trying to locate himself. He couldn't see a single one of the landmarks he had memorized before. He could do a dry night and find water the next day. But as evening descended he was still out on the *playa*, still crossing a baked flat full of furnace heat. He made the first of the gulches of the next range, and followed it upward, finding neither brush nor water. In fact, it was nothing but a rocky watercourse that once in a long while channeled tons of water off the stormy peaks and onto the *playa*. But not a blade of grass grew in any of its cracks.

He found a widening of the gulch and called it a day. He had a little water, and there would be more up in those dark slopes a few miles up. It was quiet. No breeze cooled the rock, which continued to bake him and the mule. He decided on half rations of water this eve; save the rest for dawn, and the trip up to the moist peaks. The mule licked up every drop and waited for more.

Bitter didn't eat; all a man could do was prop

himself against a rocky wall of the gulch and wait for the sun to sink and some blessed cool air to tumble out of the mountains. Tomorrow he'd find that well he'd dug in the brush-choked gulch, the well that was only a short walk from his copper and silver ore. This was the range, all right.

The mule stared at him, neck low, with blame in its eyes.

Chapter Twenty-Two

Chalk Spring wasn't much of an oasis. A dribble of slimy water oozed from an odd formation in which strata of yellow sandstone rested on gray granite in a cañon wall. The dribble sank into sandy soil, leaving no pool, so anyone using the spring had to catch the water as it leaked from its subterranean vault. Not much grew there. The water appeared and disappeared. But it was strategically located a day or so from any other water, and thus was hard used by prospectors and the occasional wild burro or even deer that survived in this naked land.

Beef Story steered his prisoner up the dry gulch, unpromising and devoid of any sign of moisture. Albert Gumz followed along, his demeanor placid and serene, which struck Story as odd, considering that Gumz faced years in the Carson City prison.

They reached the spring and stared at the dribble of cloudy water leaking down the cliff wall.

"Chalk Spring," Story said. "It's gyp water. It tastes bad and it's full of salts, and it'll give you the trots. The mules tolerate it better."

"The trots, you say? It sounds like something sent from heaven."

"Yep, it'll send you to the bushes, I guarantee it. And there's no bushes around here. The water doesn't do much for vegetation, as you can see."

"Sheriff, let me at it. For much of my life I've been bound up, for reasons unknown to me, and I've suffered at the hands of every quack in Europe, and a few on this side of the Atlantic. It's been my sorrow, the burden I bear, the misery inflicted on me. If this fine flow does what you say it will, sir, then this spring's the most merciful in the world. I would happily spend my life here."

He hastened to the spring, washed his hands in the flow, and then cupped them and began drinking handful after handful. He tackled the drinking with such enthusiasm that Story was duly impressed, and thought maybe the gyp water would improve his own evacuation. Indeed, he'd experiment. Maybe he'd take a canteen of it back to Eureka, and see if it helped him over the long term. He could even import it to Eureka. A man could make a fortune and relieve the distress of half the population with a little gyp water.

"Be a little cautious, Gumz. You've got a long

way to go, and I'll not have you stopping every half hour."

"Sheriff, it would be heaven on earth to stop every half hour and improve my comfort. I'm in paradise. I was born to wander this country. I can dodge hard work and relieve myself on schedule. When your justice system is done with me, I'll come here."

Story let the mules lap up water. They didn't mind the miserable taste, and knew how to slobber it straight off the rock into their mouths. Then Story filled the canteens and proposed to leave. This was no place to tarry. There was no wood for a fire, no place to lie down in the scree, and no place to spend a night. He knew a spot a few miles north where a delta from a gulch managed to support some brush, and a man could cook up some beans.

But just as they got ready to leave, a commotion below reached their ears. Story immediately loosened his revolver. He was escorting a bank robber to justice and company could be trouble. But what appeared down the trail did not seem menacing. A group of men in new clothing, well-groomed and prosperous, was making its way toward the spring. They were bringing some well-groomed mules, each laden with a heavy pack, some with panniers, some employing the diamond hitch. They were not wearing sidearms, though Story did see a rifle sheath hanging from the side of one of the mules.

He made sure his star was pinned to his shirt.

"Well, sirs, we seem to have company," the lead man said.

"Beef Story, Eureka," the sheriff said. "And you?"

"I'm Lester Lambeau, sir. Our pleasure. This is the Battle Mountain Company. We're mostly geologists in the employ of a mining concern."

"Mining company? Here?"

"Especially here, Sheriff. We have designs upon the water in the whole territory. We've been staking claims to all of it. See that fella? That's Horace Winfield, and his mule's loaded with the finest cartography equipment on earth. He has the finest chronometer known, and sextant and compass, and he can pinpoint our location within a few yards, given a clear night or a good noon sun. Water's the key to controlling the whole area. Once we own the water, we'll be in a position to own or discover all the minerals, because no one else can even penetrate this arid land."

"I see," said Story, feeling vast displeasure leaking up through him.

"Yep, we'll have the water located by late summer, and, after that, everything in here is our oyster."

"Can you do that? Take the water?"

"Certainly we can. Federal law. Water rights. Nevada law. Water rights. It's all perfectly legal and on the books, and once we've got the juice of life, we've got the territory."

The rest of the Battle Mountain Company collected around the sheriff, eyeing his star, and the person with him. Story absorbed more names: Elmer, Wilbur, and Magnus.

"Sheriff," said Gumz, "that gyp water. You mind if I retreat from here for a moment? It's become . . . well . . . urgent."

"Go ahead, Gumz." Story watched the young man hasten away. "Gyp water," Story said. "It gives a man a need."

"Yes, well, we'll file on it. By summer's end, the company will own the water."

"Maybe not," Story said, thinking of Wet Agnes and her double loads of buckshot. He fervently hoped she would triumph, and wondered whether she had filed for her water, or even had known what to do or how.

Albert Gumz vanished behind a boulder, so Story waited.

"What springs have you got so far?" he asked.

"Poison Springs, that's the best so far. Baker Well, Soda Seep, Missing River, and a couple more we found that no one's named," Lester said. "That's the advantage we have. We're geologists. We know a thing or two. We've also picked up some promising float, but we'll look at minerals after we lock up the water."

Story was so incensed he could hardly contain

himself, but what was legal was legal, and he didn't have grounds to do what he itched to do, which was to haul the whole lot to his jail in Eureka and see to it they spent about ten years behind bars.

They looked to be substantial men, used to outdoor living, able to survive in this country. Their mules were in good flesh, with good shoes, and were carefully loaded. There wasn't a pack askew, or a girth strap loose.

Story felt oddly helpless. Somehow this wilderness should stay wild. It shouldn't belong to anyone. No men or group of men should control it by commanding its scarce water. These men were smart, and whoever was financing them was smart, and Story felt oddly dumb as he conversed with them.

Gumz seemed to be gone a long time, and just when Story decided he'd better go after the bank robber, the young man emerged from his rocky latrine, and made his way back to the crowd.

"All right," he told Story.

"He's not alone, that spring is tonic for several of us," Lester said.

"Then leave it for the world to use," Story said.

They grinned at him.

He and Gumz retreated down the unpromising draw, and rounded a bend and were alone.

"Someone should guard the springs against

that outfit," Gumz said. "Someone clever, able to drive them off."

"My thinking's less kind," Story said.

"Mankind depresses me," Gumz said. "Some things should be held in common."

"Why didn't you make a run for it? You could have gotten away," Story said.

"And join up with them? I may be a bank robber, sir, but I have a sense of decency."

They headed out once again, pushing like ants across a vast and mysterious wasteland that was filled with surprises. Gumz was becoming an experienced desert traveler, and was learning how to care for himself in a land without comforts. The next stop would be the spring at Angel Cliff, but Story didn't say that. That one had sweet water, forage for the mules, and a few trees and brush for some firewood. And after that, a long waterless haul of some thirty miles to Eureka.

"I suppose we have a way to go still," Gumz said.

"Two days. And the last day is hardest."

"If you were to sell the revolver you took from me, it'd bring more than ten dollars, and you could return the entire amount to your bank, with no loss at all."

"I just may do that. But why do you care?"

"It brings things to a proper conclusion."

"Proper being ending the bank's loss, right? But your robbery requires its own punishment."

"I am at your mercy, sir."

"No, the mercy of the courts, not me."

They walked through heat all day, arriving at the spring just before dusk. The place exuded an ethereal beauty, with a trickle of water gurgling out of golden rock, sunlight catching distant peaks, a purple heaven, and close at hand the serenity and comfort of woods and water. There were some animal tracks in the sand, including the small imprint of desert mule deer.

Story unburdened the mules and watered them in the turquoise pool at the foot of the sheltering cliff. Gumz washed himself and found work to do, such as collecting kindling and filling canteens and starting a small cook fire. Story found a little grass back a ways, and turned the horses loose in it. They would not wander far, with forage and water so close.

A great quiet descended upon the spring, along with a cool eddy of air from some alpine place far above. The cool air comforted them, and gave them their ease. There in the harshest land Story had ever visited, he found beauty and grace, and balm for his spirit. He did not really want to go to Eureka. This place, this peace, was all that a man could want. He pushed the thought aside.

Gumz turned quiet. By this hour tomorrow, he would be locked in a cell in the Eureka court-house. And the day after, the wheels of justice would begin their long grind.

They ate their beans slowly, enjoying the lingering light. They heard the cooing of a dove. It was the first bird song Story had heard this entire trip across rock-girt land. Gumz eyed his captor now and then, and Story saw curiosity in the man's face. As if there would be decisions made, fateful words in the offing. But Story kept his silence, and let the night progress, let the stars spark to life in the bowl of heaven. They each had a saddle blanket for warmth, and this eve they might need them.

Yet there was something that needed saying.

"Gumz, listen closely. I'm leaving you here tomorrow," Story said. "I'm taking one mule, the one carrying the cash and a few things I'll need along the way. I'll add ten dollars to the Treasury notes and turn it all over. Then I'll go to the county supervisors and tell them I've gotten the money, and I'm going to resign then and there. They can appoint someone else. I have a good deputy. Then I'm coming back here. You'll either be here or not. Either you'll have the other mule, and the stuff on it, canteens, mess gear, or not. Either stay or go your own way."

"Honorable Sheriff, I am your prisoner."

"You were."

"I lack the . . . shall we say experience . . . to make my way in this hard land, sir."

"That's right. But you might want to try. You've learned a lot in a few days."

"I would perish in a week, sir. But if you return, what would your intent be?"

"Living easy. Oh, not right away. I'm wanting to clean up some odds and ends. I want to keep that Battle Mountain outfit off of Wet Agnes's back. They'll find her, and claim her spring, and push her out. I'd like to even things up some."

"Sir, it seems to me that she's a match for the whole lot."

"No, not in the Land Offices and courthouses where smart men file claims, put the law and the government to work anchoring their greed. She knows little about that, or how easily that outfit can steal what's hers."

"I would be honored to join you, Mister Story. My fate is still in your hands."

"No, your fate is what you make of it, Gumz."

Chapter Twenty-Three

Impatiently Gladstone Brass fretted time away, waiting for full dark, when a great quiet would descend upon the desert. Sylvester yawned, worked his yellow teeth around a juniper limb, mostly for something to do. Junipers tasted foul.

Finally Gladstone judged the night to be well along and slid into the crevice that would take him to Wet Agnes's lush gardens. He was getting the hang of it now, and worked his way down the cleft, dropping silently over ledges, easing over gravel. This time he had a bag, fashioned from an old shirt, and at last he stepped onto the quiet plateau, deeply shadowed from the rising moon. It would help to have a little light, but he had sharp night vision, and he knew he could find his way through the cantaloupes and cabbages and turnips.

He eyed the silent cabin, knowing its mistress lay asleep after working herself to the bone this day. He marveled that she could accomplish so much, never pausing to rest. Most of the two- or three-acre crop was hand watered, using a bucket she carried from her well. A pleasant breeze descended from the peak, bearing the aroma of juniper. The cabbages were well along, so he decided to snatch two of them, well apart so it didn't look as though the two were missing from her orderly rows through a human agency. One came loose with a smart crack, and then he grabbed a smaller one and eased it gently from the sandy soil. Two cabbages. Next, some zucchini, which he would use to feed Sylvester. He snapped several big ones from their vines, and loaded those in. It was a little early in the season for potatoes, but he decided he hankered for some spuds anyway, so he carefully pried a plant free, and with a spare stick opened up the hill and bared a cluster of small, brown potatoes. These he gathered, and decided that would be enough. His sack was full.

He started out of the potato patch when the ground came up and bit him. Or rather, some piece of steel clamped his boot and held on, hurting his calf, causing him to tumble. This thing had caught him well. It had clapped his leg in its jaws, and loudly, too. He tugged, discovered a heavy chain leading from the trap to some anchor that could not be budged.

Damned woman. He hurt. He set down his loot and began prying at the iron jaws, to no avail. This was no ordinary trap; it was intended for bears, or maybe elephants. He pulled and pried, but that only made the jaws hurt his leg the more. He was glad that it caught his boot and not naked flesh, or he would have suffered an amputation. He thought to unlace his high-top boot and slide his leg out, but the jaws were so firm that it didn't seem possible.

The more he struggled, the more he hurt, and he finally surrendered and waited for moonlight, when he could see how the trap was anchored and free himself. He raged at the woman. He was simply borrowing a few of her vegetables; she was treating it as a major crime. He wished he had never seen this corner of paradise, and had never been tempted to slide in and cop a few meals.

She loomed over him, wearing a thick robe. Moonlight glinted off the barrels of her shotgun.

"Gotcha," she said. "You weren't fooling me."

"Agnes, this thing is killing me. It's amputating me. Take it off."

"In some parts of the world, Brass, they cut off the hand of a thief."

"Save my leg, Agnes."

"I think it is serving its moral and educational purpose, just as it is, Gladstone."

"It's cut my circulation. My foot prickles."

"Then prickle away, foot. Do you think your foot's worth, let's see here, some cabbages, some potatoes stolen before they were half grown, and some turnips?"

"Agnes, help me. This is meant for bears, not mortals."

"And what will happen if I release you?"

"I'll return the cabbages. I need the zucchini for Sylvester. I will make it up with honest labor."

"You're like my late husband Jared, if truth be known. So lazy he'd risk a leg rather than work. You wouldn't be in this spot if you had a knack for getting things done. Have you ever produced anything in your worthless life?"

"Gold, madam. I brought gold into the world. Now, please release me. My leg is dying by inches."

"I'm not sure how to spring that thing, Gladstone. I don't rightly remember. So you'll have to suffer until I figure it out."

"I am doomed," he said.

She settled the shotgun on the ground, well away from Gladstone. And then she felt the trap, her fingers working around it. "There's a pin you pull that releases the leaf spring," she said.

"I'll find it!" he cried. "Agnes, you're the most beautiful, sweet, thoughtful woman on the Nevada desert."

"Since I'm the only woman, Gladstone, that's hardly kind of you. But I'll take it for what it's worth. You have a gifted mouth."

She found the pin, pulled it hard, and suddenly the jaws fell slack.

Gladstone fought back tears. His leg felt mauled and lacerated, but he could find no broken flesh or blood. He moaned, running his hand over his high-top boot, loosening it, poking gentle fingers into it to feel his outraged flesh.

"I knew it would be you. I played a guessing game. You were first choice, a few other lazy louts second or third choices. But now I have your sworn oath that you will perform honest labor, so consider yourself employed."

"I will weed your fields until daylight, madam."

"No, you will be much more useful to me in another office, Gladstone. The only flaw in this little farm is the lack of firewood. I need it for cooking, and for heat in the winter. I've made do with brush down the gulch, but that's thinning out. I need a dozen cords of good wood, brought down from above. Anything will do, even juniper, but I'd prefer the pine up there. Now that I've let your leg live, you may consider yourself obligated. A dozen cords of firewood."

"Agnes," he said cheerfully, "I have neither saw nor axe, or wagon to haul it."

"Good try, Gladstone. I will lend you the saw and axe, and you may use my mule as well as Sylvester to carry the wood to me. If you should lose or damage my tools, I will arrange for you to step into the bear trap again. Don't be clever. You'll end up doing even more work. Jared was very clever, but he died young."

Gladstone had nothing to say. This was worse than twenty years in the state pen.

Just then, Sylvester bleated, and galloped across the little flat to his master.

"He found that cleft in the cliff," Agnes said. "Now I have two mouths to feed."

The mule was industriously chomping on the zucchinis, his yellow buck teeth slicing them to bits.

"I have a softness in my heart for mules," she said. "Unlike human males, mules work hard and are loyal and smart. How did he acquire his noble name?"

"Elimination, Agnes. Nothing else fit. There is only one Sylvester in all the world of mules, and he's it."

"I lack pasture enough for two mules. You will have to work hard so we can purchase grain for him."

"He makes his own living, given the chance, Agnes. Up where the mountain goats roam."

"He's a handsome mule. I don't suppose he's all boy, is he?"

"It takes a jack and a mare to make a mule, Agnes."

"I am innocent of such things, Gladstone."

"That's why you're the most beautiful woman on earth, Agnes. Beauty and innocence go hand in hand."

"I swear, Gladstone, I will overlook your worst failings. You and Sylvester may sleep in the pen and in the morning I will send you off with a breakfast."

It didn't quite work out that way. Gladstone usually slept to 9:00 or 10:00, but she was up at first light, around 5:00, and soon had flapjacks awaiting her guest.

He wasn't half awake, but he downed the cakes while the downing was good.

Then she handed him a cross-cut saw and an axe, and pointed at a cliff. "You don't need to bring the wood clear down here. Just take it to that cliff and pitch it over. My woodpile will accumulate over there, where it'll be handy. Come in for supper, if you've earned one. Remember . . . work or starve."

That was the depressing beginning of the day. Gladstone loaded the tools on the mule, and together they toiled up to the alpine splendor above, just as the sun began to light up surrounding ridges. It was a noble sight, but Gladstone wasn't in the mood for noble. After three decades of liberty, he was trapped in a prison of his own making.

He passed the overhang where he had intended to lay about, sneaking food when he needed it. He was tempted to nap, but thought better of it, and headed upslope, finally entering dense juniper mixed with pine. He realized that for eons of time these bushes and trees had been shedding limbs. He didn't need to cut anything. He loaded up Sylvester with a bunch of dry wood, and together they retreated half a mile to the cliff, and he pitched the stuff over.

It gave him no satisfaction.

"All right, one more, and that's it for today," he said to Sylvester. "We got all summer to fix her up for the winter."

He collected another load of ancient wood, tossed it over the cliff, and then he retreated to the overhang he called home for a nap.

"Go eat, dammit," he said to the mule.

The beast snorted, headed up toward the thin brown grass above, and that was the last Gladstone would hear from him.

He studied his meager possessions. What few items he had were ragged and falling apart. His clothing was patched and torn and threatening to fall away. His ancient saddle blanket, which did double duty as his cover at night, was soaked with the sweat of several mules, the color washed out of it by sun and weather. The duck cloth of the panniers was ripped and grimy. His two canteens were battered and one didn't hold water unless it was kept upright. He usually wore it over his chest. What shocked him was Agnes's shiny tools. The axe had a shiny new handle, and the blade was good silvery steel, with a fine edge that didn't have a nick in it. The cross-cut saw was brand new, with fresh teeth that would rip through any wood. But they were hers, unless he stole them and traded them for some chow in Eureka.

He could do that. He could smuggle enough out of her garden to make a trip to Eureka, sell those tools of hers, and head out, a free man once again. He wished Sylvester were about so he could discuss the issue with the mule, who was smarter than Gladstone Brass would ever be.

He realized that this was a momentous point in his life. He could still preserve his freedom and escape this life of indentured servitude. He could start prospecting again, clean out pockets of gold, get along free as the wind. Or not. He could become Wet Agnes's slave. That's what it amounted to. Work himself to the bone for a little chow and a chance to visit with a non-woman. That's what she was. She wasn't any usual female, in flounces and straw hats. This was something else, not properly called female. He couldn't put a label to her. What proper woman would come out here and build a stone cabin and start a garden?

He decided he'd stick for a few days, fatten up on her good food, pitch some firewood to her, and then get out. And he'd take her saw and axe with him. He had earned them. And he'd outfit and return to the life he knew best, all alone, the emperor of no-man's land.

Chapter Twenty-Four

Gladstone Brass sank into woe. He went about| his toil with many a sigh and groan, and dark thoughts about being a slave to a petticoat tyrant. Here he was, in the middle of paradise, and saddled with cruel labor. He had fled her to escape the fate of other males who chained themselves to a life of drudgery to support a wife and children. He didn't want wives or children; he wanted a life lived in ease and liberty, and the Nevada desert was the perfect place for it— until now.

He and Sylvester gradually explored the wooded mountainside, gathering the deadfall, the easy pickings scattered about. He decided that when he had gathered the last of it, that would be his parting day. He and Sylvester would quit this slavery. He drew a line—when the moment came when he would have to employ his saw and axe to bring firewood to her, that was the moment, the hour he'd up and quit.

Thus did he toil for a week more, dumping

deadwood over the cliff, heading down the cleft in the cliff for a bountiful supper, which gave him the opportunity to complain that he was being put upon and Sylvester had been reduced to animal slavery.

She smiled, as if she had heard it all before, which she probably had, and served up some vegetables drawn from her blooming gardens.

"Agnes, you're the most gorgeous, wise, and delightful woman this side of the Mississippi River," he said, to keep her at arm's length. If he didn't compliment her, she'd think of new tasks for him. But that always won him a tittering little laugh, and she would clear away the dishes without asking him to do it.

He learned to vary his flattery. One day he'd tell her she was sublime beauty, the essence of womanhood. The next day he'd tell her she was the most schooled and educated and brilliant woman to cross the Great Plains. And other days he'd surprise her by saying she was sweet and tender, and would make someone a perfect wife. He didn't believe any of it, but what did it matter? All that was his only crowbar to pry her away from him. Gladstone was a man of the world, capable of dealing with anything.

He roamed farther and farther up Portuguese Peak, collecting deadwood and hauling it to her. But this slope was hemmed by gulches and ridges, and clearly he was running out of deadwood, and the great red-line moment was upon him. On his very last trip he traveled clear to a giant cañon that stretched north, and that's when he saw it. A reddish brown streak veered upward, mostly concealed by juniper. He knew the color, the rust color of iron oxide, and a potent sign of minerals in the formation. There it was, and he didn't even have a pick hammer to explore it, but those were not far away. A wave of delight coursed through him.

"Sylvester, we have toiled our last hour. We have hauled our last stick of wood. We have reached the promised land," he said.

Sylvester yawned. The wise mule knew that Gladstone's rhetoric was premature. He had yet to examine the lode, which could just as well be a dud as a bonanza. Mules had a way of humbling a man.

Gladstone hurried back to his overhang where his pick hammer and sample bag rested. He collected these, while Sylvester eyed him as one would eye a person gone berserk, and soon enough they were back at this amazing ledge, which stretched as far as Gladstone could see at a crazy angle upward along a giant fault with cliff on one side and a steep slope covered with scree on the other.

"This is it, Sylvester. This is the Holy Grail. This is the Pearly Gates. This is life in the South Seas surrounded by maidens in grass skirts."

Sylvester clamped yellow incisors over Gladstone's waving arm, to quiet him.

"You're right, you ornery mule," Gladstone said.

He eased out upon the scree. For the first fifty yards or so he could reach the quartz vein. He was all a-tremble, his lungs heaving, as he made his way out upon the treacherous scree, eyeing the quartz. At first it was plain brown translucent crystals, quartz laced with iron. But then it turned whiter and clearer, and that's when Gladstone saw it—wiry gold threading the quartz, pure gold easily knocked out of the crystallized mineral. He whacked a piece loose and licked it, which improved the view. Sure enough, the threads of gold retreated into the quartz, but there were nodules, too, nuggets of pure glowing gold shining in the desert sun.

"Eureka!" he said.

He didn't know where the phrase came from, but it was what finders of bonanzas were supposed to utter at the moment of discovery. A whole town named Eureka lay fifty miles north.

Sylvester yawned. For once Sylvester was dumb as a stump. Gladstone gloated. He wouldn't need to show any respect to a mule like that.

Gladstone continued to edge out on the scree, fearful of falling backward and tumbling down the brutal incline hundreds of feet. But gold made a man reckless, and Gladstone didn't mind risks for a discovery like this. He gingerly made his way out, taking samples every little while, pausing in awe when he found a formation of solid white quartz a yard high, all of it laced with native gold. He chipped off a few pieces and popped them into his sample bag. He felt half crazy, and if he had wings for arms he would have flown. But there came a point when the vein angled sharply upward, where the earth's upheavals had snapped the ledge into a new vector, and Gladstone could no longer reach it.

But he was not through. He gingerly worked his way out upon the treacherous rubble, looking for float. And there was plenty of it. Lying loose amid the country rock were pieces of the ledge, milky quartz, there for the plucking. He snatched this piece and that, working out upon the rubble, until at last his sample bag could hold no more. He collected a dozen more pieces, stuffing them into his worn shirt, and finally surrendered to reality. He was a walking rock pile, and if he wasn't careful, he'd stumble in the scree, tumble down-slope, and kill himself at the very moment of triumph.

Sylvester had wisely stayed back, and now awaited Gladstone as he gingerly retreated back to safe turf where pine and juniper struggled to survive. He made it without disaster, and sat, shaking, while he recovered his wits.

"Sylvester, we can retire," he said.

But the knowledge of the ledge was also the knowledge that it could be staked, claimed, and stolen by anyone. He sighed. There was brutal work ahead. He needed to measure the claims, three hundred by six hundred, federally-mandated dimensions, build cairns at the corners, place his written claim in a waterproof container, and then go file his claims at the nearest federal Land Office.

The task filled him with foreboding. The moment he filed, his secret would be public, and the schemers would soon be looking for ways to rob him. Indeed, some would show up well armed, and simply clean out all the quartz in sight, no matter whose claim it was.

He would need to keep it secret. He would need to clean out a fortune before anyone else knew of it. He would need to work in silence, secrecy, gouging the vein, storing the ore, hidden from view.

That would take work. The thought made him ache. He wouldn't quite plunge into the world of lifelong leisure without doing a heap of work.

He poured the rock out of the sample bag, arms a-tremble, and began licking and picking at his lode. Some of the wire gold he could simply pluck out of the decaying quartz. Other samples yielded to a tap of his pick hammer, which shattered the quartz and freed the gold. In a few minutes he had a pile of free gold, and there were tons of quartz waiting.

Time vanished. He popped open quartz, pulled the freed gold out of it, and then suddenly it was twilight. He should have been at Agnes's long before. He packed up reluctantly, not wanting to leave this place, but his stomach was interfering with his ambitions, and he grumpily retreated, and found his way down the cleft to Agnes's fertile fields.

"I put the food away," she said. "You're out of luck."

"But, Agnes . . . I'm hungry."

"Go wash. I don't lack water. You have a week's dinners in your scruffy beard. Your hair hasn't seen soap for years. It sticks to your head like you'd rubbed bag balm over it. I shall have cleanliness at my table, or no one at my table."

"But, Agnes, I don't like water. It damages my flesh. I've spent years in this climate perfecting my flesh, which now needs nothing but sun and air."

She did not move. He was suddenly hungrier than he had been in a long time.

"You can quit the arrangement, Gladstone. I believe something has changed. A little ledge? A little quartz?"

"Agnes, never. One day is like another. I pick up deadwood and deliver it hour after hour, trying to keep you happy. But you never have enough.

You always want to extract more from me, as if I were your indentured servant."

"You hungry?" she asked.

"Yes, I found a little mineral, but don't you make much of it. It's a little quartz, so high up the slopes it's hardly worth digging out."

"A bonanza, then," she said. "All right. Lay out a nugget or two, and I'll dish up some stew."

"But, Agnes, I put in a hard day's labor. I loaded Sylvester and brought him to the cliff. Really, you are cracking the whip when you should be filled with gratitude."

She sighed. "We've come to a parting of the ways. Thank you for bringing me some firewood, Gladstone. You may fill up your canteens, water Sylvester, and take one zucchini each as a token of my gratitude."

"But, Agnes . . ."

He had yet to sink his teeth into a turnip, and his belly was howling.

She reached for her scatter-gun, lowered it until both bores poked at his stomach, and gestured. In an instant, she had turned into a wall of basalt, and Gladstone knew there would be no more dickering.

"Very well, then, madam," he said, mustering his dignity. She nodded. He retreated from the cabin. She followed. He retrieved Sylvester under the bores of her cannon. She marched them to the zucchini patch and plucked two and tossed them to him. He collected each. She motioned them to the pool, and watched while the mule drank and Gladstone filled his canteens. Then she motioned them toward the cleft in the cliff, and when they had finally begun their ascent up its troubled slope, she discharged a load of buckshot into the cleft. He did not miss the stern warning.

He and Sylvester hastened up the twisty defile, and reached the top. A spot there afforded a view of the flat below, and he paused a moment. The green gardens, the orderly cabin and livestock pen, the gate leading down the mountain, and Agnes, empress of no-man's land, still staring at the cleft. Then she turned and went inside her cabin, as twilight settled.

It was the end of something but he wasn't sure what. But did it matter? He was two days from Eureka, had a zucchini for each day. The mule could forage tonight and would manage. He had enough threaded and nodule gold in his shirt pocket to outfit. He'd come back with plenty of beans and flour, a water cask, lots of stuff he needed including paper and pencil to write out the claims that would go into the cairns he needed to build at the corners of his bonanza.

The thought of leaving this fortune unguarded for even a few days gave him the fits, but it had gone undiscovered for millions of years, and it would go undiscovered a few days more. He didn't need Wet Agnes. He was on his way to heaven, and nothing would slow him down now, except building those cairns. Those would be a lot of work, but maybe they could be small, with just a few rocks in them. The smaller the better. He didn't want wandering interlopers to see them. Yes, that would do. Little cairns the eye would miss.

Chapter Twenty-Five

The uproar at the pole gate was like nothing Agnes had ever heard. Her mule, Toledo, had heehawed, and several mules coming up the gulch had responded. There was a mule choir carrying on. That was enough for Agnes to collect the shotgun and head for the gate.

When she got there, she discovered five gents, all fancy dressed, and seven mules milling about, uncertain about the pole that blocked passage. The men were studying her sign.

She did a swift count.

"That'll be twelve dollars, the same for man or beast. And I can't let you in for long. Your mules will eat my garden."

"That's a little steep, madam," said one, who wore wire-rimmed spectacles.

"I charge whatever I feel like. There's no other good water for fifty miles, so I got the advantage over you. And by the looks of you, you can afford it."

"A public spring, madam, is available to all."

"I settled here, fella. If you don't like it here, go somewhere else."

She watched the men glance at one another. They wore well-washed flannel shirts and clean canvas britches and boots barely broken in. They all wore beards, carefully cropped, and clean straw hats with wide brims against the desert sun. The mules were sleek, and carried packs that were straight out of an outfitter store.

They eyed her, and her double-barreled shotgun, and her bib overalls, and hair bound up and tied in a ponytail, and a scowl that brooked no nonsense, and the lead man, the one doing the jabbering, said they would agree.

"Not that we think it's a proper price, but we're peaceful men, and we need water. I am Lester, by the way, and this is the Battle Mountain Company."

"Agnes here, though some thoughtless locals call me Wet Agnes, because I'm the only thing wet in fifty miles. All right, show me your coin, and I'll let you in."

He found a billfold and extracted six $2 Treasury notes and handed them to her.

"Now that's entertaining," she said. "Battle Mountain, you're welcome here."

She pulled the pole aside, and they trooped in, eyeing her, spotting the verdant gardens tucked into this tiny flat surrounded by towering cliffs. They spotted her rock cabin, her pen with Toledo in it, and above all were drawn to the fabulous spring gurgling out of a fault in a rock wall, tumbling into a fine pool before sliding into the earth and down the gulch well below the surface.

"Nice little place here," Lester said.

"I did it myself," Agnes said. "There's not a worthless man on the place."

The men swiftly headed for the pool and let their mules lap up the water, and then some of them began filling casks at the spring, which conveniently tumbled over a ledge and into the bungholes.

"So what's the Battle Mountain?" she asked.

"We're an exploration company, looking for assets here in an uncharted land," Lester said. "We're geologists, a cartographer, a chemist, and we've two muleskinners."

One of them was pulling out brass and glass instruments from his pack, and began things that Agnes couldn't comprehend. "What's he doing?" she asked.

"Oh, that's Horace. There never was a better man with a sextant. He's taking a reading on the noon sun, and with your permission, if we stay the night, he'll shoot the stars as well, and come up with an exact reading of latitude. He also has the finest chronometer money can buy, which gives him longitude, you know, distance west from the Greenwich Meridian, which is about 115 degrees here."

"That's about the temperature, all right."

"No, ma'am, the earth is divided into degrees and minutes, and that's how we know where we are."

"Well, I sure know I'm right here."

"Well, when Horace is done, we'll give you the coordinates, and you will know just where this place is, and you can finger it on a map."

"I suppose you want a meal," she said. "That's two bits each, but I can't feed all those mules. They'll have to go into my pen, or my garden's done for."

"I think it can be arranged, Agnes. Now, this is Elmer, and that's Wilbur, and over there is Magnus. And we're really explorers, on the look-out for items of value."

"Like gold and silver?"

"That and anything else the country offers that might yield a profit for our employers."

"And who's that?"

"Oh, some financiers, some based in Tonopah, some in Carson City, some in California."

"You ain't easy on names, I take it."

"They prefer to work quietly, madam."

She watched Horace do stuff with the sextant. He had to get it level with the horizon, but there wasn't any horizon in this cañon, so he was using a regular little thing that worked like a level, with a bubble in the mercury he was lining up on a tripod.

She sure didn't know what that was about.

"Well, I've got lots coming along, but it's still

early. Too soon for potatoes, but there's some squash I got going right after the frost, and I've got turnips and some onions and carrots and some cabbages. How about cabbage?"

"Cabbage would be splendid, madam. We've not had fresh vegetables for weeks."

"You know, the one thing I'm short of here is firewood. How about you fellers going down the gulch and getting me some?"

"At your service, madam."

Lester designated Wilbur and Magnus to do the job, and the pair retreated from sight.

"You got people that work? That's not the usual around here."

"Every man here works hard, madam. The success of our enterprise depends on it."

"Most prospectors I've seen are the laziest bunch on the planet." She saw Horace messing with something else. "Now what's he up to?"

"He's measuring altitude by the air pressure method, Agnes. Since air pressure varies, it's not as accurate as working from some known base-line with a transit, but it serves our purposes. You're at about five thousand here, a mile high give or take."

"What does that do for you?"

"When we file, madam, we want to be as accurate as possible. The Land Offices require it. You know how the government is. Get it all right, and in triplicate."

"Beats me," she said. "I'll get my tin stove going, and we'll get some cabbage boiling. It'll take some time. Meanwhile, if you'd keep all those mules out of my cucumbers, I'd be grateful."

"We'll do that, Agnes. May I call you that, ma'am?"

Lester and Elmer began corralling the mules, which were starting to roam, and led them into the pen. They'd be crowded there, but seemed docile enough. Every one was so sleek they shone in the sunlight, unlike Toledo, who was scruffy and a typical male.

It sure was nice to have some industrious males around. Maybe she could give them a few more tasks to do, like watering her gardens. She got three big cabbages and cut them up to save some boiling, and soon had a good lunch started, so long as no one wanted meat. She didn't have any. But these gents seemed content with whatever she could dish up.

"You mind watering my gardens?" she asked. "I've got the bucket there. That's my biggest job."

"We've got two canvas camp buckets. I'll show you," Lester said.

They were cloth, all right, but they snapped open and held water, even if it sweated through a bit, and pretty soon some of the fancy gents were carrying the canvas pails and dumping load after load on her potatoes and young stalks of corn and all the rest.

She marveled. There were these industrious gentlemen, patiently watering two acres of garden, bucket by bucket. The unending task consumed her time more than anything else, but for a moment she had respite. It was all good fortune.

"With a little engineering, you could water some of this flat by gravity," Lester said.

"If you want to try it, go ahead and give her a shot," Agnes said.

"No, madam, we're pressed for time. Our task is to map every asset of this sort in the central Nevada basin and range country."

"What'll you do with all that? Make a big map?"

"Oh, we'll see," Lester said, and Agnes thought he wasn't leveling with her.

In time she filled their own mess bowls with a good vegetable stew. Her vegetables were not as filling as bread or meat, but that was what she managed in this remote place, and she could buy flour and sugar and spices in Eureka, and even some tinned beef now and then.

The gents ate appreciatively, commending her use of spices, and she enjoyed the flattery. She cooked plain, and they ate plain, and all the rest was blarney. Afterward, they cleaned their own mess kits and restored them to their packs. What sort of males were these? She thought maybe they were from New Zealand, where males were supposed to be more civilized than the Yank variety. She thought they could be Swedes, but they all spoke English.

As soon as the meal was off the table, Horace was outside with that device on a tripod, doing something. Another of the company was holding a pole over near a cliff.

"What's he doing?" she asked Lester.

"He's getting the size of your flat here, from wall to wall."

"Why would he do that?"

"This might be the most valuable property in central Nevada. I suppose you're squatting, right?"

"What's that?"

"That's settling on land without claiming it."

"It's mine. I built everything here. When I came there was no one here."

Lester smiled, nodded, and wandered about, examining the crops, the stone cabin, the pen. Agnes watched him with a deepening sense that something was not on the up and up. When Horace was done, so was the Battle Mountain Company.

"Got it all in the ledger," he said. "Had to estimate the flow, though."

"Did you put that I built it with my own hands? That I plowed most of that land with a mule and a stick? That I planted it all and watered it, and weeded it, and made it work, dawn to dusk, every day I've been here? Put that in your ledger, sir."

"It will be something to tell our employers, madam," Horace said.

She eyed him. He was almost fashionable. He kept his boots shiny, had someone shear off his hair, wore a tight-clipped mustache, and had a fancy pocket watch on a ribbon. That sure was a first for the middle of Nevada.

They departed as cheerfully as they had arrived, with many a thank-you to their hostess. She was richer for it, and the money would be spent in Eureka soon. It'd buy her new duds, spices, canned goods, tools, a shovel, a new rake, and some jars for canning. She felt uneasy about it all, but they certainly were gentlemanly, unlike half the brutes who wandered into her little oasis.

She felt oddly lonely now that they were gone. She had booted Gladstone out, and maybe she had been too hasty. He was a sponge, soaking up the fruits of her work, but she sort of enjoyed that. She was born to toil, and at the end of most days she felt pleasure in her achievements. It did her heart good to feed someone who was too lazy to feed himself. Sometimes, such as when she was laying up the walls of her cabin using loose rock off the cliffs and mud mortar, she had felt a kind of ecstasy. If a wall rose two feet, she felt she had done something good and true.

She had come a long way. She had started with no life of her own, and now she was commanding her life, and finding daily joy in it.

Next time someone came by, she'd ask about squatting. She stood upright; she never squatted, except when weeding radishes or beets, but the term haunted her. Lester was talking about something else, something about taking up land, and as dusk settled that evening, she couldn't get the word out of her mind. She wished that sheriff, Beef Story, would stop in. He would know.

Chapter Twenty-Six

Bitter Bowler swirled his canteen, aching to hear water slosh around in it, but it was silent. And dry. He had licked away the last drop. His mule stared desolately at him. He was perishing of thirst, and his mule was no better off. The sun bore in from a brass sky, and sapped the last moisture out of him.

His throat ached. His face burned. He did not know where he was. He was surrounded by barren rock. This was another of these low ranges, mostly naked of brush, that failed to claw water from high-flying clouds. He had spent a crazy morning hunting for that elusive gulch, filled with brush and promise that would take him up to that hole he had carved in sand, the hole that had filled with clear water. The hole close to the bright copper float, and the black silver ore. But this was not the place, and he knew that he was done for. He would die a miserable death in an hour or two, roasted and tormented by the merciless sun. And he'd shed no tears. He was too parched for tears.

His pulse raced as his heart worked harder to pump thick blood. He sat down in shade, but shade did him no good now. And waited. That was all that was left—the waiting. His mule waited, head down. This was the end of Bitter Bowler, born Ransom Bowler, soon to be bleached bones in a gulch half a hundred miles from anyone.

Then up in the sky he saw the men and mules marching across the heavens, several men, more mules, two mules carrying big casks of water. They were crossing the heavens, left to right, mostly single file, high above the surrounding horizons. He saw the mirage and scorned it, and cackled at it. It was the delusion of a desperate man. But the mirage kept marching across the cloudless sky, a trick of light, a phantasm. He stood, clawed his way to his feet, shouting at the passing men and mules. And below, on the flat, were the men and mules, no trick of light, far away, big hats protecting their heads, walking across sage-dotted bottoms.

He cried, and his cry didn't escape his dry throat. Then he remembered his ancient revolver, grabbed it, lifted it high, and fired. The shot shattered the desert silence. No one paused. He shot again, and this time they paused and stared his way, far distant. He shot again, and again, and now the men and mules turned his way. He would save the last shot for himself if they couldn't find him.

But they did see him now, saw his sagging mule, saw him clinging to the shady stone of the gulch, and hastened toward him. He didn't know if he could survive that final few minutes, but he willed it, willed himself to live, and then they were standing over him, and one was lifting a canteen to his throat, and he felt the warm water slide into him, and he drank it as fast as he could and began shaking violently, and emptied much of the canteen into his belly.

His mule nosed in, and they poured water into his felt hat and let the beast drink, and the mule made a strangled noise, and lapped it up.

He finally steadied enough to sit up, and beheld several men, all staring at him.

"Had enough, fella?" asked one.

"More," Bitter said. His first gulps scarcely set his body right or quieted his heart, and he wondered if it were too late. But after a few more sips, his body rallied.

"I was done for," he croaked. His vocal cords were not functioning.

"Glad we found you in time, old fella," said one in wire-rimmed spectacles.

These were rich men. Or at least they had

money. There they were, well equipped, sleek mules, trimmed beards, washed and cleaned clothing. Good boots. He didn't care who they were; they had saved him. He stared up at them, feeling the shame of it. He, a desert rat from the time he fled home, rescued by these rich men with their fancy outfit. He felt bitter about it, and hid his shame from them.

"Yeah, I made a wrong turn," Bitter said. "Got the biggest strike I ever seen, and lost it."

He could hardly make his throat work and the words scraped out like sandpaper on iron.

"How did you see us, fella? We couldn't see you."

"You was marching across the sky. I watched the parade."

The men eyed one another, doubt subtly forming on their well-groomed faces.

"I don't care what you think. Mirages, I've seen them lots of times," he croaked.

"What are we going to do with you, old man?"

"Keep me alive, me and the mule, and I'll make it worth your while."

"Neither of you are fit to travel, sir."

"Then dammit, leave me something, water for the beast and me, and something to settle our stomachs."

"Do you know where you are, sir?"

"Haven't a notion, but I'll get my bearings tonight."

"You're on the edge of the Monitor Range."

"That ain't where I am. I'm two ranges east."

The men stared at one another. Then the spokesman said it plain. "If we leave you here, without help, you'll not be rescued a second time."

Bitter was about to explode, but he quieted himself. He was too weak to stand, too weak to walk.

"Maybe we can put you on your mule, sir. He seems to be stronger now."

Bitter hated it, hated being beholden and shamed by this bunch. Hated being rescued. But he nodded.

"I'm Lester, sir. Battle Mountain Company out of Tonopah. And you?"

"Bill Bowler," he said.

"We have a way to go, sir. There's a seep at the north end of this range. We'll get you there and talk about your future."

They moved his ragged pack off the mule, and lifted him on. The mule side-stepped, and then accepted Bitter. His few possessions we removed to one of the mules carrying two oaken casks.

Bitter didn't remember much of that trip. The company was solicitous, and gave him water again and again, and more for his mule, and toward the end of that desperate day they swung into a cañon and headed straight toward a shadowed wall that had a dark streak where the seep surfaced. Bitter had been there many times. But this time he didn't even know he was half a day away.

So picayune was the seep that it took an hour to restock the casks and canteens, and hours more to water the mules. Each man in the company had assigned tasks. One of them, introduced to Bitter as Horace, was operating a sextant and examining a chronograph, plainly taking coordinates and recording them in a ledger. Bitter knew a little about that.

"What's that for?" he asked Lester.

"We're mapping every known asset in this back country," Lester said. "The company is interested in potential properties."

"Like water?"

"Especially water. It's the rarest asset of all."

Bitter nodded. The lack of it had led him to the brink of death, and even now his body was far from vital again. It was as if the great thirst had robbed him of energy, or left poisons in his blood.

There was no wood for a fire, but this disciplined company had prepared for that, and had a container of cooked beans that could be served and eaten cold. One of them handed Bitter a tin plate piled with them. Salted and seasoned, they went down well, and Bitter began to feel he had life ahead of him. They asked nothing of Bitter, and left him to his own devices, and when he felt refreshed, he filled his own canteens, and saw to it that his miserable mule had its chance at the seep, which was dripping water so slowly that the mules lapped it as fast as it leaked out of the strata.

Then, at last, the toil seemed to be done, and the men collected under the wall of rock, which still radiated the day's heat.

"I believe you have some decisions to make, sir," Lester said. "You are welcome to come with us. We're winding up here, and should be in Eureka in three or four days."

"Haven't got a choice, have I?" Bitter asked.

"We always have choices, sir. We could grub-stake you, at least for a week or so. Nothing long term. It's all carried on the backs of our mules. Or you could come with us."

Lester seemed oddly intent, and was watching Bitter closely. Horace was fussing with his navigational equipment, preparing to shoot some stars. There was a good view of Polaris from this place.

"What's your price for the grubstake?" Bitter asked.

"Well, sir, you mentioned you got lost looking for a discovery you'd made."

"I said that, did I? Well, there's no discovery. Must have been outta my head."

"Very well. We'll take you into Eureka. You can repay us by whatever means."

"What do you want for the grub?"

236

"Half. That's a lot, sir, but I believe we are running a risk, staking you to anything."

"You want half? Of my ledge? If I find it again?"

"You are a man of honor, sir, and we would trust you, and will put it in writing, two copies. We have paper in the ledger book, fortunately, and can draw up a simple contract. We supply you for a week. You give us half of your claim or claims."

"That don't make a bit of sense to me," Bitter said. "Half's not the regular stake."

Lester rose, peered about the camp, and studied the place. "It's your life, which we restored to you," he said.

That sure made Bitter mad. Getting a new lease on life from these greenhorns was more than he could bear. And half? A grubstake was usually for a quarter, maybe a third if grub was supplied the second or third time out. These crooks wanted to bleed a man of every drop of blood in him.

The whole bunch was listening in but pretending not to. Horace was busy with his sextant, and using some kind of level so he could get a true horizon. Wilbur and Magnus—he thought those were the names—were feeding the mules using nose bags. Elmer, another one with well-washed clothing and clean boots, was sitting and listening, sort of like he was a witness.

Bitter itched to escape. He didn't like a one of them. He didn't like the Battle Mountain Company. Well, he'd do it, whatever it took.

"All right, gents," he said, offering a gap-toothed smile at the lot. "Write her up."

Elmer tore two pages from the ledger book, and put a pencil to use. No ink pen this far from anywhere. "What did you say your name is?"

"Bill Bowler. William."

"And how do we contact you?"

"I don't contact. I'm here. Or just put Eureka. I go there for stuff."

"Then we will trust you to contact us. In Tonopah, of course."

With a bull's eye lantern, Elmer drafted two brief contracts that simply stated that William Bowler, in exchange for supplies, agreed to give a half interest in any discoveries current or in the future, to the Battle Mountain Syndicate, Tonopah, Nevada. There were two lines and a witness line and a date.

Elmer handed the document to Bitter, who could barely move the pencil in the right direction, it had been so long since he had written. Then he signed the other sheet. Then Lester, whose last name was Lambeau, signed both, and Elmer signed as a witness. Then Lester handed a sheet to Bitter, who stared at it, tucked it into his shabby pack, and slumped against the rock wall to await dawn, with a week's supply of beans for himself and oats for his mule.

"Seals the deal," Lester said, offering a hand-shake.

"Sure does," Bitter said, taking Lester's hand and discovering a hard clean grip, much harder than Bitter's own scaly grip.

"I hope the arrangement's mutually profitable," Lester said. "Welcome to our company."

Chapter Twenty-Seven

Beef Story pushed steadily toward Eureka, wondering whether he would actually go through with it. He had a cushy job, scarcely a job at all, and now he was thinking of ditching it. He got paid for snoozing; paid for meandering around town; paid for wandering into saloons at night and looking over the clientele; paid to rattle merchants' doors; paid to wear a star and act important and stare down ruffians. It was all he was fit to do. He had shunned real work all his life. He hadn't thought much about that until now, when Wet Agnes accused him of being even lazier than prospectors. He hadn't thought of it as laziness. It was easy. He liked an easy job. And being sheriff of Eureka County was the easiest job he'd ever had.

The feisty little burg lay between gloomy ranges of mountains, and was so isolated it felt disconnected from the rest of the country. Mail took an extra day or two to arrive in Eureka. There was so little pasture that bringing in hay and grain was a major operation there, and added to the cost of everything else.

But he was bored. He could only take so much of doing nothing. The paradox was, that back country with about twenty people in it was much more entertaining than Eureka. He could not explain it. Just as he could not explain to himself, or to anyone else, why he let the bank robber, Albert Gumz, go loose. He could be a hero hauling in the little Frenchman. But for reasons behind fathoming, he liked the wayward Frenchman. The man didn't deserve liking. He was lazy, looking for an easy way out of debt, and pulled off a heist and did it brilliantly except for underestimating the perils of the desert.

It all made Beef uneasy. He hiked past the high ridges guarding Eureka to the south, rounded a long curve, and walked into town. His progress was not noted. He was just another man leading a horse. He passed his own sheriff's office and jail, and decided not to stop there. The brick Eureka Miners and Merchants Bank lay a block ahead. It was an empire in itself, the fiefdom of James Lotus Garwood, self-made frontier magnate. He divided his time between the bank and a mansion in Carson City, where he guided the legislature toward its decisions.

Beef trudged through the sleepy, sun-bleached town at a time when most people hid indoors, and tied his horse to a hitch rail before the bank.

He hefted the canvas Wells, Fargo bag from his pack, and entered, making his way past the two tellers who eyed him and that sack, and straight into the office of the president, who on this occasion was sipping crème de menthe and reading the New York *Herald Tribune* ten days late.

"You could knock, Sheriff."

Beef yawned. "There it is. Minus ten dollars."

"You didn't get it all? What's the matter with you?"

"Count it."

"I will have a teller do it. Blake, come in here."

A young man with hair parted in the middle and an acned face appeared instantly.

"Count it and avoid your usual mistakes."

Blake opened the sack, pulled out packets of Treasury silver certificates, and began counting the packets.

"No, not by packet. You are lazy, Blake. Count the bills," Garwood said.

"I'll want a receipt," Beef said.

"Where did you get it?" Garwood said.

"It was hidden outside of Tonopah."

"And you have the criminal locked up?"

"No, sir."

"We need a new sheriff," Garwood said.

"I agree with you, sir."

"Coming up ten dollars short. You should have brought it all in. What excuse have you for that?"

"Water, sir. It costs money in the desert."

"There's a fellow named Sigmund Freud you should talk to," Garwood said. "He's expensive, but effective. In Vienna."

Blake was mumbling his way through the packets, keeping a running count, while the two men stared at him. Small bills slowed him down. But the pile of counted bills grew steadily.

"You could have washed before polluting my office," Garwood said. He sipped his crème de menthe from a crystal glass.

"He's right. Ten dollars short," Blake said, stacking the bills.

"You should have done better, Sheriff. I'm not saying it's a bad job, and I'm grateful to have some of the money back, but a sharp man is needed for this sort of thing," Garwood said. "And you were a little lax."

"I will add the man's revolver, which I possess. You can sell it."

"But that's evidence," Garwood said.

"Your choice," Beef said.

"I'll take it. Stopping loss is a sublime good. Higher than retaining evidence. I am made whole, except for the interest lost on the cash the bank could not lend."

Story pulled Gumz's little five-shot out and| laid it on the bank president's shiny desk.

"Write him a receipt for both, Blake, and sign it for me. I don't like ink-stained fingers."

Beef collected the receipt, read it slowly, and

then walked away and into clean air. He felt blue. He unhitched the patient horse and took the half-starved animal to the livery barn, and told the hostler, Jefferson, to give the animal some grain, and clean him up, and keep him near fresh water. The horse had earned a break.

"You catch that bandit, Sheriff?" Jefferson asked.

"I've just come from the bank, where I gave them the loot."

"Too bad," Jefferson said. "I was rooting for the bandit."

Beef lumbered slowly to the sheriff's office and found no one around. He still had a decision to make. He could quit or not. Go talk to the county supervisors or not. And he still didn't know what he'd do if he quit. Or even why he had told Gumz to wait for him, when there was a chance he'd not head into the desert at all. He didn't know what to do, or when, or why.

He slept hard that night in spite of oppressive heat, and the next morning he was no more certain of his future than he had been upon his return to town. When he got to the Beanery for his usual ham and eggs, the owner, Madhouse Morton, accosted him.

"You got the money but not the man," Morton said.

"Most of the money."

"Well, I suppose you done what you could."

"No, I could have done more."

"That's what everyone's saying," Morton said.

That decided Story. He lapped up the chow, laid two bits on the counter, and headed for the courthouse and a visit with Packer Flowers, chairman of the supervisors.

"Just like that?" Flowers asked, a few minutes later. "What'll we do now?"

"You have a good deputy. And lots of able men, all good at taking a nap."

"Are you insinuating something?"

"Sleepy job," Beef said.

"You made it so. I hear you got the loot but not the robber."

"Got the itch to travel, mostly."

Flowers smiled. "All right, Story. They come and they go. I have a nephew who'd fill the bill if he'd learn how to shoot. And I can start him at a good salary."

No sooner had Beef abandoned the supervisor than he encountered a few gents in the hallway, one of them in wire-rimmed spectacles. It was Lester Lambeau. He'd met them before at Chalk Spring.

"This way to the county clerk and recorder, Sheriff?"

"Down the hall there."

Beef left the little courthouse and the members of the Battle Mountain Company, left his badge in the sheriff's office, and headed into the unknown. He'd quit just in time. He'd likely be carrying an eviction notice to Wet Agnes if he stayed on as sheriff. There were better things to do with his life.

He headed for his room, collected his few things, including a tintype of his parents and sister, told his landlady he was leaving, and headed into the sun-blistered streets of Eureka, suddenly feeling that the place had spit him out. He would not be missed.

He had some pocket change, not enough to outfit himself or his friend Gumz, but enough to buy them a few days. He collected his horse, loaded up with some beans and flour, and left town, feeling as empty as a kettledrum. He wondered what the hell was wrong with him. He had no ambition. He worked as little as possible. He had no large goals. He wasn't climbing any ladder or dreaming dreams. All he could say was that the desert lured him, enticed him, drew him into its dangerous wastes, and if there was no reason for it, then that made his life all the more mysterious. He was returning to the province of failed men.

His trip back to the seep was uneventful, and Albert Gumz greeted him quietly. Oddly, he knew Gumz would stick it out and not head into the blue.

"I can keep us fed for a week, Albert. That's time enough for you to get to Tonopah and start up a life of your own."

"I have no ambition," Gumz said. "One day is the same as another. Once I was desperate to get ahead, and now I'm as comfortable as a bull-frog on a water lily. I'll snap at passing flies. It's called waiting for opportunity."

"Yeah, but there's the small matter of beans and spuds and bread."

Gumz shrugged. "Consider the lilies and how they grow," he said.

"We won't last for long here. I ran again into the smart men who are about to lock up all the water in central Nevada. They were in the courthouse, looking to file on it. That's governed by Nevada law. But they are also going to file federal land claims, too. You know they said that whoever controls the water owns much of Nevada. Once they've got the water, they'll go after the minerals. The area's hardly been explored, and those gents have the education to do it."

Gumz stared. "Then, my friend, life has given us purpose, after all."

"Such as?"

"I believe they have just stolen Agnes's water and land."

"So what? She can manage her life. Can you imagine trying to manage Agnes?"

"I believe we are about to become an army of righteousness."

"You mean, like stopping their lawful and legal acquisition of desert assets?"

Gumz smiled. "Do law and justice always coincide, Mister Story?"

"I've been on various sides of the law, but never on the side of righteousness," Beef said. "How am I supposed to feel?"

"Righteous," Gumz said. "The main question is how we feed ourselves while we connive against this company invading no-man's land."

"I think we should go talk to Agnes and offer our services. She has no idea she's about to lose her place."

"And maybe she'll pay us in cabbages?"

"It's a thought," Beef said.

They loaded the horses, headed out, both of them uncertain why they were alive, what they should do, what the future might bring, and how to put food into their stomachs. There never was a sorrier pair, but that was how things had always been in the empty stretches of Nevada where men went to disappear from the world.

Chapter Twenty-Eight

The Eureka Mercantile peeved Gladstone Brass. Its white-aproned, bony proprietor wouldn't pay more than $14 for Gladstone's wire gold, even though it wasn't dust; it was pure gold Gladstone had knocked out of quartz. He had brought over five troy ounces of it, expecting to collect

$100 and re-supply, but all he could get was $70.

Gladstone intended revenge; he would soon buy the mercantile, or start a rival Monkey Ward and run this old vinegar-lipped man out of business. Still, it bought him plenty. He loaded ten pounds each of flour, rolled oats, barley, and cornmeal into the panniers, and added two tins of lard, five pounds of sugar, five of coffee, and then added new britches to replace his knee-sprung ones, a chambray shirt, two bars of soap, a box of Fels Naptha flakes, a corrugated scrubbing board, a two-gallon canteen, a woman's straw hat with silk roses, ten yards of blue cotton muslin, an apron, and sundry other items.

Sylvester despised the load and hunched his back, but Gladstone quieted him down.

"It's only for two or three days. And I'll carry some of it. And if things go right, you'll be in the clover."

Sylvester humped up, and then settled down for the ordeal. All in all, Gladstone had spent only a few hours in Eureka, and awakened no curiosity, which was what he wanted. He was just another desert rat who'd found a good ledge.

The trip back to Portuguese Peak went swiftly because Sylvester was in rare good spirits and trotted right along beside Gladstone, rarely resisting or rebelling. Gladstone fed him an occasional piece of rock candy to keep him cheerful. When they reached the foothills, Gladstone headed straight up the brushy gulch to Agnes's place rather than cutting around to his high-country camp. He arrived at the pole gate late in an afternoon, when the heat was bad, and hollered. Over in his pen, Toledo blatted at the visitors.

Agnes appeared promptly, shotgun at the level, its bores aimed straight at Gladstone.

"You, is it? You are not welcome."

"I've been to town and I brought you gifts. Take them or leave them, I don't care," he said.

"I wouldn't touch your gifts with a ten-foot pole."

"Very well, I will leave them for whoever wants them."

He opened the panniers, and lifted out the ten-pound sacks of grains and flour, the cans of lard, the soap and soap flakes, the bolt of blue cloth, the hat, the apron, and some lesser delights.

"There you are, dammit, and now I'll go."

"I won't touch a one until you leave," she said.

He decided to stand there a while, while she eyed the stuff. But she wouldn't touch it.

"Agnes, you are the world's most beautiful and accomplished woman, worthy of a president, worthy of a king, worthy of the pope, or whatever."

"You really think so, Gladstone?"

"You mind if I fill my canteens before leaving?"

"A dollar for man or beast," she said. "But I will make an exception this one time. Help me carry all this."

The pole slid open, and Gladstone and Sylvester were admitted. Then the pole slid shut behind them. Gladstone pushed all that stuff onto Sylvester's back, and the mule hauled it the last forty yards, where Wet Agnes promptly relieved the animal of its burden and hauled her loot into the cabin. When she emerged, she was wearing the hat.

"It's not very becoming," she said. "But I'll use it anyway. On rainy days. I don't like red roses."

He let Sylvester drink, and then filled his three canteens and hung them on the mule.

"You may put him in with Toledo," she said.

"Why is he named Toledo?" he asked.

"Because women may not be profane," she said. "When I am in danger of being uncivil, or unfemale, I say Holy Toledo, and pretty soon that was his name."

He penned Sylvester, entered Wet Agnes's humble cabin, and sat at the table she had fashioned from the materials at hand.

"Lard! How did you know I needed lard?" she asked.

"Because you had none."

"And cloth. How did you know I like delft blue?"

"It's all you wear, Agnes."

"And soap. Now I can scrub you clean."

"Only if you blindfold me first, Agnes. I wouldn't want to see it."

"And soap flakes. You have made this a memorable day, Gladstone."

"It never occurred to me," he said.

"I'm sorry you didn't bring any baking soda," she said. "And I needed salt, and some vinegar, and a bottle of molasses."

"That's why I never married," he said.

"I have some beets soaking. I won't charge you for a meal if you wish to stay. But if you'd chop some firewood, I'll start the beets boiling."

"Maybe me and Sylvester should climb outta here."

"You can do that later, Gladstone. I don't allow men in my cabin after sundown."

He chopped the wood, watched her whirl through the cooking, and finally had a dark red meal before him, sliced beets on purple cabbage surrounded by red lettuce. He wasn't partial to beets, but she had seasoned them with something acerbic, and they tasted fine. She wore her new straw hat through the meal, and when they were done, she waited, expecting something, and he finally figured out that he should clear the dishes and scrub them up. He managed that in the waning light, and then it was time to enjoy the twilight.

"Well, I'll fetch the mule," he said, hoping she would invite him to stick around. "You're the best cook I've ever met, Agnes," he said.

"That's because I don't run from hard work," she said, "unlike some people I know."

He headed across the quiet flat, found Sylvester in a bad mood, put the pack on him, with the remaining stuff he would use himself, and headed through the quiet of a serene summer eve toward the cleft, and up to his own bailiwick above.

"How did that go, Sylvester? Do you think she'll give me some chow now and then?"

Sylvester grunted. That was an ominous sound.

Everything was fine. He was the Bonanza King of Nevada.

His camp at the overhang was undisturbed. He unloaded the last of the stuff from Eureka, and turned Sylvester loose.

"Tomorrow we start a new life, Sylvester. Tomorrow, we're in the clover."

Sylvester disagreed and departed into the night.

Gladstone slept soundly after all that labor, and awoke to a sunny dry day. He breakfasted on the hard candy he had bought, and then headed upslope and off to the south where his bonanza lay. Twenty minutes later he gazed down on glory. There it all was, the quartz outcrop stretching across and up a giant cañon, riches unimaginable. Much of it would be hard to reach, but who cared? A lot of it was handy to his every whim. Did he want a yacht? All he had to do was dig a little. Did he want to visit Peru? No trouble at all, just whack the gold out of that quartz, which lay glowing in the morning sunlight. He could even afford Wet Agnes's prices for her garden meals, but he would stop that as soon as he could import meat and dine like a bonanza king.

The next step would be daunting. His task was to lay claim to this bonanza, and that required locating and measuring the claims he would file with the federal government. He couldn't remember what the proper dimensions of a claim might be, but three hundred by six hundred feet stuck in his head. He could claim one of those and get another one as the discoverer of the lode. That would be dandy. And he'd need to locate the corners of each, build cairns there, and additional cairns in the middle of each claim, with a notice concealed from the weather in each.

The very idea was exhausting. By rights, the corner cairns should be located in the bottom of the gulch, several hundred feet down, and the lines should extend up the cañon wall, past the ledge, and out on top somewhere. And then he needed to add the cairns located in the middle of each claim. And then he needed to do location work, ten feet of excavation, and register the claim within thirty days of discovery. At which point there would be a gold rush, with hundreds of eager prospectors and geologists and mining magnates flooding in.

It made him ache. But so did letting the bonanza lie there unclaimed, vulnerable to anyone who came along and spotted it. He sat down on a rock to contemplate this difficulty. It was proving to be more of a problem than he had imagined. He finally summoned the courage to descend the slope and choose a corner, indeed two corners, and erect cairns there. The problem was not only erecting the cairns, but measuring the claims. He had nothing more than a four-foot boot lace to help him.

Heart pounding, he slid and scrambled to the cañon floor, narrowly avoiding some tumbles, and finally found himself staring upward at the ledge, far above. He wanted to choose the best ore, the widest vein, but he could barely make it out. He studied the gulch, hoping someone would build his cairn for him, but no one showed up. Plenty of rock was available. All he had to do was lift chunks of it, one by one, and make a little pyramid.

He patrolled the base, finally decided where to put a cairn, and began hauling rock. The pieces he selected weighed more than he thought, so he chose smaller pieces, and collected three before his back started tormenting him. He was determined, so he carried two more chunks of tan rock to the pile, and then realized that his heart was hammering dangerously, and he dared not continue. And he had the awful task of climbing up that vertiginous slope. Still, he had not lived in the Nevada desert for all these years for nothing, so he tackled the dizzying slope with bravery, and eventually reached the top.

He sucked on his canteen, worn out by the grim experience, and pondered what to do. The plainest choice was to hire Agnes to do it. She had built her rock-walled cabin without difficulty; surely she could build some cairns. And he could pay her with a claim, one with a less promising lead, of course, but a claim. He arose, heartened by the plan, and explored the tilted country above the quartz outcrop, an area of violent upheaval and slippery slopes. He would need to build discovery cairns there, too, but she could do that. He could hire her to write out the claim and put it in a bottle and place it in the cairn. And she had a measuring tape for sewing, so that would give him his corners.

But the more he pondered that, the less he liked it. The moment he brought anyone else in on the bonanza, word would escape, and he'd be out of luck. There were some things a man should keep to himself, and gold quartz was one of them. He examined the country above the cliff, and found it treacherous, and several times he almost slid toward the cliff edge to his certain doom. Building any sort of discovery cairn in terrain like that, high on the flank of Portuguese Peak, would place his life in peril.

He eased his way back to his canteen and sucked on it, having sweated away a lot of liquid in his examination of his bonanza. He eyed the whole scene, realizing that scrub juniper concealed most of the quartz ledge, and it was in little danger of being discovered.

Why file a claim at all? He could live happily the rest of his days just gouging what he needed out of the vein, and taking his bounty to Eureka now and then. If he still wanted to go to Peru, all he had to do was chip away with his pick hammer, and pulverize the quartz. Nothing could be easier.

He wasn't entirely happy with the decision. A part of him yearned to file the claims good and proper, keep them from being stolen, and maybe sell them off to a syndicate for a million or two. But that just made him ache.

Instead, in a rare moment of industry, he began prying out the weathered quartz nearby, and when he had a good pile of it, he began shattering it, and pulling out the wire and nodule gold, piece by piece. In short order, without much effort, he had several troy ounces. He also had Agnes. And what more did a man need?

Chapter Twenty-Nine

Gladstone Brass slept through the afternoon, his gold in his shirt pocket, and when the time seemed ripe, he hunted for Sylvester, who appeared miraculously, being thirsty and ready for whatever Gladstone had in mind.

Gladstone was in a rare good mood. His kindly feelings overflowed in Sylvester's direction, and he took time to scrape the dirt out of the mule's shaggy coat. The more presentable Sylvester was, the better for Gladstone's ripening plans.

"Come along, then," he said, and the mule followed obediently toward the cleft in the cliff, leading down to Wet Agnes's cliff-hugged flat. When the pair of them reached bottom, there was Agnes, her shotgun leveled.

"Don't think I wasn't expecting you," she said. "Coming in to steal my squash."

"Now, Agnes, I didn't have a thought in my head like that."

"You stay put," she said. "I will let Sylvester have a swallow or two, because I'm kind to animals, but don't you move a muscle."

"But, Agnes, if I can't move a muscle, how will I be able to pay you in gold for the meal you'll give to Sylvester and me?"

"What gold?"

"My shirt pocket. See for yourself."

"I have scruples," she said. "Touching your shirt is the last thing I would do. Slowly lift your hand and dig out some gold in your pocket and show it to me."

Gently, slowly he raised his right arm, pulled out some wire gold and some nodules, and showed her the gold resting in his horny hand. She stared suspiciously.

"How do I know that's a dollar's worth for each of you?"

"It's about ten dollars of gold right there, half an ounce."

"Don't you go cheating me. I'll take it all, just to keep you honest, and feed you both."

"I won't give you all of it. I won't pay ten dollars for two meals."

"I don't want gold. I want greenbacks. I know greenbacks."

"Agnes, gold is worth twenty dollars an ounce. The crooks in Eureka will give only fourteen for it, because they say it's not refined. But this is pure gold, knocked out of weathered quartz, and if you won't take gold, I'll go elsewhere for my food and water."

"Fat chance," she said.

"And besides, Agnes, you are the most beautiful and sweet woman in Nevada."

She waved the shotgun at him. "I don't know why, but I will trust you this one time. You give me two dollars of gold, and I will feed the pair of you lazy boys."

Thus was the bond formed. He had no scale, but if she had a $10 gold eagle, weighing half an ounce, or a $20 double eagle, weighing an ounce, he could satisfy her. But it turned out she had no coin at all.

"Very well. I will give you ample gold, and you can keep it against the time of reckoning, when we take it to a scale."

She glared at him, looking for faults in that, but couldn't find much. "You're going to cheat an innocent woman," she said, tucking the gold in a handkerchief, which vanished into her bosom.

With her new flour and lard and firewood, she had baked sourdough bread this day, and that suited Gladstone just fine. He had bread once or twice a year. It wasn't something commonly found in the wastes of Nevada. But on the occasions when he had cleaned out a ledge and traded the mineral for cash, he had gorged on bread.

Sylvester was enjoying the company of Toledo, and they were being fed with garden greens. Squash leaves made good mule fodder, according to the mistress of this manor.

In a quiet peace that settled over the flat, Agnes stared at Gladstone until it dawned on him to scrub the dishes. The task was so onerous that he steeled himself for it, but with a few soap flakes he got the job done, more or less, although she squinted at each vessel, and returned one or two for more massaging. But the moment came when they could both sit outside in the shadows, watch the sinking sun gild the peaks, and wait for cool air to roll down the mountain.

"Agnes," Gladstone said, "I wish to hire you. You're good with rocks. You built the cabin. I'd like to have you come up the mountain and build a few little rock piles for me. Some markers here and there."

"What for?"

"Oh, just because I want you to, and would pay you in gold. You'd profit from the work."

"Why don't you pile up the rocks yourself?"

"Oh, I'm involved with more important things."

"You haven't told me what they're for."

"I'm thinking of homesteading, get my one-sixty acres, and it would be good to mark the corners."

"On a mountain top?"

They fenced like that for some while, but Agnes ended up turning him down. "I don't care if it's got a little gold . . . I've got more important things to do," she said.

He was feeling grumpy. "If that's how you feel, then I won't share my fortune with you. I'll be rich as King Midas, and you'll spend the rest of your life on this little flat, suffering from hard work and aching back and bad elbows and bunions, too."

That silenced her. She sat, staring. Then she smiled. "If I were a man, I'd use the proper language for my sex. But I'm a lady, so I can only use the first word, which is *bull*."

"Agnes, you are the most attractive woman on the planet, and if you were the marrying kind, I'd be first in line."

She sighed, plainly pacified. A quivery little smile lifted the corners of her mouth.

"Agnes, I've found gold just up the mountain. I

was looking for firewood for you when I found it. There's a certain cañon south of here, drops right off, and angling up the wall of that cañon is the biggest quartz seam I've ever seen. I dug out some gold, which is free and clean in decaying quartz. That's what I took to Eureka. There's tons more. Tons, not ounces. Tons and tons of gold, so much gold that I'm a millionaire, maybe ten times over. I'm the richest man that ever you met. That seam is hidden from view, and only I can find it, so don't you go hunting, because you'll never locate it."

She sighed. "Now we'll be overrun."

"No, it's invisible, almost. Agnes, you can have anything you want. I'll dig up the gold and get it for you."

She didn't respond, but stared into the lingering summer twilight for a while. And then she turned to him.

"Oh, Gladstone, I already have everything I want. I've made the earth bloom, and have made my way without a bit of help, and have found my strength, and have learned to enjoy this life in the desert, and my life as a woman alone." Then, quietly: "But thank you, Gladstone, for thinking of me. No one ever has."

"I sort of thought you'd like to have me around. I can pay for everything. I'll pay you more gold than you ever dreamed of having."

"You're welcome to be here, Gladstone. But I

have no need of a fortune. Just a little to buy a few things, that's all. I have most of what I need, and I can simply be myself. I made my own heaven."

He couldn't quite fathom it. He was offering to shower gold on her, and she was saying no, she had what she wanted. It was making him itchy.

"Here's the deal, Agnes. I can knock gold out of that quartz in no time. Just a few minutes. I hardly have to work at it. I've been looking for this all of my life. It's like it fell out of the sky."

"It fits," she said. "But it won't last."

"No one's gonna steal it from me, Agnes. I've got the secret."

She smiled and said nothing. She thought he was balmy and that annoyed him. He was offering her gold for free, or for food anyway, and she was getting uppity.

"Maybe I should file claims," he said. "I'll hire you to build the corner cairns. They're a lot of work. Then I'll file, and there'll be a claim for you, and you'll file, and then we've got it all in the bag."

"You are very innocent, Gladstone."

"Innocent? Innocent? I've been around the block, Agnes."

"Virginal, Gladstone."

"I offer you gold and you call me that?"

"Perhaps it's time for you and Sylvester to go up the mountain, Gladstone. I'm ready to call it a day. There's light enough for you to go up to your lion's den, or whatever it is."

"Sylvester won't be happy. He likes Toledo."

"Scoot!" she said.

He rose reluctantly. He'd been a loner all his life, and couldn't say why he was reluctant to abandon her company.

A ruckus at the gate drove away such thoughts.

"Some blasted loafer wanting water," she said, reaching for the shotgun. She stormed toward the pole gate, and he tagged along behind.

There were two men and two horses waiting outside, in the soft light.

"I'm closed," she said.

"Agnes, it's me, Beef Story. And you remember Albert Gumz?"

"The sheriff and the bank robber."

"I'm no longer sheriff, and Mister Gumz is thinking about reforming."

"Lazy, that's what. You're both lazy. It's late and I'm not going to let you in."

"How come you're here?" Gladstone asked, priding himself on his curiosity.

Beef Story eyed him gratefully. "We have news for Agnes. Important news."

"Four dollars for two beasts and two men," he said.

"I have one dollar. That should buy our horses half a drink each," Story said. "And we'll stick with our canteens."

"Four dollars," she said, wagging her shotgun.

"I'll pay, Agnes," Gladstone said.

"Not you. They've got to. Lazy people need lessons."

He dug into his pocket and extracted some nodules of pure gold and dropped them into her free hand. She sighed, opened the pole gate, and let the interlopers in.

In the thickening dusk the horses lapped water from her pool, and Story began telling about some outfit in Eureka called the Battle Mountain Company that was filing water claims in the courthouse, and would soon file land claims as well. "Including yours," he said.

"What does that mean?" she asked, suddenly paying close attention.

"It means they're claiming your spring, all the water coming from it, and your land, too."

"But I was here first. I got here and built here and it's mine."

"And they made the claim first," the lawman said. "They've recorded the locations of every watering hole in the area. They're filing on them all. They told me that's the way to control every-thing here, including mineral rights. Water's the key. They're heading to Carson to file federal claims on the land, and after that they've got much of central Nevada locked up."

"Then what?"

Story shrugged. "Nothing much. They're not

going to put armed guards at every watering hole to keep people out. They're not likely to come here. No one's going to show up with an eviction notice, at least for now. But someday, sometime, some year someone will show up here with papers and try to boot you out. They'll claim it when they need it."

"Over my dead body," she said. "They'll get both barrels."

"Well, that's where Albert, here, and I come in. I have a little experience with weapons, and Mister Gumz is a quick study. We thought we might protect you from interlopers, in exchange for a home-cooked meal now and then. Just a pair of desert rats watching over you, is all."

"Now it all comes out," she said. "I shouldn't have let those Battle Mountain people in here to begin with, and I'm not going to let you in here. So, out you go."

"Agnes, stop that right now," Gladstone said. "They've come a long way to give you word about this."

"And you can get out, too," she said, lifting up the shotgun.

The barrels pointed at him were persuasive.

Chapter Thirty

Bitter Bowler exulted. He had food and water. He had been yanked from the pits of death. His skinny carcass still pumped blood. He had conned some suckers out of food and drink with a few scribbles of a pencil.

By dawn, much restored, he hobbled up the nearest ridge to take his bearings, figured out where he was, and headed due east. He'd trekked this country for decades, and now the map in his head came to life. He still limped, but no longer needed a ride, which pleased the ugly mule. During that hot day he progressed steadily toward the north end of the next range, and straight into a gulch he had traversed only once, a gulch that took him past a seam of black silver ore, and, later, an outcrop of brilliant green copper salts. He eyed them lasciviously, but didn't stop until he had reached that brushy narrows where he had scraped a hole in the gritty sand, and discovered sweet water slipping into it.

And it was there, exactly as he remembered it. He let the mule push its snout in, and then he filled his canteens, and sat refreshed during the hottest hours of the day. He had a future. He was a king. He could take his millions and go to Buenos Aires, and do the tango. Long ago, some sailors told him about the tango. There was no dance on earth as volcanic as the tango. It was worth moving to Argentina just to see the girls tango. Or do the tango himself.

Refreshed, with his bonanza rediscovered, he headed for the ore bodies. At the copper outcrop, he first collected float that had fallen from above, and then climbed through scree, carefully favoring his bum ankle, until he got to the seam, with its satisfying complex mix of native copper, green and azure, all mixed together in some primeval cauldron. He took several pounds of the stuff, examined the ledge, which ran fifty yards east and west, and then carefully descended to the patient mule, and headed down a steep and cloistered narrows to the black silver lode, another formation entirely, where giant forces had shoved one sort of rock into another and upended both.

He followed the same routine there, collecting black float from below, and then clawing fresh glinting ore out of the thick seam, until he had several pounds of that, too. That seam ran a vast distance, more than he could claim, so he took a few samples farther down, and stuck them in his pocket. His heart raced. If he wasn't a millionaire, then he had badly fooled himself. He was reluctant to leave such a fortune unclaimed, but the prospect of anyone else finding it was so small that he knew he was being foolish to worry about it.

Next, that assayer in Tonopah, the one who grubstaked him $20 against $200 in ore. It peeved him to surrender even a nickel to the man, but in fact he needed to have these samples assayed, and there was no escaping that. And he needed a new grubstake. That Battle Mountain cheapskate outfit had given him barely enough grub to get him to a safe place. Well, he'd deal with them, all right. Mostly by putting a match to that contract.

He pushed south and east, this time knowing exactly where he was, not quitting when the heat was high, and resting only briefly at the wells. The mule had nothing to eat, but Bitter pushed him along anyway, just as he ignored his own limp and put as much weight as he dared on his bum ankle.

Tonopah was lively that afternoon, with the mines going full blast. He saw the Desert Queen's boilers pumping smoke, and the Burro looking busy. Both were located next to the Mizpah. The Lynch and O'Meara and the Brown and Cutting were pulling up ore, and others that sprang up overnight.

He passed the Tonopah Club, where all the swells collected, and a place called the Northern, run by some hooligan called Earp, out of Tombstone. He'd like to wet his whistle, but business came first, so he turned up the hill to the Mizpah, and the little shed where Walt Wacker ran his assay operation.

"Sorry," he said to the irritated mule, "you gotta wait."

The packs were heavy with rock, but he yanked them off as if they were feathers, and lumbered into the one-room laboratory.

Wacker was tending an assay furnace, but finally peered behind him from his wire-rimmed spectacles.

"You, is it?" He eyed the heavy canvas bags. "All right, just a minute while I pull this."

He donned heavy gloves, opened the door, and with tongs he pulled out a dish and set it to cool. There was a metal button in its center.

"Mister Washington, or whatever. You've been to your ledges?"

"Look at this, will you?" Bitter said, emptying one sack of copper ore.

"Pretty fancy stuff there," Wacker said. "You want me to run assays on all these?"

"No, you decide what's what. Some's float, some's chipped out, and you can tell the difference. Do what gives me the story."

Next Bitter unloaded a load of the black silver ore, which glinted brown in the window light. Wacker examined these pieces, too. "Same here, I see. Some float, some fresh out of the vein. You want samples?"

"I got to pay for these out of this," Bitter said.

Wacker grinned. "A lot of assays cost a lot of cash."

"Well, I'll go somewhere else, is what I'll do."

"Come back tomorrow."

"I need some spending money."

"Two dollars."

"More than that, Wacker."

"A dollar boards and feeds your mule, and you got a dollar to drink up."

"You got a pile of ore there. You'll coin money."

Wacker smiled, opened a drawer, extracted two singles, and gave them to Bitter.

Euchred again. Bitter stormed out, grabbed the suffering mule, headed for the livery barn, and accosted the hostler. "Overnight, still a dollar?"

"You're in luck. Seventy-five cents, fella. We've got a narrow-gauge bringing in feed now."

That was the first good news Bitter had heard in Tonopah, and it gave him $1 and a quarter to drink up.

Bitter cussed the sunlight and headed for the Northern Saloon to subdue his thirst. He found no customers at all in the gloomy place.

"Lay a shot of whiskey before me, friend," he said to the barkeep, who had huge mustachios and black hair parted in the middle.

The barkeep looked him over, saw the quarter in Bitter's hand, and poured one. The place was hot. The glass was warm.

"Water?" the barkeep asked.

"Neat," Bitter said. "You the proprietor?"

"No, I'm the day shift."

"I haven't had a sip since childhood," Bitter said. "My mother fed me by the bottle."

The barkeep was waiting for Bitter's quarter.

"Start a tab, boy," Bitter said, sipping rapidly.

"House policy, it's pay as you go if we don't know you, sir."

"I'm George Washington, and now you know me."

The barkeep didn't move. Bitter grumbled and laid out the dollar, which the barkeep inspected and accepted.

"A rich man shouldn't have to do that," Bitter said. "I'm a millionaire. I've got the biggest deals cooking you ever heard of. I've got better silver ore than all the mines in Tonopah put together. And when I'm tired of that, I'll start in on my copper holdings. And along the way I'll buy this two-bit saloon."

"The owner would gladly sell it, sir, if the price is right."

"I'd give him the wrong price and make him sell it, or face a bigger thirst parlor next door, with drinks at half the tariff."

"Mister Earp would be entertained, I'm sure, Mister Washington."

"Fill her up, boy. What did you say these run?"

"Twenty cents, sir."

"This Earp is a crook, I'd say. He's a nickel above the going rate."

"You're welcome to look for a fifteen-cent whiskey elsewhere, Mister Washington."

The barkeep carefully refilled the glass, and marked a tab.

"You could've filled it fuller," Bitter said. "Just remember when you first met me, and what I said, because you'll be telling the story to all your customers for the rest of your life. I hit it big. In a few weeks you'll be calling me the Silver King. And when I own the town, I'll start hiring and firing, mostly firing."

"I'm glad you have a plan of action, sir. In fact, I agree with you. A lot of men around here need firing."

Bitter was all aglow. "You say so? You give me a firing list in a few days, and I'll make all your dreams come true, boy."

The afternoon progressed just fine, at least until the dollar ran out and the barkeep shook his head. "Good to see ya, friend, and come again," he said.

Bitter was outraged. "You're at the top of the list!" he shouted.

"What's the trouble, fella?" a sandy-haired man asked.

"I've been denied my constitutional rights," Bitter said.

"This is George Washington, Wyatt," the barkeep said.

"Where's your mule, sir? At the livery barn? I'll take you there."

"I'm not ready for bed, you knucklehead."

"But, Mister Washington, bed is ready for you."

"I'm the new Silver King of Nevada. I have a strike that makes Rockefeller look like a piker. I'll own this town. I'll own you. What's your saloon worth? I'll buy it."

"I'll sell it to you tomorrow, George. Say, watch your step. That's a bad leg you've got there."

"Yeah, and that bad leg cost one man his burro and another man his life. If Gladstone Brass wanders in here, tell him that Bitter is a Silver Baron. That'll fix his wagon."

"I'll do that, Mister Butter."

Bitter didn't remember much else of that escorted trip to the livery barn, but he awakened in the night and found himself lying on hay, and smelled the acrid and pleasant odor of horses. He wakened at dawn with a headache, and found two bits in his pocket, his ugly mule in the livery yard, and the hostler eyeing him with steely eyes.

"You puked on my hay," he said. "Out. Right now."

Bitter was affronted. "I can buy and sell this barn and you, fella. Just give me a week or two, and you'll see."

Bitter collected his mule, looked at the two bits in his pocket, but didn't feel like coffee or pancakes. He stepped into a cool and quiet morning, and decided to head directly to the assayer's office. He hiked up the grade to the

Mizpah, found the assayer's door locked, and settled down to wait. The cool air did him no harm, but the mule was restless.

"We'll have shut of this town soon as I collect," he said to the mule.

Wacker finally showed up and let Bitter in.

"I'm only half done with all these samples," the assayer said. "I've got notes here, but your ore is holding up. Some's even better than the first samples you brought in."

"I'm a millionaire," Bitter said. "I've got a whole mountain of ore. You ever heard of Butte, Montana? I got Butte beat. Meanwhile, I need a grubstake again."

Wacker shook his head. "You've a lot of copper here, but it's pennies on the pound. And the silver ore barely pays my assaying costs. There's time and labor, fuel and chemicals, all of that in any assay, plus my labor and paperwork. This is a lot of rock here, but it isn't going to do much. And there's the two hundred you owe me."

"Wacker, I knew you'd think of some song and dance to rob me blind."

The assayer didn't say anything for a while. Then: "I can get the Mizpah management in. Show them my notes here. They might be willing to buy you out if you've filed on your claims and want to show them what you've got so far."

"I'd rather jump off a cliff," Bitter said.

Chapter Thirty-One

Bitter fumed. He was hurting. He had no grubstake. The cheapskate would not stake him. He had to get back out to the bonanza gulch to stake his claims. And he had no way to do it.

Wacker eyed him quietly, and then excused himself. "Wait here. I'll be back in a few minutes," he said.

Bitter wandered the assay lab for a while, looking at the various glass bottles full of chemicals, the two furnaces, the equipment to crush a sample of rock to powder, and all the samples of ores that lined a shelf. And then he sat down. His ankle hurt.

Cheapskate. All he needed was a grubstake.

Wacker returned with a man wearing a suit and cravat, carrying some large sheets of paper.

"Mister Washington, this is Sam Butler. He's the manager of Mizpah Mining Company. I've showed him your ores, and the results of the assays so far, and of course he's very interested in dealing with you."

"I don't deal," Bitter said.

"Pleased to meet you, sir. I'm always looking for ore, and silver ore in particular, and thought you'd like to deal. I gather from Mister Wacker you'd like to go back to your ore and do some location work, and get your claims lined up. We could do that for you."

"Fat chance I'd come out of it with anything."

"Well, that's your choice. I've been thinking to offer you a thousand dollars for your properties, sight unseen, if you'd like to tell us where they are. Now, we have a subsidiary, Battle Mountain Company, that's been out doing some surveying and mapping, and they've got these preliminary maps of the area, with accurate mileages and so on. You seem to have a game leg, Mister Wacker said, and we could spare you the hard trip. If you like, of course."

"A thousand dollars?"

"A hundred right now, and nine hundred when the ore's located and the claims are in."

"And I wouldn't have to go?"

"You can stay right here. We'd enter your discovery claim in your name . . . or whatever name you wish, Mister Washington. I believe the Battle Mountain Company has a claim to half of that, and our thousand-dollar advance would purchase your half. That document is signed by Billy Bowler. And of course we would stake our own claims on the lode, next to yours."

"A hundred dollars right now?"

"And you wouldn't even have to leave Tonopah, Mister Bowler."

"How long would this take?"

"Maybe ten days . . . two or three days out,

two or three back, three or four on the site. We'd send a large crew for the fieldwork. And we'd get wagons out there with supplies. But that depends on the location. If it's farther, it'd take more days."

"It's three days walking."

"Well, you think about it. I've got some preliminary maps here, mostly penciled in by our map people, and we think they're detailed enough so you could steer the party, and a good description of what to look for on the ground. Of course, if they don't find the right gulch, or ridge, you wouldn't get your payment."

"I can have a hundred dollars right now?"

"After you sign a little agreement."

"It beats walking three days on a game leg," Bitter said. "But I'm not putting my finger on any map until I have it in writing and the bills are in my pocket. That's good ore, and it's rich copper ore, too, and I won't give you a peek until every-thing's proper."

"Mister Bowler, we'll treat you to breakfast . . . here's a dollar. Come back in an hour or two, and we'll proceed."

"I don't know if this is a good deal," Bitter said.

"Neither do we, sir," Butler replied. "But no one gets ahead without taking chances. Here. I'm going to roll out the maps. Don't tell me where to go . . . just look at them and see if they make sense to you, so we can be guided if you decide to accept my offer."

Butler and Wacker unrolled a stiff sheet of butcher paper on a table. It was a rough map, largely sketched in pencil, and covered country north and east.

"My men have been working on this," the manager said.

"Not this one," Bitter said. It was too far south.

They unrolled the next one, and Bitter swiftly saw the low, anonymous range north and east of Tonopah, actually closer to Eureka than this place. A range with no name he had ever heard of, no great altitude, no peaks, no defining ridges. The place where his bonanza gulch worked eastward from the bottoms was blank, and that suited him fine. If he chose to reveal it, they would find it. If he didn't like the deal, they'd never figure it out.

"Maybe it's this," he said.

"Close enough so our party can locate it?"

"I ain't saying."

Butler smiled. "Enjoy your breakfast. Come back in a couple of hours, and we'll have something written up, and you'll put a hundred in your pocket."

Bitter nodded and bolted into daylight. They'd euchre him, but he'd been around the block and he'd make sure it didn't happen. $1,000 was pocket change, but he'd make sure they would sweeten the pot. His hangover vanished, and he ordered eggs sunny-side up and side pork at the local beanery, and bought a cigar, and watched the world go by for a while. Then he marched up the hill, still puffing on the good Havana, and found them waiting in the assay office.

They handed him the agreement, scarcely a paragraph long. It was as Butler proposed, and not loaded with fine print. He read it again, puffing on the stogie, and nodded.

Butler handed him a nib pen and ink bottle. Bitter dipped it, and signed both copies.

"Unroll that sucker," he said.

They did. He put an X on the spot.

"It's a narrow gulch, doesn't even show here, rises from the flat here east to the ridge, some brush on it. The silver's halfway up on the north side, the copper's farther up, also north side. Where's my hundred?"

They made some notes, and added some small marks at the points where he said the lode would be.

Butler smiled. "Join the company," he said, and offered his paw.

"How soon do I get the nine hundred?"

"We'll have a party on the road by noon. What else can I say?"

"Well, you could advance it."

Butler pulled an envelope from his breast pocket, and handed it to Bitter. "Ten tens, all yours, fella," he said.

"Folding money," Bitter said, snatching it. "I'll be around town. And checking on you."

He marched out, dizzy with delight, and headed first for the livery barn, where he accosted the hostler.

"Sell my mule and keep the change, boy."

"Yes, sir, but I'll need a bill of sale from you, sir."

"Draft one and put my name to it, boy. William Bowler."

Next he headed for the Tonopah Mercantile, and headed for the men's clothing.

"Show me the fancy stuff," he said to the acned clerk. "I'm a millionaire, starting in a week."

He bought a checkered jacket with wide lapels, brown and tan with a thin green stripe running through it for $9, a black derby for $3.50, a white shirt for $1.50, a bow tie, stiff brown shoes, a wallet, into which he stuffed his change, and a Waltham pocket watch on a brass chain that looked like gold.

Next he visited a tonsorial parlor and ordered a hair trim, a beard trim, and an extra dose of witch hazel.

"I'm the next bonanza king," he said. "Do a good job, if you want a tip."

He eyed himself in the mirror and was satisfied. The desert rat had vanished. The new Beau Brummel of Tonopah had emerged. He looked natty in his outfit. His beard lay smoothly cropped and close over his weathered face. His hair was neatly trimmed.

"You should have a handkerchief in that breast pocket," the barber said.

"Good idea, man, that's worth a dollar," he said, and tipped the barber extravagantly.

He dined on steak and spuds that eve, and avoided the temptation of the Northern Saloon. That would come later. Instead, he strutted the town, keeping a sharp eye out for admiring glances. There were plenty of glances, all right, and people on the street registered the newly minted mining king.

When that got tiresome, he walked the mining companies, studying the head frames and boilers and shafts and ore cars and heaps of tailings. A mining king had to know mining, and he intended to know mining better than anyone.

That night he stayed at the Tonopah Inn, spending a dollar, and then booking the room for a week. That's how long it would take to become the next bonanza king.

"Start a tab," he said, but the clerk demurred. "In advance, sir, that's our policy."

So Bitter laid out $7 more. "I'll buy this place, and then you'll learn some manners," he said to the clerk.

Over the next days, Bitter became a man about town, tipping shoeshine boys, lifting his derby to the rare lady on the street, buying hard candy to give to children, studying the narrow-gauge California train that had become Tonopah's lifeline to the rest of the world.

And each day, he made his ritual walk up the long grade to the busy Mizpah Mine, admiring the sturdy buildings and the aura of prosperity. He stopped at Wacker's assay office, and the assayer simply shook his head.

"Too soon," he said.

"Well, then they're incompetent," Bitter said. "Bunch of know-nothings."

One day he headed straight to Butler's very plain office, and confronted the manager, who replied calmly.

"Mister Bowler, it's been eight days. Hardly enough time. Be patient. We'll send for you the moment we have word."

Bitter laid out $3 for three more days at the hotel, noting that he was going dry fast, and waited some more, his irritation rising with each dawn.

But then one afternoon things changed. He saw the mules lined up at the manager's suite, saw rough-dressed men milling about, and beelined in that direction, pushing through the crowd.

Butler eyed him at once, and waved him in with a hearty smile.

"Well, Mister Bowler, my congratulations. The news is excellent."

Just as Bitter had said, there was silver and

copper ore under the X he had put on the map. The exploring party had easily found both lodes, confirmed their size and richness, staked out claims, including Bitter's discovery claim, located a dozen additional claims filed in the name of the company and various trusted employees, erected corner cairns and discovery notices, brought back some samples systematically chipped from the lodes, and had taken every step to ensure legal ownership of the bonanza.

"So, then, Mister Bowler, we owe you nine hundred dollars," the manager said. "Here's a draft over my signature. Take it to the bank. This pays for your half share in your claim . . . the Battle Mountain Company, our subsidiary has the other half, right?"

"You've bought me out?"

"That was the agreement, sir."

"I'd prefer cash, pal. Cash on the barrel head."

"We have it in our safe, if you prefer." He nodded to a clerk, who soon brought Bitter a stack of bills, and counted them out before Bitter, and had him sign for them.

"I guess you owe me two hundred," Wacker said. "The twenty-dollar grubstake, remember? Against any claim?"

Annoyed, Bitter unloaded two hundred of his bonanza, and marched out. He didn't like being surrounded by parasites.

He made his way to the Northern Saloon, where

the stocky barkeep was wiping glasses, and a dozen patrons were sipping, and that Earp fellow was watching from the rear.

"Set 'em up! It's on the house all night!" Bitter Bowler yelled, flashing his wad of cash. "The silver king is buying."

Chapter Thirty-Two

There was something in her voice Gladstone had never heard before. Something metallic and wounded. He stared at her, slowly headed for the pen to release Sylvester, and felt the shotgun dog his every step.

"And you, too," she said to Beef Story and Albert Gumz. "Out. And don't come back."

"But, Agnes . . ."

"Out!" The twin barrels swung around toward the visitors, and lowered.

"We're going," Beef said.

He and Gumz collected their horses and hastened into the gulch, and vanished in the twilight. She slammed the pole into place behind them, and turned to monitor Gladstone's exit.

He carefully released Sylvester, who needed no halter or lead line, and gently made his way toward the cleft, carrying his truck, mostly the filled canteens.

"And don't come back," she said. Her voice

was so low it sounded like the whirring of a rattlesnake.

He hurried into the declivity, grateful to be protected from a lethal charge of buckshot, and made his way up the steep trail to the slopes above, feeling winded. He couldn't understand it. The news she had received was like a dynamite cap exploding on her temper. But she'd get over it. Tomorrow would be fine.

"That was one mean woman, Sylvester," he said.

The mule remained uncommonly quiet.

He spent a troubled night under the overhang, and resolved to go down and make peace, which he did as soon as daylight permitted. He left Sylvester above, to guard his few possessions, while he stumbled down through the defile to Agnes's little paradise.

The shotgun blast barely missed him. Buckshot shattered on rock a few feet from him, the moment he stepped onto her little flat.

"I told you, and I won't tell you again," she said.

"What can I do to make things good?"

Another shot rattled rock near him, an angry whir of lead caroming in all directions.

He ducked back into the defile. "I'll come some other day," he said.

A third shot sent buckshot into the defile, but over his head. One ball grazed his pants. He scrambled backward. This was not a morning to visit Wet Agnes. He hastened upward, exhausted by the steep climb and the urgency of his ascent.

"She don't like us," he said to his patient mule. "And we've got a problem . . . food and water for the both of us."

Chalk Spring seep was a long day's walk west. And from there it was a day and a half to Eureka. And it was hot. And he hadn't dug any gold out of his seam. An all-day walk to water made it impossible to stay here, at his gold seam. And the lack of food made the problem worse.

"I've got to dig up some dinner," he said to Sylvester. "We're going to vamoose."

The mule sighed, bared yellow teeth, and wandered into the juniper slopes, looking for stalks of grass to murder.

"Damned witch," Gladstone said.

He gathered his pick hammer, a bag, and a pry bar, and headed for his gold mine, arriving a half hour later, charged with a rare burst of energy. He began a frenzied effort to loosen weathered quartz and put it all in a heap. Fresh quartz, deeper in, was solid rock and hard to break free, but where sun and wind and water and freezing had fractured the quartz, it pulled free with less effort.

He lost track of time, and next he knew the sun was high and hot, and he was thirsty, and he was a long way from more water.

But there was a lot of quartz in his pile. He sucked at his canteen, and then began reducing the quartz with his hammer, carefully picking the wire and nodules out of each piece. Time slid by, but he was oblivious of it, and kept shattering the milky matrix and freeing more native gold. He felt the load in his shirt pocket grow heavy. It was pure gold, and so heavy it didn't take much space. He felt fevered, some lunatic force driving him to clean this great heap of shiny mineral of all its treasure.

Sylvester appeared and plainly wanted water.

"I'll save some for you," Gladstone said.

By midafternoon, amid great heat, Gladstone had reduced his heap of quartz. He had more gold than he could carry in his shirt pocket. He transferred it to his canvas sack, making sure there were no holes in the sack, collected his tools, and headed for the overhang where Sylvester was waiting, head low.

Gladstone let him have half of the canteen. They started down Portuguese Peak when the temperature was high, but the sun was plunging, and the high desert began to cool. He walked deep into the night, his bag of gold over his shoulder, Sylvester trailing along. Both of them were eager to reach Chalk Spring and a blessed drink.

Damned woman. What got into her?

Sometime after midnight, Gladstone arrived at the cliff, and found no one there. He had worried about that, because of the gold he was carrying.

They drank gratefully, even though the water was alkaline. He rested there, while Sylvester foraged, and late the next morning, after sharing some hardtack with the mule, he headed north up the long basin to Eureka.

It took all that day and into the eve, but early in the night he and Sylvester had reached civilization, if that was the word for it. He had gold but didn't know who to trust, and finally headed for Beef Story's jailhouse. No one was around, but the door wasn't locked. He watered Sylvester at a trough, and found an empty cell, and went to sleep.

When he awakened, he found a stranger peering down at him. A star was pinned on his shirt.

"This ain't a hotel, fella. Best you up and git out."

"Nice bunks here. Beats hard ground," Gladstone said.

"That's not the usual sentiment," the lawman said. "You got a name?"

"Gladstone Brass."

"You're not wanted. I ran through all the dodgers. It was handy. There you were, sleeping, and there I was, looking at portraits."

"Nope. Just an old prospector with woman trouble."

The lawman thought that was pretty entertaining.

Sylvester was much put out, so Gladstone led him to a livery barn, where the hostler accepted him without asking questions, such as whether Brass could fork up some cash. Sylvester grinned, baring yellow buck teeth, and headed for the feed. This was a spa, as far as he was concerned.

Gladstone was damned if he'd trade gold at the mercantile for $14, but didn't quite know where to go, until he thought of the mines. They produced silver and lead, but maybe someone there would buy the gold.

He was in luck. At the Richmond Mining Company, out of town, he found himself talking to the superintendent, who was also a mining engineer.

"I've got this pure gold, dug out of a ledge, and at the mercantile they want to give me fourteen for it. You interested?"

The burly man studied Gladstone and nodded. Gladstone pulled open his sack and extracted some wire and nodule gold.

"You're right," the man said. "Native gold. Unusually clean. How much you got?"

It turned out to be thirty-seven ounces, without a speck of country rock or quartz in it.

"Seventeen an ounce?"

"Eighteen."

The man shook his head. "Cost of processing this and selling it, seventeen tops."

"Oh, all right. I've got no choice."

Gladstone Brass walked out with a bank draft for $629. And the amused superintendent gave him a silver dollar for good luck. But that didn't allay Gladstone's sense that he had been euchred. Those mining companies, they were all alike.

He didn't trust banks for an instant, and cashed the check instead of opening an account, stuffing the wad of bills into his pocket, and making sure he wasn't being followed.

So there he was, in Eureka, with only his mule for a friend. The town was fading; the silver and lead mines were yielding less. The bonanzas were elsewhere. Now there was Goldfield, exploding into a gold town, not far from Tonopah. Even Tonopah was fading, its mines past their prime. It sure was a puzzle.

He bought a fancy lunch—oysters on the half shell, imported from New York, they said. He didn't care for them, but got them down. That and all the frills with them cost him half of his silver dollar. The rest would redeem Sylvester.

He didn't know how to spend his cash. He had never had so much of it, and didn't want anything. The mercantile, solid and respectable, was full of sturdy clothing and household items, and shoes, and dry goods. The opera house was running shows nightly. The hotel, with its fancy ginger-bread, looked prosperous and busy.

The Low Dog Saloon, a board and batten

building on a side street, was for sale. A sign in the window announced it. He had never tended bar before, but he didn't doubt he could learn the trade. It looked to be hard work, pouring, washing glasses, keeping tabs, ordering, and all that. But the thought intrigued him. He circled around the block a few times, thinking it over, and finally got up the nerve to enter.

The place was dark and dank, lit only by light filtering through small windows on the street. There were no customers.

A burly barkeep rose from a chair. "What'll it be?" he asked. "Don't ask for it cold."

"This place for sale, it says. How much?"

"Five hundred, including stock."

"What do you take out of it?"

"Depends. Some days, ten clear. Some days, five. That's enough. I live in a room at the rear, so I don't need a lot. It's a living, and I'm not ragging you."

"I don't know nothing about saloons. Is that good?"

The barkeep shrugged. "It could be built up some. You gotta be dedicated to do it."

"You own it? How long have you worked it?"

"Oh, maybe two, three years. I got it from a bum who drank himself under."

"And you're getting out now. Why's that?"

"Beats me. I'm tired of it. This place is the middle of nowhere."

"You need to give me better reasons than that."

"Mister, you think running a thirst parlor's easy? Especially in a town that's fading away? It's hard work. They come at you with a tax or license for everything. The suppliers, they cheat you. You got to wash it down, swab the floor, clean the ashtrays, buy oil for the lamps, and throw out the drunks. I got tired, that's all."

"And what did you like about it?"

"I get to tell my stories. I stand here and tell my yarns. I worked in the mines until I wrecked my back, and I got more stories than I got time to tell them. But all I did was drive away the trade. They come in to talk, not to listen. If you ain't a listener, and I'm not, you lose the trade. Got it?"

"All I do is listen," Gladstone said. "What's your bottom price, no dickering, cash on the barrelhead."

"Four-ninety," the barkeep said.

"You own this clear, with no debt on it, no taxes owing?"

"I do."

"Write her up," Gladstone said. "Date it today, four seventy-five."

Ten minutes later Gladstone Brass owned the Low Dog Saloon in Eureka. Twenty minutes later, the barkeep, one Dan Deutsch, was packed up and gone, leaving an odd odor behind him. Gladstone moved into the little room at the rear, which had an iron bed with a cotton-stuffed mattress, a novelty for him. He summoned some energy, washed the front windows, mopped the floor, surveyed his stock. The bottles were mostly empty, and he'd need to refill. He pulled the FOR SALE sign from the window, wrote NEW OWNER on the back, and put it up again.

He was open for business. It wouldn't take much work.

Chapter Thirty-Three

The good thing about running a saloon was the company. Miners drifted in, and they bought Gladstone's wet goods, ate his peanuts, and he listened to their stories. He liked some of them and tolerated the rest. In a way, they shamed him. He would never get into a cage and go underground, but these men did every day, and lived to tell about it.

The Low Dog paid its way, and Gladstone Brass settled into a peaceful life. He never saw Agnes again, though once he heard a story about a woman dressed as a man who bought some shotgun shells and other stuff at the mercantile. And then, a couple of years later, someone told him that no one was present at the well at Portuguese Peak and the stone cabin was forlorn, occupied only by pack rats. There was no sign of her. But someone had found a gaunt old mule living there on the flat.

Gladstone never saw Beef Story or Albert Gumz again, but one day someone told him that both of them were night watchmen at the booming mines in Goldfield, perfect work for men who had no desire to exert themselves.

He never figured out what got into Agnes that day, and he never stopped missing her.

About the Author

Richard S. Wheeler, born in Milwaukee, Wisconsin, emerged as an author of the Western story at the age of forty-three with *Bushwack* (1978) followed by the highly praised *Beneath the Blue Mountain* (1979). Already this early his work was characterized by off-trail storylines, avoidance of any appeal to myth or legendry, and a rejection of upbeat resolutions. Following a hiatus of a few years in which he published nothing, Wheeler brought out what remains his masterpiece, *Winter Grass* (1983). It was finalist that year for the Spur Award from the Western Writers of America. It was, however, his later novel, *Fool's Coach* (1989), that earned him his first Spur Award. His more recent work, *Cashbox* (1994) and in particular *Goldfield* (1995), has been more ambitious, taking a wider spectrum of history into account in narrating the complex lives of his characters set against distinctive historical backgrounds. The period between 1989 and 1993 was an extraordinarily productive one for Wheeler during which he published no less than eighteen novels and averaged 250,000 words a year. He also deserves recognition for his special talent as an editor—for eight years he worked for Walker and Company for their Westerns line and brought a number of notable writers to the fore by recommending their first novels for publication.

Center Point Large Print
600 Brooks Road / PO Box 1
Thorndike, ME 04986-0001 USA

(207) 568-3717

US & Canada:
1 800 929-9108
www.centerpointlargeprint.com